If there was one thing Toby Bishop didn't crave, it was responsibility for other lives.

He'd traveled that route more than once, though never as a landowner, and the results were mostly negative.

Tonight, he had first watch, along with Curly Odom and Deke Sullivan. He'd caught a break when Graham Lott drew an assignment to the second shift, sparing Bishop from uninvited monologues.

Three drovers at a time kept eyes on Mr. Dixon's stock for a three-hour turn, then packed it in when their replacements came on duty. During those three hours, men on watch spread out and circulated, singing to the animals if they felt like it, otherwise just watching out for danger in the dark.

A threat requiring action might be animal or human. Coyotes and the like would be repelled by any means required or shot if they refused to take a hint. A human prowler, on the other hand, shouldn't expect a chance to cut and run.

There was no good reason for anyone to sneak around a herd once it was bedded down. Therefore guards on night watch assumed that any trespassers were armed and nursing bad intentions. Rustling ranked first among the possibilities for devilment, but Bishop had heard tales of drifters looting chuck wagons — and once about a drover who was stalked and murdered on a cattle drive by the brothers of a girl he'd left with child.

Orders were simple when it came to lurking strangers. Order them to stand fast for a meeting with the trail boss, tossing any weapons that they might be carrying. A prowler who attacked or tried to flee was forfeiting his life. Cowboys who couldn't bring themselves to pull a trigger normally weren't hired.

Bishop had no qualms about shooting if it came to that, no fear that it would spoil his sleep, but as he mounted Compañero, he was hoping that his shift would pass without that need.

An hour into it, he thought his luck had soured.

Deke Sullivan was crooning to the herd, an off-key but passable "Oh! Susanna," circling around to Bishop's south, some eighty yards distant. Curly Odom was riding to the east of Dixon's lowing herd, marked by the glowing ember of a hand-rolled smoke.

So, who or what was moving in the brush ahead of Bishop and a little to his left?

RALPH COMPTON

THE BADLANDS TRAIL

A RALPH COMPTON WESTERN BY
LYLE BRANDT

BERKLEY
New York

BERKLEY
An imprint of Penguin Random House LLC
penguinrandomhouse.com

Copyright © 2020 by The Estate of Ralph Compton
Penguin Random House supports copyright. Copyright fuels creativity, encourages
diverse voices, promotes free speech, and creates a vibrant culture. Thank you for buying
an authorized edition of this book and for complying with copyright laws by not
reproducing, scanning, or distributing any part of it in any form without permission.
You are supporting writers and allowing Penguin Random House to continue to
publish books for every reader.

BERKLEY and the BERKLEY & B colophon are registered trademarks of
Penguin Random House LLC.

ISBN: 9780593100776

First Edition: July 2020

Printed in the United States of America
1 3 5 7 9 10 8 6 4 2

Cover art by Steve Atkinson
Cover design by Steve Meditz
Book design by George Towne

For Harley

THE IMMORTAL COWBOY

This is respectfully dedicated to the "American Cowboy." His was the saga sparked by the turmoil that followed the Civil War, and the passing of more than a century has by no means diminished the flame.

———◆———

True, the old days and the old ways are but treasured memories, and the old trails have grown dim with the ravages of time, but the spirit of the cowboy lives on.

———◆———

In my travels—to Texas, Oklahoma, Kansas, Nebraska, Colorado, Wyoming, New Mexico, and Arizona—I always find something that reminds me of the Old West. While I am walking these plains and mountains for the first time, there is this feeling that a part of me is eternal, that I have known these old trails before. I believe it is the undying spirit of the frontier calling me, through the mind's eye, to step back into time. What is the appeal of the Old West of the American frontier?

———◆———

It has been epitomized by some as the dark and bloody period in American history. Its heroes—Crockett, Bowie, Hickok, Earp—have been reviled and criticized. Yet the Old West lives on, larger than life.

———◆———

It has become a symbol of freedom, when there was always another mountain to climb and another river to cross; when a dispute between two men was settled not with expensive lawyers, but with fists, knives, or guns. Barbaric? Maybe. But some things never change. When the cowboy rode into the pages of American history, he left behind a legacy that lives within the hearts of us all.

—Ralph Compton

PROLOGUE

"FULL NAME?"

"Terrell Tobias Bishop. Most folks call me Toby."

The foreman had a sheet of paper on the card table in front of him, a pencil in his left hand, and wrote with a funny kind of slant. It made a scratching noise like spiders walking.

"Where you from?"

"All over," Toby Bishop said. "If you mean born, that would be Cairo."

"Cairo, Illinois?"

He thought of Egypt and restrained an urge to laugh. "That's it."

"More recently?"

"I drift around. Last place where I spent any length of time was Mason County. That's in Texas."

"Doing what?"

"Odd jobs. Whatever paid."

He didn't feel like mentioning the Hoodoo War, saw nothing to be gained from it.

"Not wanted anywhere, meaning the law?"

"No."

Bishop had cleared out before it came to that, losing his last week's pay. If the court had papers on him now, he didn't know it, so he wasn't lying.

"Ever been locked up?"

"No."

"We can check on that, you understand."

"Answer's still no."

"What brings you to the Circle K?"

He had an impulse to say his horse but played it straight, with money riding on the line. "The same as everybody else. I heard in town that you were hiring for a drive."

"'Town' meaning Atoka?"

"Right."

The foreman wrote it down, then raised curious eyes to study Bishop's face. He said, "The boss likes hearing 'sir' from drovers."

"Does that mean I'm hired, sir?"

"Not yet. And I ain't the boss."

"Okay."

That would be Gavin Dixon. Bishop hadn't seen him, but he knew the name from talk around Atoka's main saloon, the Dry Gulch, which was anything but dry.

"You ever worked a cattle ranch before?" the foreman asked, his pencil poised.

"I have. Last time in Mason County, on the Sutter spread. Before that, Winston's, up in Barber County. That's in Kansas."

"Ever on a drive?"

"Not yet," Bishop replied.

"It ain't the same."

"I figured that."

"We've got about two thousand longhorns heading for St. Louis. That's five hundred miles and change northeast of here. With any luck, we ought to make it inside seven or eight weeks, but luck ain't something you can count on, driving steers."

"You're saying anything could happen."

"That's the ticket, and it likely will. Weather aside, times past, we've had to deal with rustlers, hostiles, damn near anything."

"Sounds fair to me."

"And you can spare that kind of time?"

"No problem."

"Only, we've had so-called drovers quit a drive before and leave us wanting. Understand, the boss don't pay until the herd's delivered and he sells 'em off. You drop out anywhere along the way, you ride off empty-handed. You can't come back later, asking for partial compensation. It's an all-or-nothing deal."

"I get it."

"Same thing if you make trouble anywhere on the drive and Mr. Dixon has to let you go. Get fired and it's on you."

"Seems plain enough."

"You've got a horse."

That didn't come out sounding like a question, but he answered anyway. "The snowflake Appaloosa tied outside."

"There'll be replacements out of the remuda. Give your animal a rest on night patrols and such."

"As long as no one else tries riding mine."

"Not much for sharing, then?"

"I was thinking of my horse. He doesn't take to strangers."

The foreman considered that, then said, "I see you wear a Colt."

Bishop didn't respond to that. The Peacemaker was holstered on his right hip, in plain sight.

"Well, are you any good with it?"

"I've held my own so far." He let it go at that and hoped the foreman would as well.

"You have a rifle?"

"Winchester. The Yellow Boy."

"Might come in handy sometime on the trail."

Bishop expected to be asked if he had ever shot a man, was calculating how to answer, but the question didn't come.

"The job pays forty bucks a month and found. We'll feed you meat, bread, taters, beans, and bacon. Nothing fancy, but our cook's all right."

"I'll take it, if you're offering."

"I am, under the terms I just explained." He pulled another sheet of paper out from underneath the one on top, spun it around, and pushed it toward Bishop, pencil extended. "Sign or make your mark on the fifth line."

Bishop wrote out his signature, refrained from adding any kind of flourish at the end. When that was done, the foreman shook his hand. Said, "I'm Bill Pickering, but you can call me 'Mister.'"

"Duly noted."

"Nothing much for you to do, rest of today. We start first light tomorrow, and I mean first light."

"Got it."

"Breakfast is half past four. Get used to it."

And that was it. After the bloodiness in Mason County, riding for the past month up from Texas, killing time and spending most of his remaining money in Atoka, Bishop had another job.

He hoped that it would turn out better than his last.

CHAPTER ONE

B REAKFAST CAME EARLY, as the foreman had promised: bacon, beans, and bread. It wasn't gourmet fare, but Toby Bishop had survived on worse.

From time to time, he had survived on nothing much at all.

The other hands seated along the outdoor trestle table, ten in all besides Bishop, spared time to introduce themselves, most of them shaking hands. Toby was good with names and filed them in his memory, matched up with faces, guessing that he'd find out more about them on the trail.

The only one who stuck out, for a start, was Graham Lott, a sometime preacher, likely self-ordained. A rangy man with thinning ginger hair, left eyebrow interrupted by a scar, he advised that those who felt inclined could call him "Pastor." He said grace over their tin plates piled with food and claimed that he'd be offering a Sunday service in the evenings, for anyone who felt the need after ten hours herding beef.

For Toby's part, he couldn't picture spending any downtime on his knees.

It wasn't that he spurned religion altogether. He'd been "raised right," as the folks in Cairo used to say— meaning brought up to be a rock-ribbed Baptist, though in Toby's case it felt more like a superficial coat of paint that weathered down with time.

When Illinoisans spoke of Cairo as the lowest city in the Prairie State, they mostly meant geography. It was the farthest south, as far as Toby knew, located at the confluence of the Ohio and the Mississippi Rivers, also with the lowest elevation in the state and prone to flooding, ringed around with levees in a bid to hold back nature's inundations. But there was a certain meanness to the place as well, and throughout Alexander County as a whole, particularly when it came to white folks versus blacks. People of color in the neighborhood kept to themselves whenever possible, free state before the Civil War or no, and on occasions when a young man might forget "his place," he sometimes wound up stretching rope.

That was one reason Bishop hadn't gone back home since lighting out at seventeen, the better part of sixteen years ago. But if he'd been expecting other states or towns to demonstrate more tolerance, they'd come up short so far.

While Toby cleaned his plate, he glanced around the table, firming up the link between faces and names. Foreman Bill Pickering was absent, busy elsewhere, but that still left ten hired hands besides himself and Pastor Lott.

On Toby's left sat Boone Hightower, forty-something, with a weathered air of weariness about him, focused on his food without contributing to conversation. Close on Bishop's right, Deke Sullivan was roughly half Hightower's age, maybe three-quarters of his weight, and wore his pistol holstered for a cross-hand draw that struck Toby as awkward.

Moving on from Sullivan, he came to Leland Gorch, the oldest drover in the bunch, somewhere on the high side of fifty, with a permanent black smudge at his jawline, which looked to Bishop like a gunpowder tattoo. It wasn't close enough for an attempted suicide, more like a remnant of some long-ago near-death experience.

To Gorch's right, down at the table's end, sat Curly Odom, obviously named in jest. He wore a slouch hat now, but if glimpsed without it, he was bald on top, with long hair down below the arid pate that draped his collar all around. He smiled a lot, maybe too much, and had no qualms about intruding on a conversation if he spied an opening.

Facing him sat Paco Esperanza, sole Latino riding for the Circle K on this trip, traces of his breakfast clinging to a handlebar mustache he'd cultivated to enhance his narrow face. To his right was Isaac Thorne, their only black companion on the trail, full-faced and sporting a goatee shot through with flecks of gray. Scarred knuckles marked him as a brawler at some bygone time, and maybe not that long ago.

To Thorne's right, facing Bishop, Estes Courtwright kept his head down, shaded by his hat's brim, fully focused on his food. He hadn't spoken yet in Bishop's presence and appeared to be a slacker when it came to making small talk. That was fine with Toby, since he hadn't joined the drive to pad his scanty list of friends.

That still left two. Beside Courtwright sat Abel Floyd, the Circle K's horse wrangler, who would keep and care for their remuda on the trail. That meant the blond late-twenties cowboy would be watching over thirty-odd replacement horses day and night, instead of babysitting some two thousand steers.

Across from Floyd, to Boone Hightower's left, sat Whitney Melville, tallest of the lot at six foot five or six, tipping the scale at around two hundred pounds. To that weight, add a fancy gun belt holding up a Colt Dragoon that had to measure nearly fifteen inches overall, more than four pounds of steel, together with a Bowie knife protruding from his boot.

Bishop felt sorry for his horse.

Bishop had finished his breakfast when a clanging racket echoed from the main ranch house. All eyes turned toward that direction to behold the foreman beating on a metal triangle suspended from a porch rafter, demanding their attention.

"Rally round!" he called. "We're burning daylight!"

Some of the hands were grumbling as they got up from their benches, but they clearly didn't mean much by it. Young or old, raring to go or halfway broken down, even if you'd done it all a dozen times before, there was a certain energy about the start-up of a trail drive that no free spirit could ignore.

A T FORTY-SEVEN, COMING up on forty-eight that autumn, Gavin Dixon knew that he could stand to lose some weight. His wife had mentioned it in passing and he couldn't argue with her, tried to make his peace with smaller portions at some meals and cut back on his alcohol intake, but so far he had nothing much to show for it.

That was the thing about prosperity. When he and Maryanne had started building up the Circle K—named for their daughter, Katherine, who'd died before she reached her second birthday—it had been hard work from dawn to dusk, with little in the cooking pot but prairie stew. Once they had made a decent go of it, the spread still made demands, but they had help around the place, the number of their hands increasing as the herd grew and their bank account kept pace. Dixon wasn't retired, by any means, but there was marginally less to do that forced him to complete each job himself.

Now he was older than his father ever lived to be, and it occurred to him that most folks—in Atoka, anyway—regarded him as wealthy. Sometimes, facing his reflection in the mirror, Dixon reckoned it was mostly true.

Which didn't mean that he could stay home, rocking on the porch, and let Bill Pickering command the trail drive to St. Louis. Dixon wasn't *that* old yet, and when the time came, if he lived that long, he just might sell the spread and find a city place, maybe in Dallas or its new neighbor Fort Worth.

But not just yet.

He scanned the upturned faces of the drovers ranged before him, wishing he could pick out anyone among them who was likely to go sour on the trail. He'd trusted Pickering to hire them, but that didn't mean that all of them would go the distance without problems. Every drive he'd been on, there were quarrels that had to be resolved and some that couldn't be, so that he had to part with badly needed hands. He hoped there would be less of that, this time around, but Dixon never liked to bet on human nature to come shining through.

You could have heard a pin drop when he started speaking to his men.

"We've got a long trip waiting for us," he reminded them. "Five hundred miles and then some till our payday in St. Louis, and I hope to get there with the herd intact. Remember that your pay depends on it. Each steer we lose along the way, and any weight loss by the ones that make it through, comes out of my pocket, and that means less for each of you. I can't predict what we'll run into down the road, won't even try. It calls for every one of us to stay and do our very best, no matter what the job demands. Focus on that, we ought to be all right. Questions?"

No one spoke up or raised a hand, which suited Dixon fine.

"Okay, then," he concluded. "Stash your bedrolls on the chuck wagon, mount up, and get these critters on the trail. Time's money, gentlemen."

L ONGHORNS WERE DIFFERENT from other cattle Bishop had worked on other spreads in Texas, and particularly farther north. First, their horns could reach a two-yard span or half again that much on ancient bulls, and served as deadly weapons if the steers were riled. A drover caught in a longhorn stampede might wish that he was facing hostile Indians instead.

Another thing: they were descended from the New World's oldest cattle, spawned in far-off Arab lands and shipped across by Christopher Columbus, their numbers mounting with the Spanish colonists who'd followed him long before the Pilgrims got around to fetching up on Plymouth Rock. Predominantly white and dark red, they were a hardy breed, resistant to the Southwest's frequent droughts and scarcity of feed, in the sixty-pound range at birth, up to five feet at the shoulder in maturity, weighing from fourteen hundred to twenty-five hundred pounds.

The trick was keeping most of that weight on their bones while traveling five hundred miles or more across rough country, over hills and valleys, fording rivers as required, and always stopping where the herd was free to graze all night. As Gavin Dixon had reminded them, each steer they lost along the way—from snakebite, broken legs, or rustling—meant their payoff at trail's end would be reduced.

Their boss couldn't hand over money that he hadn't made.

The drovers weren't guaranteed to reach St. Louis either. The Circle K provided no insurance if one of them died along the way or got stove up somehow and couldn't pull his weight. Dixon was required to pay a cowboy for the time he worked, not for being dragged along on a travois through trail dust. Dead men were worth less on a trail drive than a wagon with a busted wheel, since that could be repaired.

If one of them died en route, their payout was a prairie grave, trampled into invisibility by longhorns' hooves.

The steers were penned in large corrals and well fed in close captivity so they'd start the drive with weight to spare, then closely examined to make sure that none of them were lame or otherwise injured. Once they were on the move, nature would take its course over the next two months or so.

It was like gambling, in a way, except the stakes were life and death for all concerned.

Riding his snowflake Appaloosa stallion, christened Compañero—"Partner"—by the Mexican horse trader in Nogales he'd bought it from sometime back, Bishop kept pace with Mr. Dixon's other drovers as they nudged, cajoled, and cursed the longhorns from their pens and into a formation that he knew would bear consistent watching once they left the Circle K.

Drovers would have to watch for any strays while traveling by daylight, and the men assigned to riding herd at night were duty bound to keep the steers from spreading out too far, while also remaining alert for any predators, whether the ravenous four-legged kind or bandits bent on rustling cattle any way they could.

In that case, Toby knew there would be gunplay, and while that was nothing new to him, he didn't relish it.

The whole point of his ride across the line from Texas was to leave all that behind him if he could.

WHERE'D YOU SAY you come from?" Pastor Lott inquired.

"I never said," Bishop replied.

They were together on the herd's southwestern flank, Lott riding on a chestnut gelding brought from home—described to anyone who'd listen as a little Texas town called Bitter Root. They both had sandwiches prepared by Mel Varney, the drive's trail cook: cold roasted beef on buttered bread and not half-bad.

"That's right, I recollect now," Lott said, talking with his mouth full. "Must have mixed you up with someone else. But now you mention it—"

"I didn't," Toby said.

"All right, then. I apologize for being nosy, son. Don't mean to pry."

"It's not that," Bishop answered back, although it was precisely that. Then said, "Most recently, I'm out of Mason County."

"Texas?"

"That's the one."

"That rings a bell," Lott granted. "Something I should know about." He chewed and swallowed, then came out with it. "I've got it now. The so-called Hoodoo War."

So-called was right. There wasn't a thing about Mason County's troubles that had to do with voodoo.

"I never understood that name," Lott said, as if reading his trail companion's thoughts.

"From what I hear," Toby replied, "it had to do with

vigilantes wearing masks when they went out to hunt for rustlers."

Steers were at the bottom of it, countless head stolen by rustlers and sold across the Rio Grande in Mexico. No herd was safe from depredation, though at first it seemed the county's German immigrant homesteaders suffered greater losses than their Anglo neighbors.

The conflict between the rustlers and vigilantes hunting them had turned into a chauvinistic thing, Germans against "Americans." Toby had departed from the war zone after a few months of gunwork.

In any case, a recent arson fire had razed the Mason County courthouse, taking with it all official records of the Hoodoo War, sparing participants who'd managed to survive from the embarrassment of being charged and facing trial.

"I hope you didn't get mixed up in that," said Pastor Lott.

"I try to mind my own business," Bishop replied, thinking it wasn't quite a bald-faced lie.

WATCH OUT FOR them steers straying over there!" Bill Pickering commanded, pointing toward a trio of longhorns who seemed about to lose their way and wander off westward.

"We're on it," Whitney Melville told him, riding off with Boone Hightower to retrieve the truant steers.

So far, so good, thought Pickering, but it was still day one, another four, five hours until dusk, and anything could pop up to surprise them in the heart of Indian country.

From what Pickering knew, the problems with that unofficial territory spanned three-quarters of a century, without considering the wars and massacres that started almost from the day England's first colonists set foot on the East Coast. The native tribes, present for umpteen thousand years before white Europeans first "discovered" the Americas, resisted being driven from their homes and hunting grounds as anybody would, but always wound up on the losing end. By 1803, tribes were ceding their ancestral lands and trekking at gunpoint to dwell on "reserves" set aside to protect them—white leaders claimed—from mistreatment by westbound settlers.

When Fort Sumter set America on fire, most of Indian country's reluctant inhabitants belonged to "Five Civilized Tribes": the Chickasaw, Cherokee, Choctaw, Creek (or Muscogee), and Florida's Seminole. In short order, all five tribes signed "friendship" treaties with the breakaway Confederacy. Most sat out the bloodbath if permitted to, but some donned Rebel gray and fought against the Union, not defending chattel slavery but striking back at Uncle Sam, who'd forced them into exile from their homes.

In June of 1865, two months after Appomattox and Lincoln's assassination, the last Rebel commander to surrender on American soil was Brigadier General Stand Watie, commanding the Cherokee Nation, driven into exile and death. The postwar Reconstruction treaties hammered out in 1866 and '67 granted amnesty to ex-Confederate Indians and "promised" Washington would keep hands off their tribal organizations, while tribal leaders ceded rights-of-way for railroad and telegraph lines cutting swaths through Indian country for corporate profit.

Most recently, in March of 1871, another Indian Appropriations Act broke Washington's four-year-old promise of relative independence, formally dissolving all Indian "nations," making individual tribe members "wards" of the federal government, claiming more land from various tribes, and barring red men from voting, buying liquor, or in any other way offending whites. Transgression prompted U.S. troops to chastise those who broke the rules, sometimes with help from gunmen hired by white land barons.

It was no surprise, therefore, that certain tribesmen fled their reservations, taking to a last-ditch warpath when and where they could, inflicting damage on their longtime persecutors before tumbling into shallow prairie graves. Bill Pickering could sympathize and see their side of things, but only to a point.

When push came down to shove, he stood with other members of his race, holding the line for what some folks called civilized society.

More movement on the herd's flank caught his eye. He zeroed in on it and counted four more straying steers.

"Floyd! Esperanza!" he shouted. "Wake up there, will you? Get those dogies back in line!"

A FTER A FEW miles, Bishop realized that Pastor Lott couldn't rein in his gabbling. As they rode along, he talked about the landscape, its flora and fauna, his background, and what he called his "ministry." From what he said—at least, the parts Bishop absorbed—said ministry consisted of an endless circuit through the South and border states, sharing "the good news" with anyone who'd hold still long enough.

When he'd exhausted those topics, Lott came around once more to Bishop, asking him, "Are you expecting any kind of trouble on this drive?"

"I haven't really thought about it," Bishop said.

Which was a lie, of course. He had been bucking trouble ever since he'd fled the worked-out family farm, and seldom failed to find it anywhere. He'd killed his first man at eighteen, a clear-cut case of self-defense against a drunken bully, but the local law had kicked him out of town regardless. Since then, he'd been drifting aimlessly, his overriding goals being warm weather, peace, and quiet, until Mason County's war soured all that.

"I wonder about injuns," Lott confessed. "I suppose they're mostly on one reservation or another now, but still . . ."

"As long as you're aware of it," Bishop replied, "just take things as they come."

"That's sound advice, friend. Thing is . . . well . . . I've never had to harm another person, much less killing."

"There's no reason to suppose you ever will."

"I'm hoping not. You know, the Sixth Commandment says—"

"I've read it," Bishop interrupted him. "From what I understand, it's meant to say, 'Thou shalt not *murder*.' Going back to Cain and Abel, nothing that I know of in the Bible bars a man from self-defense, and they were always fighting wars. God ordered lots of those Himself."

"You know your Good Book, son."

"I wouldn't claim to be an expert, but I'd say I've got the basics down."

That silenced Lott, but only for a minute, give or take. "I've prayed on this," he said, no longer able to contain himself. "I've asked the Lord to keep us all from harm and lead us not into temptation."

"You reckon he was listening?" Bishop replied, only half-serious.

"He always listens," Lott replied. "He doesn't always *answer*, though. And when he does, it might not be the answer you were hoping for."

"Amen to that, Preacher."

It was the major reason why he'd given up on praying altogether. Never quite convinced that anyone could hear him, or was interested in the first place, he had learned to deal with problems as they came, not begging help from Someone he could neither hear nor see.

Bishop was hoping for some relief from fighting, at least until they reached St. Louis. Failing that, he would meet trouble in the only way he knew.

Head-on.

CHAPTER TWO

SUPPER THEIR FOURTH night on the trail was pretty much the same as every other meal served from the chuck wagon so far: a slab of meat, some beans, with bread and coffee on the side. In place of beef this time, however, Mel Varney had given them smoked pork.

The kid who came around collecting plates and silverware was Rudy Knapp. Known to the other hands as Varney's "hoodlum" or his "little Mary," he was tasked with chopping firewood, peeling spuds, and washing up after their meals. Bishop surmised that he was fifteen, maybe sixteen years of age, longing to be a cowboy but diverted to the role of kitchen help.

Still, for a boy fed up with school, it just might prove to be a start.

At what?

Droving wasn't a life Bishop had ever pined for, though he didn't mind hard, honest work. It beat plowing and planting, hoping Mother Nature would be kind and let a decent crop survive, instead of blighting it with too much heat, too little rain, and pests that lived for ruining a hard-luck farmer's dreams.

In Bishop's mind, it also beat owning a spread, trying to raise a herd for profit, nursing them through sickness—hoof-and-mouth, whatever—and patrolling to defend stock against predators, supplying feed and water during droughts and shelter during winter storms. On top of that, finances needed reconciliation, and you always had at least one bill collector knocking on your door.

If there was one thing Toby Bishop didn't crave, it was responsibility for other lives.

He'd traveled that route more than once, though never as a landowner, and the results were mostly negative.

Tonight, he had first watch, along with Curly Odom and Deke Sullivan. He'd caught a break when Graham Lott drew an assignment to the second shift, sparing Bishop from uninvited monologues.

Three drovers at a time kept eyes on Mr. Dixon's stock for a three-hour turn, then packed it in when their replacements came on duty. During those three hours, men on watch spread out and circulated, singing to the animals if they felt like it, otherwise just watching out for danger in the dark.

A threat requiring action might be animal or human. Coyotes and the like would be repelled by any means required or shot if they refused to take a hint. A human prowler, on the other hand, shouldn't expect a chance to cut and run.

There was no good reason for anyone to sneak around a herd once it was bedded down. Therefore guards on night watch assumed that any trespassers were armed and nursing bad intentions. Rustling ranked first among the possibilities for devilment, but

Bishop had heard tales of drifters looting chuck
wagons—and once about a drover who was stalked and
murdered on a cattle drive by the brothers of a girl he'd
left with child.

Orders were simple when it came to lurking strangers. Order them to stand fast for a meeting with the
trail boss, tossing any weapons that they might be carrying. A prowler who attacked or tried to flee was forfeiting his life. Cowboys who couldn't bring themselves
to pull a trigger normally weren't hired.

Bishop had no qualms about shooting if it came to
that, no fear that it would spoil his sleep, but as he
mounted Compañero, he was hoping that his shift
would pass without that need.

An hour into it, he thought his luck had soured.

Deke Sullivan was crooning to the herd, an off-key
but passable "Oh! Susanna," circling around to Bishop's
south, some eighty yards distant. Curly Odom was riding to the east of Dixon's lowing herd, marked by the
glowing ember of a hand-rolled smoke.

So, who or what was moving in the brush ahead of
Bishop and a little to his left?

It struck him as a stealthy kind of movement, almost
creeping, but not the sound of footsteps. Bishop, his
hackles rising, tugged at Compañero's reins and steered
the snowflake Appaloosa toward whatever might be
rustling in the tallgrass up ahead. He drew his Colt.

It was a Frontier Six-Shooter, nicknamed the "Peacemaker," its barrel shortened from the Single Action
Army model's seven inches down to four and three-
quarters. Chambered for the same .44-40 cartridges
his Yellow Boy Winchester used, the pistol saved
Bishop from carrying two kinds of ammunition and
still delivered a punch on par with the parent gun's
.45 caliber.

With luck, Bishop could drop a man-sized target

out to thirty yards or so, but in his personal experience most pistol fights were won or lost at ten to fifteen feet.

He didn't cock the Colt yet, though his thumb was ready on its hammer, index finger tucked inside the weapon's trigger guard. He'd schooled himself to draw and fire instinctively, but riding up on trouble with his gun in hand—if there was trouble to be met—gave him an edge.

Of course, nocturnal prowlers might just have the same idea.

They might have him outnumbered and outgunned.

He reached the spot where maybe-movement had attracted his attention. Compañero sniffed the night breeze, snorted once, and then stood still. Scanning the brush, Bishop saw nothing to alarm him, nothing man- or even mouse-sized moving through the dark. Regarding tracks, he'd need a lantern to survey the ground and wasn't packing one.

So, maybe nothing.

Bishop spent another moment watching, waiting, ears pricked to the prairie night, but all in vain. When he was satisfied that no threat lay in wait for him, he put his Colt away and clucked to Compañero, moving on.

TOO CLOSE FOR comfort, Amos Finch decided, letting pent-up breath escape his straining lungs. Rising from where he'd hidden when the drover nearly spotted him, he sheathed his skinning knife and eased back through the darkness, waddling in a crouch until he'd put a hundred yards between him and the herd, finding his grulla gelding tethered to a blackjack pine.

Pulling his knife had been a reflex action. Finch could easily have dropped the cowboy with his Schofield .44 revolver, but that would have brought the other trail hands down on top of him, five shots left against at least a dozen guns.

To hell with that.

Finch could be reckless when his blood was up, and understood that, but he didn't mean to die before his time—whenever that might be—if he could put it off.

This was the second night he'd sniffed around the northbound herd, not knowing who the boss man was or where they'd come from, caring even less. To Amos Finch, a trail drive was an opportunity for profit, making off with any animals that he could sell, no questions asked. Cattle were good, but there were too damned many of them in this herd for Finch to grab enough of them that it was worth the risk.

Now, horses, on the other hand . . .

He'd counted riders on the drive and checked out their remuda when they'd stopped last night. Thirty-some prime mounts he'd have no trouble selling in Arkansas, the Texas Panhandle, maybe across the Rio Grande if he felt like a long ride down to Mexico.

And once the sale was made, there'd come the sharing up.

Aside from Finch, there were six others in his gang, all thieves and cutthroats. Four of those were white, like Amos, while the other two were Mexicans with "Wanted" posters out on them back home. Six surefire killers, counting Finch, and one convicted rustler who'd escaped from custody before a sheriff in New Mexico could string him up.

Division of their spoils should be as usual, one-third for Finch, the rest of it split up six ways. If they pulled down a thousand dollars, say, he'd have $334, rounding it up, each of the others pocketing $111.

That was about the limit of Finch's arithmetic, but if some others didn't like it, he could always thin their numbers. Knock off one, the other shares increased to $133.20 and so on.

Fewer mouths to feed meant more for Amos Finch, and that was all he had to know.

Well, not quite.

Before anyone got anything, he'd have to hatch a decent working plan, and there was no time like the present to begin.

HOW MUCH LONGER, do you figure, till we cross the line into Missouri, Bill?"

Gavin Dixon had an answer roughed out in his mind, but sitting with his foreman by the campfire, sipping strong black coffee out of metal cups, they needed something to talk about until they both turned in.

"To reach the border," Pickering replied, "another two weeks if we don't run into any trouble. If we do . . ."

He let it trail away and sipped his steaming brew. The coffee wouldn't keep Dixon from sleeping through the night, but he'd remain alert enough to pick up on the first hint of a problem with his stock while they were bedded down. One of the side effects of bossing any trail drive that he'd ever been a part of, going back to when he was a teenager.

"I hear you," Dixon said. "I want to bypass Joplin City, if we can. Don't want our drovers getting liquored up and mixing with those miners, much less cardsharps and fancy ladies."

"That could be a hitch, all right," said Pickering.

Joplin City, occupied by lead miners and those who serviced them, was named for a parson who had tried to save their wayward souls some twenty years before the Civil War. Once upon a time it had been "Union

City," signifying merger of the mining camps that sprouted up along Joplin Creek Valley, before dreamer Patrick Murphy filed a city plan and named it for himself. That didn't stick, and later on the growing settlement was christened after Reverend Harris Joplin, dead these many years and pretty much forgotten by the folks he'd left behind.

The pastor wouldn't recognize Joplin today—or, if he did, would likely call down fire and brimstone on the nest of smelters, rough saloons, and brothels that bore witness to his fading memory. Today there were some seven thousand full-time residents in Joplin, a majority of them men still mining lead, still single, working shifts around the clock by lamplight, blowing off what steam remained to them when they returned aboveground at ramshackle pleasure palaces, outnumbering the city's churches ten, maybe fifteen, to one.

That would attract trail-weary cowboys, naturally. Dixon had discussed it with them once already, but he would reiterate the ground rules when they'd closed the gap to one day's travel. His hands were free to spend their pay however they desired, but only when it was their time to waste, not his. He wasn't bailing any drunks or brawlers out of jail, much less advancing anyone's pay.

Bill Pickering, his coffee almost gone, was still computing miles that lay ahead of them. "Once we're across the border," he observed, "we've got another four weeks, easy, till we hit St. Louis. That's if nothing holds us up, o' course."

"Of course," Dixon agreed. "And wouldn't that be nice?"

A veteran of many drives, both as a drover and the boss, he'd never seen one yet that ran according to a master plan without some unexpected hurdles to be cleared. He hadn't liked the clouds that afternoon, maybe a storm front building up to the northeast. They might mean rain, or even lightning that could spook a herd into stampeding. Hell, he'd even seen bolts from the heavens fry a steer from time to time—and once, a grim surprise, take down a horseman on the open prairie up in Kansas, three days out of Dodge.

So, maybe rain and maybe worse, or it could still be snow. Forget the fact that it was April. Freakish weather came around when least expected, never welcomed by dirt farmers, cattlemen, or anybody else, and there was nothing they could do but drive the herd on through it, holding to whatever schedule nature might allow.

"Shift change," said Pickering, checking his pocket watch to verify that drovers from the first night shift weren't skimping on their duties. "Reckon I'll be turning in, boss."

Dixon was about to second that when one of his hands stepped into the firelight, still trailing his mount before he dropped it off at the remuda for a rest. Dixon immediately recognized the snowflake Appaloosa and matched it to the drover's face.

"Toby," he said in greeting. "Something on your mind?"

"Yes, sir," Bishop replied. "It's likely nothing, but I thought you ought to know."

I T WAS CLOSE there for a second, but he didn't see me," Amos Finch assured his men.

"Good thing for you, *ese*," Jaime Ybarra said.

"Good thing for all of us," Reed Dyer chimed in.

"Easy as pie," Finch said. "The bum never came close."

Okay, that wasn't strictly true, but why raise apprehension for his men, who were erratic at the best of times, easily thrown off stride. The kind of thugs that he'd recruited were, by definition, hell-raisers and misfits, always contrary and sometimes cowardly. The last thing Amos needed was to give them any reason to back out.

"So, when you plan on hitting them?" Bert Fitzer asked, before he scooped more beans and rice into his maw.

"There's no rush," Finch replied. "We've got a couple weeks, and likely more, before the herd gets to Missouri. I just want to eyeball them another night or two, get their routines down, then we'll make our move."

The faces ringed around him in firelight were dissolute, world-weary, from the late teens to early forties in age. Most of them had been in jail at one time or another. Those that hadn't done time yet were either lucky or were faster on the draw than any lawmen who had tried to take them in. None would have raised an eyebrow in a gambling hall, saloon, or whorehouse, but they'd all stand out like sore thumbs in a Sunday congregation.

Finch's second in command was Shelby Gretzler, thirty-one, an inch taller than Amos but a few pounds lighter. Fitzer was a redhead, freckled, also in his thirties. Dyer was in his early forties, with a harelip some sawbones had tried to fix in childhood, leaving him with a speech impediment that prompted fits of rage whenever some fool joked about it to his face. Earl Mullins might have been their oldest, but he swore the gray had started showing in his hair when he was just a sprig. The Mexicans, Ybarra and his sidekick, Mariano de la Cruz, were cutthroats from Juárez and looked enough alike for rednecks to mistake them for brothers.

Six thieves, drunkards, and killers, temporarily allowing Finch to lead because his reputation put them all to shame, at least until some bigger, tougher hombre came along.

Between them, they had guns enough to start a small war, but Finch hadn't planned their current job to be a bloodbath. It was different from taking down some small town's bank, where it made sense to let a few rounds off at the beginning, cow the locals, maybe even kill one or two of them to make the point that they could get along without a sack or two of gold.

By contrast, tapping a herd was stealthy work; going in at night and stealing stock without a lot of racket, slipping off into the dark with animals enough to sell for profit.

"We're still just goin' after the remuda?" Mullins asked.

Finch nodded and leaned across to pour himself another cup of coffee from the tin pot on the fire. "It's like I told you. Too much trouble drawing steers away without stampeding them or catching lead from the night watch."

"I like a nice stampede, me," Mariano said, and chuckled to himself.

"It ain't good business," Finch reminded him. "They keep their mounts tied up together, so they don't stray in the dark. We slip in, cut the line, and lead them off. Be quiet doing it, and there's a chance to pull it off without them noticing."

"And if they do," said Gretzler, "all but three or four of 'em will be on foot."

"Still shooting at us, though," Dyer reminded them.

"That's where the quiet part comes in," Finch said. "But if we're under fire . . ."

"We shoot back, right?" asked Mullins.

"Same as always," Finch assured him.

"Shoot to kill?" asked Fitzer.

Nodding, Finch responded, "Is there any other way?"

I'M HEARING THAT you didn't really see this whatever-it-was," the foreman, Pickering, remarked.

"That's true enough," Bishop allowed. "It started with a feeling, then there was a shadow, something moving, but I never got a look at it."

"Coyotes?" Gavin Dixon asked him.

"Could've been, boss. But I haven't heard them calling any night so far."

"We've got a waning crescent moon tonight," said Pickering. "On top of that, coyotes put a lid on all that yipping when they hunt."

"Makes sense," Bishop acknowledged. "But the shadow, what there was of it, seemed . . . bigger, somehow."

"Just this shadow, though," Dixon replied. "When you rode up on it, you saw nothing?"

"Maybe I wasn't quick enough."

"You felt no need to shoot, though."

"No. I didn't want to spook the herd or ruin anybody else's sleep until I had a clear target."

"And as it is . . ." The boss had made his skepticism plain enough, without elaborating further.

"Right. I said it might be nothing, boss."

"You did. And since you tipped off the new shift, which was the right thing, you can pack it in and put your mind at ease."

"Yes, sir. Good night to both of you."

"And you," said Dixon.

Pickering sat staring at the fire and kept his mouth shut, likely pondering another cup of coffee, but he hesitated when his hand was halfway to the pot and drew it back.

Bishop retreated to the place where he'd deposited

his bedroll after he unsaddled Compañero, lightly tethered him with tallgrass all around to graze on overnight. The snowflake Appaloosa knew when it was time to sleep and Bishop left him to it, thinking of himself now that their working day was done.

Or so he hoped, at least. If he had missed a lurker in the night . . .

Forget about that now, he thought.

Tents weren't carried on a cattle drive, due to their extra weight and taking up space better used for packing food. A cowboy's saddle served him as a pillow, and Toby's bedroll consisted of a rubberized ground sheet and a wool blanket. That was better than what drovers called a "Tucson bed," meaning no pad beneath them and no blanket over top.

Keeping his saddle close wasn't for comfort only. If any kind of problem roused him in the night, Bishop would need to mount up in a rush, no wandering around in darkness looking for his tackle. Like most other cowboys he had known, Bishop had spread his lariat around his open bedroll, hoping to keep snakes away from him. That might be simpleminded superstition, but he'd learned to do it as a youth, and he'd been spared from rattler bites so far.

If something worked, why change it?

In final preparation for shut-eye, Bishop took off his boots and stood them upright to his left, decreasing odds that some nightcrawler would climb into one of them. Next, he removed his gun belt, curled it within reach of his right hand, his holster's hammer thong released. The Winchester was tucked under his blanket, right hand resting lightly on its walnut stock and well back from its trigger.

Now all Bishop had to do was shake the nagging sense that something—or someone—was watching from the outer darkness, sizing up potential prey.

* * *

I'M NOT SO sure about the boss," Mariano de la Cruz remarked, keeping his voice pitched low to stop it from carrying.

"He's just another loser gringo," said Jaime Ybarra in reply.

"I think he's more than that. Maybe a fool who'll try cheating us."

Ybarra tilted the bottle in his hand to take another swallow of mescal before he passed it back to Mariano. "How he's gonna do that when we're with him all the way? We get the horses, kill anyone who tries to stop us, then we sell 'em. Stand right there and watch him count the buyer's money out. We take our share and go our own way if you still feel bad about it."

"But suppose he tricks us? Leads us into an ambush, eh?"

"Who has he got to ambush us?" Ybarra asked. The liquor had begun to make him feel light-headed, which was, after all, the point of drinking it.

"He don't need anyone but who we've met already," Mariano said. "Five gringos against two of us. You know damn well that none of 'em like Mexicanos, eh? They won't think twice about killing us and splitting up our shares amongst themselves."

"That's if we let them," Jaime said, grinning.

"You got a better plan, then?" Mariano prodded him.

"Maybe I do," Jaime answered back. "Maybe I do."

"Is it a secret, then?"

"No secret," Jaime said. "Look, we need them till we get away with the horses, yes? That's work for all of us. But when we're done with that . . ."

"Then kill them," said de la Cruz. "I'm liking this idea, my friend."

Jaime heard the scrape of footsteps first and cleared his throat, alerting Mariano just as Amos Finch came up behind them, backlit by the dying fire.

"Making a night of it?" their Anglo leader asked, trying to make a joke of it.

"Just passing the mescal, *jefe*," said Mariano. "You want some?"

"No, thanks. I'm turning in. Long day tomorrow, shadowing the herd without them spotting us."

"We both be ready," Jaime said. "How do you say it? All bright-eyed and bushy-tailed."

"That's how we say it," Finch agreed. "See you at sunup, give or take."

Jaime and Mariano watched him go, waited until they heard Finch settling down into his bedroll. When Ybarra spoke again, his voice was lowered to a near whisper.

"Bright-eyed and bushy-tailed . . . Sounds like a damn skunk to me."

"A skunk or a gringo," muttered de la Cruz, taking another hit on the mescal. "I never saw much difference between the two."

Ybarra would have laughed at that comparison, but worried that the sound might carry to the spot where Finch was lying now, still wide-awake and maybe listening. He would assume that any laughter coming from the two Mexicans was aimed at him, and there was nothing to be gained by rousing anger or suspicion in their leader's mind.

Leader for now, that is.

Between the two of them, Jaime and Mariano had four pistols and two rifles, plus a sawed-off double-barreled shotgun de la Cruz kept handy for emergencies. That hardware gave them fifty-six shots without having to reload or pull a knife, against five men who wouldn't be expecting any treachery. Or, even if they were halfway expecting it, they still couldn't know exactly when and where their double-crossing "friends" would strike.

That gave Jaime and Mariano all the edge required to pull it off . . . as long as no one beat them to the draw.

CHAPTER THREE

THE SNOW BEGAN an hour after breakfast, their fifth morning on the trail. It started with a chill wind and a few stray flakes, then thickened through midmorning, spreading white drifts on the open prairie and collecting on the drovers' hat brims.

Toby Bishop reckoned only children truly love a snowfall, most particularly when it canceled school or their outside chores. He hadn't met a farmer yet who welcomed it, nor townies forced to shovel sidewalks granting access to their shops. Granted, some people felt obliged to comment on a snowfall's beauty, till it turned to grimy slush and ice, but he suspected few of those honestly felt that way.

And April snow, defeating spring's advance, was worst of all.

His coat and gloves were warm enough so far, the woolen scarf around his neck helping repulse a measure of the chill, but every now and then he had to doff his flat-brimmed hat and shake it clean. His Appaloosa offered no complaint—as if it could—but Bishop felt the longhorns growing restive as the falling snow occluded vision, building up like dandruff on their necks, withers, and rumps.

More steers tried straying from the herd than any other time within the past four days, and Bishop couldn't figure out if they were trying to escape the snow by breaking out of line or if the swirling flakes caused problems with their depth perception, dicey at the best of times.

The snow slowed progress and it also strained the drovers' eyes, watching for any predators along their route of march. A pack of coyotes or wolves might pass unnoticed with the morning sun obscured by clouds, snow coming down and camouflaging furtive movement on the ground. It might have been Toby's imagination, but just scanning the horizon, what there was of it, seemed to demand more energy than simply following the herd, retrieving strays.

Inevitably, he thought back to last night's incident, if he could even call it that. Dixon and Pickering seemed unconcerned by what he'd told them, and in truth it might be nothing. Getting spooked by shadows was a common problem on night watch, and he admitted to himself that he'd seen nothing sinister—just a sense or feeling that he'd interrupted something, maybe some-*one*, lurking in the dark.

So, how had it, or *he*, eluded Bishop when he'd moved to get a closer look? By stealth, perhaps. Or maybe there'd been nothing in the tallgrass after all.

Still . . .

In addition to watching for truant steers, Bishop peered farther off into the falling snow, until their moving backdrop lost all definition at a hundred yards or so. He searched for anything resembling a man on horseback other than his fellow drovers. More than once he caught himself counting the riders who be-

longed around the herd—the boss and foreman, with
nine other cowboys and the wrangler in charge of their
remuda—till it made his temples ache and he had to
stop himself.

And what if trouble found them on the snowy trail?
Bishop could draw his Colt all right with gloves on,
pull the hammer back to cock it, but he wasn't sure his
padded index finger would fit through the pistol's trigger guard. And if it did, he ran the risk of squeezing off
an accidental round. Cut back on the six-gun's relatively short effective range to thirty feet or so, and he'd
still have to hope he didn't drill one of his fellow riders
from the Circle K.

All things considered, Bishop figured it was better
if he didn't have to fire at all.

He hoped the snow would keep any potential enemies at bay until the drovers pitched camp. Then, all
he had to think about was shadows reaching out to
spook him in the long, dark night.

C AN YOU BELIEVE this crap?"
     Finch glanced over at Shelby Gretzler, riding to
his left on a cremello gelding, swiping vainly at the
snowfall with a gloved right hand.

"Seeing's believing," Amos said.

"I mean, it's almost Easter," Shelby groused.

"That's still another week. You've seen it snow this
late before."

"And didn't like it then neither."

"It helps us, in a way," Finch said.

"Dogging the herd, you mean? I get that, but I'd
rather do without it all the same."

Finch half turned on his hand-tooled saddle, stolen
with the horse that he was riding, six months back in
Santa Fe. Their five companions, all looking bedrag-

gled, rode in silence for the most part, huddled in the coats they hadn't planned on needing for the job at hand. One or another of them cursed the snow and wind from time to time, but conversation wasn't suiting them this morning.

Softening his voice a bit, glad that the prairie wind was blowing from behind him now, Finch asked his second in command, "What do you know about the Mexicans?"

"Our Mexicans?"

"I don't mean President Díaz."

"About as much as you do. Claim they knew each other in Chihuahua, growing up without a peso to their names in Ciudad Juárez. They've both done time in Texas; two, three years apiece for having sticky fingers."

"I'm not sure I trust them," Finch said.

"Anything particular?"

"Can't put my finger on it. Just a feeling like I get sometimes."

Gretzler narrowed his eyes at that. "I've learned to trust your feelings, Amos. Do you want to weed them out?"

Finch thought about that. Said, "Not yet. Not here. I want to put this job behind us first."

"And split the take like always?" Gretzler asked him.

"That's another question. Do you reckon any of the rest would side with them, were we to weed them out?"

Shelby mulled that one over for a minute, then said, "Nope. I doubt it, anyway. Jaime and Mariano mostly stick together, jabbering between themselves."

"Something to think about," Finch said.

"I'll back you if it comes to that," Gretzler offered. "Can't say I ever cared much for them, anyway."

"As long as no one else jumps in on their side."

"I'd bet against it, if I was a betting man."

Finch laughed at that. "Bearing in mind that I've played poker with you."

Gretzler shrugged. "Figure of speech," he said. Then asked, "We get the horses first, though, right?"

"Most definitely. Otherwise, we've got nothing to split."

"Except, if you thought they were gonna make a move on you . . ."

"I couldn't prove it. Just a feeling, like I said before."

"No need to drag it out if you think they've been scheming against you."

"Understood. But I've been counting on this score. My pockets are next door to empty, and that ain't a neighborhood I favor."

"Same here. Just saying, you can tip me off at any time. A high sign, anything at all. I'm there."

"Appreciate it, Shel. You'll be the first to know."

I TRIED SAYING A weather prayer," said Pastor Lott. "Asking to stop the snow and clear our way."

"Doesn't seem like it worked," Bishop replied.

"I've always thought there's no such thing as wasted prayers. They all get answered sometime, one way or another, even if it's not the answer you were hoping for."

"You mean, like wishing for a pet and waking up to find a rattler in your bedroll?"

Lott forced a laugh at that but clearly didn't see the humor in it. "More like asking for prosperity and being shown a way to earn your daily bread through honest toil."

"Most people find that going door to door or reading advertisements in a newspaper."

"But who delivers them to certain doors or sets the ads in front of them?"

Rather than drag it out, Bishop replied, "You've got me there, Parson."

"For instance—"

"Up ahead there," Bishop interrupted him. "Two strays."

They caught up with the longhorns, Bishop hoping that his Appaloosa wouldn't step into a gopher hole concealed beneath the snow. It only took a moment, heading off the strays and staying well clear of their horns, driving them back to join the larger herd.

"Where would they go, I wonder, on a day like this?" Lott mused.

"Most likely off to freeze somewhere," Bishop replied.

"Five days," the preacher said. "We haven't lost one yet."

"Don't let the others hear you say that. Tempting fate's supposed to bring bad luck."

"I don't believe in luck, Toby."

That figured. Bishop took the preacher for one of those folks who claim that everything is part of some vast plan, mysterious, unsolvable until the afterlife, when everything was suddenly revealed.

Fat lot of good that did, in Bishop's way of thinking, when no one who'd solved life's riddles ever had a chance to bring the answers back.

Bill Pickering rode up behind them, paused to shake snow off his hat, and told them both, "Good catch. We don't need any strays, weather like this."

"No, sir," Lott answered. Bishop settled for a nod.

He hadn't shared last night's event with any of the other trail hands. First, he had no proof and didn't need them snickering at him behind his back, claiming he jumped at shadows like a child. Second, even if his suspicion was correct, what of it? Bishop couldn't turn the clock back now and take another run at finding out what had disturbed him in the first place.

There was nothing he could do, in fact, but wait and see what happened next.

At least he'd passed the word along to Pickering and Mr. Dixon, for whatever that was worth.

When Pickering had ridden off, Lott asked, "How long you figure till we cross the line into Missouri?"

"Given normal weather, I'd have said another couple weeks at least," Bishop replied. "If it keeps up like this, even if nothing else goes wrong, we'll likely add a week or more to that."

"Too bad."

"Somewhere you have to be?"

"I wish," Lott answered, sounding vaguely wistful. "Nowhere special, now or later. I was hoping, once we're finished in St. Louis, I might look around, try scaring up a church in need of clergy for the summer, anyway."

"No long-term plans, then?"

"Not at my age. I just wait and take things as they come."

"It could be worse," said Bishop, thinking back to Mason County. "Take my word on that, Pastor."

B ILL PICKERING WAS angry at the weather as he rode away from Graham Lott and Toby Bishop. He had witnessed springtime snow before, though rarely, and it seemed to him that Mother Nature had a dark, contrary sense of humor, throwing roadblocks in their way for no good reason.

And if that weren't bad enough, they had a river coming up that they would have to cross somehow, before they even reached Missouri's southern border. That was the Canadian, a tributary of the Arkansas, though how it got that name was anybody's guess. No part of it was anywhere near Canada, flowing nine-hundred-odd miles from Colorado, through New Mexico, the Texas Panhandle, and Indian country. Crossing it would call for barges near a settlement the Creek tribe called Tallasi—meaning "Old Town"—where they'd spent some time along the so-called Trail of Tears while traveling to reach their designated reservation.

Fording the river would consume at least a day and maybe longer, stretched out by the storm if it kept snowing. A normal river barge could carry twenty-odd longhorns at once, meaning one hundred round-trip crossings if they found only one barge available. Bad weather would slow things down, and whoever owned the watercraft would likely hike his charges, recompense for weary hours working in the cold and snow.

Pickering knew that Gavin Dixon carried cash enough to swing it, but if he got gouged on price, it had to be deducted from their payoff at the stockyards in Missouri. With each drover who survived the trip expecting forty bucks per month, that whittled money off the top of Dixon's profit from the drive and left him starting off next year under a cloud.

Pickering eyed the gray mass overhead and saw no glimmer of relief. The good news, if it *was* good: he could only see a half mile up ahead, or less as the snow thickened. Maybe they could catch a break by nightfall, coming sooner on a day like this than normally, when sundown beat the clock and they pitched camp and bedded the longhorns down.

Thinking ahead to camp, Pickering thought about the story Toby Bishop had relayed to him and Mr. D last night. He hoped the drover was mistaken or had simply glimpsed a coyote fleeing from the sound and smell of his approach. If that was not the case . . .

Ranchers from the Pacific Coast back to the Midwest and across the South all had their stories about rustlers, bandits, thieves, and brigands. Spreads closer to Mexico endured twice the risk from their proximity to territory rife with banditry and revolution. No one moving stock across long distances could shrug that off and trust to happy thoughts.

Suspicion was the rule of thumb, and with so few lawmen spaced out along their route of march, a trail boss had to make his own rules. There was no such thing as taking prisoners alive and wasting precious time to drop them at the nearest small-town jail, where justice might be heavy-handed or ignored entirely, on a whim.

The rule on cattle drives was to shoot first and skip the questions. Anyone who threatened stock or personnel had bought himself a one-way ticket to a Boot Hill, without a marker to commemorate his wasted life.

Pickering hoped it wouldn't come to that, but if it did . . . well, it was nothing that he hadn't done before.

I HATE THIS DAMN snow," Jaime Ybarra said.

"You never saw it in Chihuahua?" Mariano de la Cruz inquired.

"One time, high up in the Sierra Madre Occidental," Jaime answered. "And I hated it back then. Same thing today."

"It slows the herd down," Mariano said. "Maybe it's easier to get their horses, then."

"One of their cowboys almost caught Amos last night."

"Maybe you wish they had?"

Ybarra shook his head. "Not yet. We still need the horses. Without money in hand, it's all for nothing."

"I doubt he'll try to take them while it's snowing.

Some of these fools would get lost and wander off to freeze or starve."

"On top of which, the gringos will be more alert when weather blinds and deafens them."

"More waiting, then," said Mariano.

"We have time, *ese*. The herd cannot go far."

"But they have us outnumbered more than two to one."

"I don't count the cook or his helper. Did you know the gringos call him Pequeña María?"

Jaime and Mariano had been riding at the rear of their short column, but Ybarra saw another of their number coming back now, drawing closer through the snowfall.

"Quiet!" he cautioned de la Cruz. "It's Gretzler."

"Damn spy," Mariano swore, spitting onto the snowy ground.

Gretzler was smiling when he reached them, but Ybarra didn't trust his show of friendship. "Everything all right back here, hombres?" he asked.

"As fine as—how you say it—frog's hair?"

"That's one way of putting it. You had me worried. Thought maybe the cold was getting to you."

"We're fine," Jaime replied. "*Gracias* for your kind concern."

Beside him, Mariano had the good sense not to laugh, although he raised a hand to mask his smile, feigning a breath to warm his fingers.

"You're welcome," Gretzler said, without a hint of irony. "Might want to close it up a bit so we don't lose you, coming up on dusk."

"Sí, *jefe*," Jaime answered. "After you."

As soon as Shelby's back was turned, Ybarra glanced across at Mariano, raised a hand, and drew its index finger left to right across his throat.

That brought a smile from de la Cruz as they followed Gretzler on the northbound trail toward a horizon none of them could see. The gray day streaked with white closed in around them, drawing closer, until Jaime felt that he was riding down a tunnel to some unknown destination, his surroundings screened from view on every side.

It must be an illusion, he supposed, that they had found themselves upon a road descending into hell. A stray line from a book he'd never read, but must have heard somewhere, perhaps in church, echoed unbidden in his mind: *Abandon hope all ye who enter here.*

THE SNOW STOPPED falling close to sundown, not that Bishop had a chance to see it with gray clouds obscuring the distant west. One minute, flakes were swirling as they had all day, and then they petered out as if someone had closed a window high above and kept the storm from dumping any more on top of them.

It wasn't long before Bill Pickering rode back along the column, passing word that Mr. Dixon had selected campgrounds for the night. The tallgrass was exposed to some extent, with snow and slush around its roots, but ample for the herd to graze on overnight. On top of that, the boss had found a stream, name unknown, that wasn't frozen over, a feeder of the larger waterway they'd have to ford on barges.

"One change," Pickering announced, before he moved on. "Mr. D needs four men on each shift tonight, with the poor visibility and all. Figure on wolves and whatnot being hungry in the cold. Don't hesitate to drop one if you see it. Just call out to warn the camp after you fire."

"Will do," said Bishop, hoping he could pass another night without having to use his guns.

Graham Lott rode up about five minutes later, calling out, "O ye of little faith!"

"How's that?" asked Bishop.

Whipping off his hat and waving it toward dark storm clouds, the preacher said, "My weather prayer! Looks like I got an answer after all."

"One possibility, I guess," Bishop replied.

"I guess that makes you Doubting Toby," Lott said, grinning with a strained fervor.

"I tend to think of weather as a thing apart. It comes and goes. Snow starts and stops. Same thing with wind and rain, twisters and drought, whatever."

"All part of the plan," Lott said.

"Maybe he'll clue us in on that someday."

"It's in the Good Book, plain for anyone to see."

"I don't recall spring blizzards, but I might have missed that chapter."

"Bill told you about the added guards tonight?"

"He did." The foreman's first name sounded funny, coming from Lott's mouth. Some people, Bishop knew, aspired to bosom friendships that they never quite attained.

"Which shift are you on?" Lott inquired.

"I didn't ask. Reckon they'll tell us over supper, same as always."

Lott nodded. Said, "I'd better get a move on, then. We've got another mile or so ahead to where Rudy and Mel are setting up the camp."

"I'll see you there," said Bishop, hoping that he wouldn't be assigned to the same watch as Lott. There'd be no time for Lott to bend his ear, of course, but even so, he didn't need distractions while he was on guard, the memory of last night still fresh in his mind.

A herd of cattle is composed of many individuals, but there are times when it behaves as if responding to a single mind. Bishop knew they were nearing camp when the longhorns in the vanguard slowed, then stopped entirely, fanning out to let the rest crowd in behind them, covering the prairie for a range of fifty yards or so from east to west, and more or less the same from north to south.

Some may have seen and smelled the nearby creek, or else the chuck wagon, with woodsmoke rising from its stovepipe. Bishop wondered if their bovine brains rebelled against the smell of roasting meat, or if they took it all in stride, oblivious.

He finally decided that it didn't matter, either way.

WE SHOULD BE safe here," Amos Finch advised his men. "Make sure you cut some brush and build a screen for that campfire and keep the noise down. Even on a night like this, it travels."

Shelby Gretzler trailed him to the copse of limber pines where they'd tethered their animals. "When are you riding up on them?" he asked.

"I'll eat first. Let 'em have a couple hours to relax and post their guards. I want the lookouts bored and sleepy when it's time."

"Unless it snows again tomorrow, they'll be coming up on the Canadian," Shelby observed. "I know a guy runs barges over to Missouri there."

"A friend of yours?" Finch asked.

"I wouldn't go that far. Was living with his sister for a little while, until she run off with a snake-oil salesman. He knows well enough he shouldn't cross me."

"How long since you've seen him?"

"Going on a couple years, I'd say."

"But he'll remember you?"

A nod and smile from Gretzler. "If he don't, I'll have to whip his ass again and help remind him."

"Fair enough."

"So, what's the plan, Amos? The rest keep asking me."

"I haven't made my mind up yet," Finch said, keeping his voice down, glancing at his other riders grouped around a crackling fire. "I'm thinking if it snows again and they sit out a day to rest the herd, we'll grab their mounts tomorrow night. If they move on and cross the river, that should take most of the day. They won't get far without another overnight. We'll get your guy to ferry us across and come up on them unawares."

"You want me to, I'll fill the others in," said Shelby.

Amos thought about it, shook his head. Replied, "Not yet. The two amigos might try something premature, before we pick up the remuda. Tell 'em I'm still undecided and you couldn't get it out of me. They ought to swallow that."

"Okay. But if the Mexicans get antsy . . ."

"Then we'll handle it, and anybody else who sides with them."

"Right." Gretzler considered that, adding, "You know the two of us can't make off with the horses on our own."

"It shouldn't come to that," Finch said. "But if it does, we'll think of something else."

"And these boys?"

"Buzzards have to eat, the same as anybody else."

Shelby nodded. "Just one more thing before you head out."

"Yeah?"

"Say that we follow them across. That puts us on the wrong side of the river, running from a bunch of drovers madder than an old wet hen."

"I thought about that, too," Finch said. "You ever heard of Willow Grove?"

"Nothing that comes to mind right off," Shelby replied.

"It ain't much of a town, but it's across the line there. Something like a couple hundred people and some scattered farms. We make it there with extra mounts, should be no trouble selling them."

"No law around?"

"There wasn't, last time I passed through. If they've hired someone in the meantime, we can reason with him."

"Right." A knowing smile. His sidekick sniffed the air and told him, "Coffee's on. You want a cup or two before you go?"

"Sounds like exactly what I need," Finch said, and trailed him toward the fire.

CHAPTER FOUR

Bishop was coming off his watch at midnight when the sky released more snow. It kept up until sunrise and beyond, when Mr. Dixon made a judgment call to keep the herd in place and hope the weather broke next day, their seventh on the trail.

Around midafternoon Toby saw Graham Lott in earnest conversation with Bill Pickering. The preacher held a Bible in one hand and gestured with it while he blathered on a mile a minute, doubtless filling in the foreman on his weather prayers. Avoiding the two, Bishop stopped off for coffee at the chuck wagon, exchanging pleasantries with haggard-looking Rudy Knapp.

"Sandwich?" Mel Varney asked, over his Little Mary's shoulder.

"Don't mind if I do," Bishop replied, then thanked Mel for a slice of pork on buttered bread.

From there, he walked to the remuda, shared a little of the bread with Compañero, and stood talking to the Appaloosa while he finished off his sandwich. Was he imagining that Compañero's dark eyes gleamed with understanding as he spoke?

Maybe. But he expected no reply and Compañero offered none, turning his full attention to the powder-dusted tallgrass sprouting up around him.

Most days on a trail drive are packed with chores, whether it be riding herd, checking equipment, helping watch the remuda, or collecting any scattered trash around the camp to feed their fire. Today, aside from Bishop's hour with Floyd at the remuda, he found the downtime tedious, wishing that they could resume their northbound trek.

The snowfall tapered off again about an hour prior to suppertime. When Bishop eyed the clouds, he saw them breaking up and scudding off eastward, perhaps to dump their next load somewhere over Arkansas. He wasn't counting any unhatched chickens yet, but while the drovers ate their pork and beans, Bill Pickering passed by to fill them in.

"Hoping we've seen the last of that white stuff," he said. "If it holds off till breakfast, we'll be moving up to the Canadian. We've got a full day on the river, ferrying the steers across, so we'll be camping in Missouri overnight, then moving on. We've lost a day already, and we can't afford too many more."

When he was done and left them, Pastor Lott called out across the fire to Bishop, smiling like he'd won a jackpot at the poker table. "See? What did I tell you? Prayer, son. Prayer!"

A couple of the others, Gorch and Odom, laughed at Lott's expense, but most ignored him. Bishop settled for a shrug and went back to his supper. He was scheduled for first watch, with Courtwright, Thorne, and Hightower, and was craving another cup of coffee first, before he put his hours in.

If he'd been a praying man himself, he might have

asked Whoever for a quiet night on guard. No shadows unidentified, no sense that he was being watched and measured up as a potential threat.

Nothing but your imagination, Bishop told himself, and not for the first time. He usually trusted anxious feelings that came out of nowhere, but in this case he was willing to admit an error. Happy to admit it, even, if that meant the drive could carry on untroubled once they made it to Missouri's soil, still better than two hundred and eighty miles below St. Louis.

Call it four more weeks after a boating day tomorrow, if they suffered no more interruptions on the trail. It was a hope that he could cling to, even if he couldn't guarantee it coming true.

So, why did Bishop feel like he was waiting for the other shoe to drop?

THE MEN WERE waiting up when Amos Finch returned to camp, Reed Dyer speaking up to ask him: "Well? What now?"

"Nothing tonight," Finch answered, face deadpan while Dyer and Earl Mullins rolled their eyes. The Mexicans just stared at him, waiting. "Unless the snow starts up again, they're bound to start their river crossing first thing in the morning. That should take most of the day."

"And what do we do then?" Bert Fitzer asked.

"We wait a spell and follow 'em across. Shelby's acquainted with the ferryman. We catch up with 'em after dark and do it then or wait another day if they're too skittish. Give 'em time to settle down and drop their guard a bit."

"Meaning they have to settle down from almost catching you?" Jaime Ybarra asked.

"Fact is, they *didn't* catch me," Finch replied. "But

if you've got a need to jump the gun, go on ahead. Take someone with you. Maybe Mariano? We can watch and see how well you make out."

"No, thank you, boss. We do it your way, just like always, eh?"

"That's music to my ears, *muchacho*. We'd all hate to lose the pair of you."

Dyer snickered at that and Mariano shot a warning glance his way. If looks could kill, Finch reckoned Dyer would be gutted on the spot.

"All settled, then," Finch said, to break the tension. "Get some rest, and if you're drinking, make damn sure you have a clear head in the morning. We're not cursing anyone who's soapy-eyed and seeing snakes. If anybody can't keep up, we're leaving him behind."

Shel Gretzler trailed Finch to the spot where Amos had his bedroll, several yards removed from their companions and the campfire. Once they had moved out of earshot, Gretzler said, "You're right about Jaime and Mariano. I wouldn't trust either one of 'em to bring in washing off the line."

"They seemed all right at first," Finch said. "But now . . . We can't keep watching 'em around the clock."

"Tomorrow settles it," Gretzler agreed. "If they don't try a move before then. Maybe—"

"I see where you're going," Finch said, interrupting. "But if we take care of 'em tonight, the others might jump sideways. If we wind up fighting five instead of two, I want to pick a better time and place. Without the horses, this whole thing has been a waste of time."

"You want me to, I'll have a quiet word with Bert and Earl? Beef up the odds."

"Leave it alone, Shel. Like as not, our two amigos would get wind of it, and who knows what they'd do?"

"Okay. I'm keeping my LeMat under my blankets just in case."

Shel's big LeMat revolver was a French creation, one of roughly fifteen hundred shipped to the Confederacy for the War Between the States. Its cylinder held nine .42-caliber rounds, while a shorter smoothbore barrel underneath the main one chambered a twenty-gauge shotgun shell. Ten shots in all, the last one spitting buckshot pellets for a bloody coup de grâce.

"Sounds like a good idea," Finch said as Gretzler turned back toward the fire.

THE WEATHER HELD come morning, the clouds mostly dispersed to eastward overnight, and when the sun made its appearance for the first time in two days, it cast the plains in rosy hues. It was the kind of daybreak where a man might wake up feeling optimistic, but the weariness induced by cold and wasting yesterday kept Mr. Dixon's hands in a subdued mood overall.

The lone exception to that rule was Pastor Lott, too cheery for his own good, acting sprightly as he stowed his gear in Varney's chuck wagon, then praying over breakfast with a special thanks to God for moving out the snow.

A couple of the other hands lowered their eyes, muttered "Amen" when he was done, but most just dug into their food, getting a head start on the slackers. Bishop was among those chowing down without attending to devotion, and he caught Lott peering at him over beans and sausage with a faintly pained expression on his face.

No convert here, he thought, and raised his laden fork in a salute that wasn't meant as mockery but felt that way.

Tough luck. He had accommodated Lott their first week on the trail, but someone had to take the starch out of the preacher's holier-than-thou routine before he talked a donkey's leg off, or irritated certain drovers to the point where they might have it in for him.

It would be meant in fun to start with, but Bishop had seen how that went. Smirking jokes evolved into insults, someone started playing stupid tricks, and spiteful words turned into fisticuffs or worse. That was the last thing any trail drive needed, when the drovers should be working in collaboration toward their common goal: delivering the herd and getting paid.

Beyond that, some might cleave to jobs around the Circle K, while others took their leave and never saw the rest again. Bishop hadn't decided what he'd do yet. With another six weeks still ahead of them, at least, it was too soon to say.

One thing, though, he could be thankful for. The night had passed without any alarms of predators or prowlers bothering the herd. He hoped their luck would hold in that regard, but Bishop had his doubts. A sense of something wicked coming down the road nagged at his mind and wouldn't let him go.

Bishop resolved that he'd be ready to react the minute something happened—*if* it happened—and do anything within his power to protect the herd, safeguard his various companions on the trail, and look out for himself at the same time.

A tall order, perhaps, but it felt better than the job he'd recently escaped from, killing for his daily bread to keep a prairie feud alive and going strong.

According to Bill Pickering, they had another eight miles still to go before they reached the southern bank of the Canadian River. Call it another day of driving longhorns over ground where snow would soon be melting, turning topsoil into muck. They would arrive too late to start the ferrying across, which meant in turn another day already spoken for tomorrow.

Bishop knew such things were built into the schedule for a cattle drive, the drovers' primary concern being delivery of the animals alive and well, with no significant weight loss. The irony of that didn't escape him, but he understood that ranching was a business first and foremost, operated for a cattleman's profit, not out of any love for animals per se.

So far this year, from what he'd read in newspapers, prime steaks sold in most butcher shops for twenty cents a pound; the price increased dramatically if you were dining in a stylish urban restaurant. A roast came in at fourteen cents a pound, while cheaper cuts of stew meat could be purchased at a nickel per.

A single longhorn weighing in at two tons, give or take, might yield five hundred pounds of meat, plus liver, tongue, and other bits. Figure two thousand head in Mr. Dixon's herd, if all of them arrived at the St. Louis stockyards, and the math began to give Bishop a headache, so he let it go.

A tidy sum, no matter how you sliced it, but each steer abandoned on the trail meant less cash for the boss, after he'd settled with his drovers and accounted for expenses. Mounting his snowflake Appaloosa, Bishop put that bloody business out of mind and focused on the trail ahead.

H OW FAR TO go yet?" Shelby Gretzler asked.
"I'd say another nine, ten miles," Finch said. "No need to push it. They'll be tying up the barge all day. Might even drag into tomorrow morning if they're slow about it, but they won't like splitting up the herd, what with a river in between them."

"And I'm guessing that their horses will be first across."

"Wouldn't surprise me," Amos said. "Might need

'em on the far side, if the stock starts getting antsy from the crossing."

"Likely split the drovers up as well."

"Makes sense. The more steers cross, the more hands need to cover them on the Missouri side. Some of 'em will be riding back and forth until they're sick to death of it."

"Wearing 'em down," Shel said. "That's good for us and bad for them."

"The way I like it," Finch agreed.

"I'm with you," Gretzler said. "You know that, right?"

Finch nodded, making sure his face reflected nothing. Asked his sidekick, "Are you sure about this Chalmers character?"

"He'll go along. Might need to let him have a little something when he's coming off a long day."

"How about his life?"

"Should do it. We can likely make it over altogether on a single run, then what's he gonna do?"

"Could talk," Finch said.

"Who to? The nearest U.S. marshal's in Fort Smith, some eighty miles away."

"Unless one of 'em is patrolling in the territory."

"Well . . ."

"I don't like thinking of them on our trail. They can go anywhere. Borders don't even slow 'em down."

"I know." Gretzler was coming around toward seeing sense.

"It's better if he can't say anything to anybody."

"Yeah. I guess."

"It might be easier, coming from you."

"I doubt he'll feel that way."

"Don't ask him, then. Just get it done."

"Sure, Amos. Don't give it another thought." Not loving it, but relenting.

"Good man. A little something extra in it for you when we dump those other two."

"Full extra share?" asked Gretzler, perking up a bit.

"Why not?" Finch said. An easy promise, coming out of Jaime's end, or Mariano's.

"Done," said Shel. "Thinking about it now, I never cared much for him anyway."

THERE WAS A single barge on hand for crossing the Canadian. It seemed in decent shape, though Bishop couldn't say the same about the ferryman.

He was a ratty-looking fellow, with a sunken chest and cheeks. Some missing teeth, and those that showed were nothing to write home about, tobacco-stained, looking worn down to stubs almost. Lank hair was thin across the boatman's pate, head mounted on a stalk-like neck, with shoulders sloping down to skinny arms. If he had bathed that month, you couldn't prove it by his smell.

For all of that, he had sharp eyes and quick hands fidgeting around the buckle of his gun belt, with a big Colt hanging backward on his left hip. From a distance, Bishop recognized the weapon as a British Beaumont-Adams double-action, made in London, one of many shipped to the Confederacy while the war was on. Once a muzzle-loading piece, most still in use had been converted to fire metal cartridges, .44-caliber, although the manufacturers in London called them .442s.

It would be deadly in a practiced hand, but Bishop knew its cylinder would only hold five rounds. Supposing that the ferryman had devilment in mind—and the ability to herd two thousand longhorns on his own—he had to know he wouldn't stand a chance against fourteen armed men.

Bishop hung back and watched as Mr. Dixon parleyed with the ferryman, discussing price. He watched the boatman take a stub of pencil from his sagging shirt's breast pocket, with a folded piece of paper, eye-balling the herd and jotting down some calculations, handing them across to Mr. D. The boss examined what he'd written, seemed to make a counteroffer, which the boatman mulled, then nodded to accept.

Some cash changed hands, not much, but likely a down payment with the balance due when all the steers had safely crossed. The ferryman tucked it into a pocket of his grubby blue jeans and retreated toward his barge.

The boat was thirty, maybe thirty-five feet long and nearly square, say twenty-some-odd feet across. Stout rails guarded its sides to left and right, while fore and aft were open, save for twin ropes tied between the side rails, like the velvet ropes Bishop had seen inside a fancy Dallas restaurant one time, used to keep customers in line while they were waiting for a table. Toby hadn't been among those diners, rather working as a bouncer on a boozy New Year's Eve, but he remembered well enough.

The trick today was guiding steers aboard the barge, already skittish when they felt it bobbing underneath their hooves, and not allowing them to gore each other accidentally with their long horns. Drovers got the beeves situated with some difficulty, one riding in front, another at the stern, leaving the farrier to man the barge's rudder.

For propulsion it depended on a thick rope strung from shore to shore, which the Circle K men hauled with gloved hands, drawing the barge across a few yards at a time. The boatman steered and kept a long pole handy for corrections if the river seemed intent on sweeping them away downstream.

It was a slow process and had to be repeated ninety-nine more times. The barge went over heavy laden and came back empty and a good deal faster, though the ferryman had to do all the work himself on the return trip.

That would be most of their day, and Bishop found himself anticipating his turn at the crossing, doing something more than sitting on his snowflake Appaloosa, making sure the dwindling mass of longhorns didn't break apart and wander off. The good news: once they'd all gotten across and pushed the herd another mile or two northward, it would be time to camp.

And the bad news: He'd have to watch the darkness close around them once again.

Surprised to see you here, Shelby," said Gilly Chalmers, reaching up to wipe his bristly chin free of tobacco juice.

"I get around," Gretzler replied.

"Uh-huh. You always did."

"So, what's the price for crossing over?" Amos Finch inquired.

Chalmers considered it, squinting one eye. Dusk crept across the prairie, moving west to east, its shadow slowly overtaking them.

"Four bits apiece," the ferryman decided, finally. "Dime each for horses."

"Jesus, Gilly." Shelby shook his head.

"Now, now," Finch interposed. "That ain't so bad. How 'bout we say five bucks and keep the change for working overtime."

The boatman smiled at that. "Suits me right down to the ground," he said. Then, looking sly, "You fellas wanna catch that herd, you're gonna have to spur your mounts."

"What herd is that?" asked Gretzler, trying to sound casual and falling short.

"I'll make believe you didn't say that, Shel. Insulting my intelligence when we've been friends so long."

"Looks like he's got our number," Finch remarked. "Can't pull the wool over this fella's eyes."

"No, sir," Chalmers agreed. "And tryin' it's a plain old waste o' time."

"Maybe we ought to add another five-spot to the fare and call it quits."

"I like the way you calculate, mister," Chalmers replied.

"Then call it done, soon as we're all across."

"We'd best get started, then," Gilly allowed, "afore we lose the light."

The boatman watched them board his craft, giving directions as they moved up toward the rope in front, without crowding too close. None of their number felt a need to test the river's chill by plunging in.

The trip across used up most of a quarter hour, with Ybarra and his buddy Mariano hauling on the bow rope, Gilly Chalmers steering from the stern. Finch kept a tight grip on his grulla gelding's reins until they'd reached the other side and had their feet on solid ground once more.

"Ten dollars, then," the boatman said when they were all onshore. "And I can say it's been a pleasure doin' business with ya."

Finch turned to Shelby Gretzler, nodding, his eyes dropping to the Arkansas toothpick Gretzler wore sheathed on his gun belt. They had already talked about the need for quiet, no gunfire to spook the drovers who were just a couple miles ahead of them and likely settling into camp.

"I've got you covered, Gilly," Gretzler said, pulling

the knife as he advanced. Departing sunlight glinted from its twenty-inch-long blade.

"Hey, now!" yelped Chalmers, going for the backward pistol on his hip, but he was too slow reaching for it, bitter recognition dawning in his rheumy eyes.

Gretzler buried his blade, or most of it, under the boatman's chin, piercing the turkey wattle there and thrusting up through his soft palate to his brain. Blood trickled from the wound at first, with Gilly going stiff, held upright by the penetrating dagger, then a gush of crimson came as Shelby gave the knife a twist and yanked it free.

Chalmers folded and dropped before them like an empty suit of clothes. Gretzler took time to wipe his blade and knife hand on the dead man's shirttail, sheathed his dagger, and stepped back, checking to verify that no gore had been spattered on his own clothing.

Ybarra swore, crossing himself.

"That ought to shut him up," said Gretzler, sounding grim.

"Had to be done," Finch told the rest of them.

"No skin off me," Reed Dyer said. "He wasn't worth five dollars, much less ten."

Shel looked as if he might respond to that, then let it go, shot Finch a look, and shrugged.

"All right, mount up," Finch ordered. "I want to catch up with them in time to scout the layout one last time before we make our play."

S UPPER WAS PORK and beans with bread again, no great surprise since fording the Canadian had used up most of Varney's time for cooking. Toby Bishop guessed they wouldn't have another taste of beef unless one of the longhorns died or came up lame and had to be put down, at which point nothing would be left to waste.

All things considered, he would rather make do with the fare on hand and spare the herd from any losses that would eat away the final payoff in St. Louis. Not that higher profits for the Circle K would lead to any bonus being passed along his way. No extras would be accrued, no handouts for performance of a job the drovers already agreed to carry out.

He had first watch, along with Isaac Thorne and Paco Esperanza, their numbers cut back to three per shift now that they'd put a river in between themselves and whatever Bishop had seen, heard, or imagined two nights back.

He wished it were that easy to forget, and yet . . .

Better to guard against a nonexistent danger than to blithely forge ahead on hope and wind up with your throat cut in the middle of the night.

Maybe the river was enough to see them free and clear until they reached Missouri's border, but he wasn't counting on it. If a herd of longhorns managed crossing over, with its drovers and chuck wagon, anybody could. The ferryman who'd served them would be open to all comers if he halfway trusted them and they had ready cash in hand.

That was the Wild West for you. Anyone who had the wherewithal to travel and put up a show of self-defense could get along, until some obstacle loomed up and blocked the way for good. Bishop had managed to avoid that sticky end so far, but everybody's string ran out sometime, someway.

The trick was doing unto others before they did unto you.

He wouldn't want to argue that with Pastor Lott, but Bishop couldn't think of any reason why it might come up between them. Every cowboy on the drive

knew what might be expected of him if the herd was
threatened. Anyone who balked at that would likely
wind up buzzard bait, or at the very least get sacked
and sent packing with no recourse.

That wasn't Toby Bishop. He'd already proved that
he could pull a trigger when the chips were down, and
if that wasn't clear to Mr. Dixon yet, it might be soon
enough.

CHAPTER FIVE

Their eighth day on the trail came off without a hitch and stayed that way until late afternoon, when one steer unaccountably collapsed and died. Cursing from Mr. D aside, that meant a feast of beef for supper after Mel Varney and Rudy Knapp were finished butchering the carcass, roasting half of it, and salting down the other half to keep awhile.

The night was undisturbed, despite a distant pack of coyotes baying at a waxing gibbous moon. None of them ventured near the herd, at least not during Toby Bishop's watch with Leland Gorch and Whit Melville.

The next morning, bright and early, they were on the move again while the chuck wagon lagged back, Varney and Knapp cleaning their cookware and stowing it away before they caught up with the herd.

Bishop could almost feel his spirits lighten, the gut instinct that he'd learned to trust relaxing as they edged within two weeks of crossing the Missouri borderline. He knew that wasn't any guarantee of safety, but at least the Show Me State had laws in place and men with badges to enforce them. True enough, Missouri had spawned countless thieves and killers starting well before the Civil War. Some of them, like the James and Younger brothers, still ran wild across the countryside, earning their native soil another sobriquet—"Mother of Bandits"—but their victims, if they managed to survive, knew where to find a county sheriff or town marshal when they needed one.

Whether or not the lawmen would respond was something else entirely. Bishop knew from personal experience that some were bought and paid for by the very felons they were meant to jail or hang. He guessed that had gone on for as long as people flocked together, choosing armed men to defend them, always hoping that they hadn't made a critical mistake.

On balance, he considered, maybe life was better on the open prairie, where an individual dealt with his problems as they came and settled them for good.

Day nine felt much the same, with clear skies overhead and nothing but a brisk north wind to conjure memories of the unseasonable snow that had delayed them earlier. Huddled in coats and scarves, the drovers pushed on through the tallgrass country, reckoning the miles they'd come without a marker to confirm their progress, leaning forward in their saddles to defeat the wind and hurry sundown on its way.

More beef and beans for supper, with potatoes for a change, and Bishop drew the middle watch with Boone Hightower and Deke Sullivan. By now, he knew that "Deke" was short for "Deacon," something pointed out by Pastor Lott over one of their meals. That hadn't won him any points with Sullivan, if looks were any guide, but when did self-anointed preachers spare a thought for anybody's privacy?

Bishop had no reason to think that he'd face any trouble on his shift tonight, but riding herd was just like anything in life. You took it one step at a time, while trying not to stumble on the path and sprain an ankle, much less fall and break your neck. With any kind of luck, while you were doing that and looking out for number one, you might just have a shot at helping someone else.

The night was fairly quiet as he started his first circuit of the sleepy herd. Somewhere above and to his right, northward, Bishop heard the high-pitched calling of a bat in flight. Farther away and somewhere east of him, a screech owl hooted twice and then fell silent.

Sunrise was just a few hours away. He would hold on to that and get what sleep he could after his turn on guard. Tomorrow was another day and there was no telling what it might hold in store.

A MOS FINCH HAD done his best to get the others ready, telling them exactly where the cattle drive's remuda was secured and talking through his plan until most of them gave up listening and started looking bored. His second in command caught Finch's eye and shrugged as if to say, *What can you do?*

Not much, when you were working with a bunch like this.

Amos knew outlaws, being one himself. He fully understood their short attention span and their need for action, whether they were pulling off a job or winding down once it was done. With most of those who followed him, he guessed inherent simplemindedness was part of it, together with a restlessness that marked them for a life outside polite society.

Still, shouldn't they at least care about whether they survived the night or not?

While they were mounting up and getting squared away, Finch took Gretzler aside and told him, "Focus on the horses, picking up as many as we can. These other sap heads want to fart around and get themselves killed, I don't give a damn."

"Leaves more for us," said Shelby.

"And I like the sound of that," Amos replied.

They rode through darkness for almost an hour before picking up the sounds and smell of longhorns, slowing down on their approach as they moved upwind from the herd. His final scouting trip had found three drovers working the night watch, random patrols around the herd's perimeter, one or another of the cowboys crooning to the sleepy steers.

That helped. A singing watchman, tired already from a long day on the trail and looking forward to his bedroll, couldn't count on registering subtle noises in the night. Unless one of the rustlers got balled up and let excitement run away from him, they had a chance to pull this off without a fight.

So why did Finch's brain whisper to him, *Good luck with that*?

Maybe because he knew the men who rode with him, and wouldn't trust five out of six to put their boots on in a rush without confusing left for right.

It started well enough, his riders slipping in toward the remuda, the horses huddled up some thirty yards from the chuck wagon and the dying campfire, nice and quiet. Over all the nights he'd scouted them, Finch hadn't seen a drover with the tethered horses overnight, and guessed that their wrangler put his trust in their proximity and caught up on his shut-eye when he could.

It was the same tonight. Shel Gretzler and Reed Dyer closed in on foot and started loosening the horses' tethers, joined by others in the task of leading them away while Finch sat back astride his grulla, Henry rifle in his hand and covering the camp.

He'd just about allowed himself to think that they might pull it off without a hitch when someone shouted from inside the covered chuck wagon, "Wake up and grab your rods! Poachers are after the remuda!"

Scrambling and cursing in the camp then, bedrolls cast aside, as Amos saw his plan start going up in smoke.

TOBY BISHOP HEARD the warning call and pegged the voice as Rudy Knapp's as he swung his Appaloosa through a tight half circle back toward camp. Some of the longhorns close at hand lowed and stirred restlessly at the alarm but they weren't truly frightened yet.

The last thing anybody needed now was a stampede.

He picked out a group of strangers—half a dozen horsemen, maybe more—preparing to abscond with the remuda, each thief clutching at the reins of eight or nine spare mounts. The horses didn't fight it, all accustomed to repeated handling by riders at the Circle K. They wouldn't break away without some help, and Bishop was the lookout closest to them presently.

Someone fired a pistol shot from camp, whether as an alarm or aiming for the rustlers, Bishop couldn't say, nor did he care. He unsheathed his rifle from its saddle boot and nudged his snowflake Appaloosa into motion toward the theft in progress.

One of the thieves fired off a shot toward camp, another miss, the gunman's aim spoiled by excitement. Bishop lined up on the weapon's muzzle flash but didn't have a chance to fire before the gang put spurs to horseflesh and began to gallop off, their living loot raising a cloud of dust to shield them.

Trusting his mount to hold a steady course, Bishop shouldered his Yellow Boy—already cocked—and sighted down its barrel toward the fleeing rustlers. It was dicey, picking out one of the thieves at random, trying not to kill or wound any of the remuda's animals, but Bishop managed, picking out a wide-brimmed hat and leading it a yard or so before he fired.

The .44 slug flew downrange at more than one thousand feet per second, found its mark, and spilled the rider from his saddle to the ground, head over heels. It looked like some of the stolen horses trampled over him, which might have seemed poetic justice if Toby had had time to think about it.

As it was, he had his hands full.

Another of the rustlers must have spotted Bishop when he fired. A pistol blazed out of the rising dust, the slug not even coming close. That was the problem with most gunfights. Whether on horseback, racing death, or standing face-to-face, combatants often let excitement spoil their aim and get them killed or maimed.

Bishop didn't return the *pistolero*'s fire, not wanting to drop any of the stolen horses accidentally. Instead, while Whitney Melville and Deke Sullivan rode in to join the chase, he sought and found the rustler he'd brought down.

The guy was obviously dead when Bishop reached him. Wan moonlight prevented Toby from examining his wounds, a bullet hole among them, his body lying twisted and broken up in places where the mounts he'd aimed to steal had galloped over him. Another of the thieves had snared them on a ride-by, the remainder of the gang escaping westward, shrouded from his view by darkness as they blazed a trail to who-knewwhere.

More shooting in the distance now, but likely all in vain.

As far as he could tell, the five or six surviving thieves had made their getaway.

* * *

BILL PICKERING WAS on his feet, pistol in hand, within five seconds after Rudy Knapp shouted his warning to the camp. A few feet distant, Gavin Dixon nearly matched his foreman's speed, clutching his Colt Open Top revolver, free hand wiping sleep out of his eyes.

"Goddammit, Bill! What's going on?" he rasped, his voice still catching up.

"You know as much as I do," Pickering replied. "Somebody's after the remuda."

Dixon started past him, barefoot, risking injury from stones and stickers.

"Gav, your boots," said Pickering.

"To hell with 'em," his boss spat back. "We lose those horses and we're screwed."

He had a point. Leaving his own boots where they stood, Pickering caught up with the raging master of the Circle K and fell in step beside him, wincing at the punishment his soles absorbed.

Gunfire was crackling in the night now, and the herd was getting antsy. If they had to suffer much more racket, some of them might start to run, followed by scores or hundreds more in nothing flat.

"Stop shooting, dammit!" Dixon bawled at no one in particular. "You're risking a stampede!"

A final pistol shot rang out, somewhere westward, then the other drovers who'd been sleeping thronged around their leader and his foreman, some without their pants, only a few with boots on, but all carrying their guns, most of them jabbering.

"Shut your pieholes!" Dixon snapped.

That silenced most of them, but Graham Lott, the nonstop talker, couldn't help himself. "What's happened, Mr. Dixon?"

"Rustlers raided the remuda," Dixon answered. "What I see from here, they got all but the two from the chuck wagon and the ones on watch."

"Speaking of those on watch," said Pickering, "here come Melville and Sullivan."

He couldn't tell if the two mounted drovers looked more furious, guilty, dejected, or a mixture of all three. As they drew closer, he asked them both, "Where's Bishop, then?"

"Back there," Deke answered for the two of them, jerking a thumb over his shoulder toward the dark. "He dropped one of them others."

"Dead?" asked Dixon.

"Yes, sir. Well, I'm pretty sure."

"Mel, fetch a couple lanterns," Dixon told their cook, who rushed off to obey. Then, to the rest, "Get your boots and trousers on. Be quick about it!"

"We might as well do likewise, Mr. D," said Pickering.

"All right. I want to see this stiff, though. Time's a-wasting."

Both were shod, with more drovers joining them as they set off on foot toward where they'd spotted Toby Bishop, still astride his mount and peering at a body on the ground. Mel Varney ran to catch up with them, carrying two lanterns, while his Little Mary trailed him with a third swinging beside him, casting freakish shadows on the ground.

WHEN THEY HAD put the best part of a mile between themselves and the longhorns, Finch reined his grulla to a halt and waited for the five other survivors of the gang he'd started out with to form up around him, with the animals they'd stolen from the drovers' camp.

Before he had a chance to tell them what his plans were, Mariano de la Cruz was whining at him, "They kilt Jaime, *ese*. We should go back right now and wipe 'em out."

"Do that your own self if you wanna," Mullins answered him. "Me, I don't plan on joining your amigo."

"*¡Maldito cobarde!*" Mariano sneered at Earl, and spat into the tallgrass.

"What's that mean?" Mullins demanded. Then, addressing all of them, "What did he say?"

"I said—"

Finch shot him before Mariano could translate the insult, one slug from his Schofield clearing de la Cruz's saddle while his mount shied for a heartbeat, then stood still again. Reed Dyer grabbed the reins of the half a dozen horses Mariano had released when he went down.

"All right now, listen up," Amos commanded, gun still smoking in his hand. "We're two men down and we've still got a job to do. Who else is in a hurry to check out?"

Finch didn't have to check on Gretzler. Shelby knew enough to draw his Frontier Bulldog double-action .44 without being instructed to, not pointing it at anybody yet but ready, just in case.

When no one answered him or made a move to slap leather, Amos relaxed a bit but didn't let his guard down one iota. "Now we've cleared up that misunderstanding, anybody miss Jaime or Mariano? Answer up now, if you do. We can work something out."

"Not likely," Fitzer said.

Dyer chimed in quickly, saying, "Hell, I never liked 'em anyhow."

"More for the rest of us, looks like," said Mullins, making it unanimous.

"You read my mind," Finch said. "I've got a town

picked out for selling off these animals. It's nine or ten miles west of here. With any luck, we should be getting there around sunrise."

"And what about them drovers?" Mullins asked.

"That's another thing," Finch said. "We left behind two horses from the wagon team, plus three the lookouts had. You all know they'll be coming after us, but we've got two advantages."

"Which are?" asked Dyer,

"First, unless they've got an Injun with 'em, they can't track us in the dark," Finch said. "And second, none of 'em knows where we're going. If we do our business quick enough, we can be in and out before they start sniffing along our trail. They get to town and find their animals, that puts them in a pickle when they try to get 'em back. They'll have to haggle for 'em and they may not even manage it."

"Which puts us free and clear," Gretzler chimed in.

"Or if we feel like resting up," Finch said, "why not? There won't be any marshal where we're headed. If we want to, shouldn't be too hard to meet the drovers and be done with 'em for good."

"Use the town like it's our fort, you mean?" asked Fitzer.

Mullins answered before Finch had a chance. "As long as that fort ain't the Alamo," he quipped.

That made the others laugh and Amos went along with it. His ears were ringing from the shot that finished Mariano off, but he was used to that. Sharing their mood for now, he said, "I reckon we can go one better than them boys with Colonel Travis." When their laughter over that trailed off, he asked them, "Any other questions?"

None came back at him, so Amos turned his grulla west and said, "Alrighty, then. Let's ride."

* * *

H E'S DEAD ALL right," Bill Pickering observed.
"A Mexican," said Estes Courtwright.

Several pairs of eyes shifted toward Paco Esperanza, who pretended not to notice. Toby Bishop kept
his focus on their trail boss and his foreman, both men
peering up at him.

"You finished this one?" Dixon asked.

"With help from the remuda's horses," Bishop said.
"Can't tell you if my .44 beefed him or they finished
him off."

"Works either way," said Pickering. "His mama
wouldn't know him now."

"When are we going after them?" asked Graham
Lott, clearing his throat to mask a tremor in his tone.

"No point to that before daylight," Dixon announced.
"Dark as it is, we'd lose 'em in the tallgrass." Looking
up at Bishop on his Appaloosa then: "You see which
way they went, Toby?"

"Due west to start," Bishop replied. "No telling if
they changed directions after I lost sight of them."

"Supposing they split up?" asked Curly Odom.

Abel Floyd answered that one. "Not how it works,
most of the time. A gang steals horses, they don't want
to sell 'em off in little bunches, three or four apiece.
Makes better sense to lump 'em all together, get a better price, then divvy up the cash."

"We can rule out a local farmer buying them," said
Dixon. "Nobody around here would have that kind of
money lying idle. Figure on a town that has a livery or
livestock dealer."

"You expect to find a town out here, boss?" Isaac
Thorne inquired, not quite a challenge.

"I could almost point to it," Dixon replied. "A place

called Willow Grove, unless they've changed the name since last year."

"I been through there," Odom said. "There ain't much to it, as I recollect. A dry goods store, saloon, and whorehouse, plus a blacksmith and a livery. Say ninety to a hundred people, if you don't count the outlying farms."

"No law, then," Courtwright said, not asking.

"No lawmen anywhere," said Dixon. "Lest a U.S. marshal happens by, running some errand from Fort Smith."

"We're on our own to get the horses back," said Pickering, "and settle with the maggots who run off with 'em."

"I'd put the horses first," Dixon amended. "I can't see a way to get along without 'em. As to punishment . . . well, let's just wait and see what happens after that."

Bishop was fine with the come-what-may approach. He'd added one more stiff in red ink to his ledger, and while running up a higher score wasn't his goal, he wouldn't shy away from it either.

Not if it meant wasting his time, drawing no pay.

And damned sure not if it meant getting killed himself.

"How long till sunup, then?" asked Odom. "Anybody know?"

Pickering checked his pocket watch by lamplight. Said, "Four hours and a quarter yet."

"First thing," said Mr. D, "we need to check the herd for any strays and bring 'em back to join the herd. With saddles left behind and the chuck wagon horses, we can field five men. Mel, get an early breakfast done so everyone can finish up by sunrise. Once we've got the light we need to track these sonsabitches, I don't want to waste it."

Everyone pitched in from there, collecting gear and

stowing it, Varney and Rudy Knapp lighting their stove
and getting busy on the food, Dixon and Pickering
mounting the two chuck wagon horses to assist in scour-
ing the night for strays. As far as sleep went, none
among the trail hands could have managed any now.

Four hours and a bit, before those still with horses
hit the trail, loaded for bear.

Bishop never considered lending anybody else his
Appaloosa. He'd already drawn first blood against
their enemies and he would see it through.

No matter what the end might be.

T HE HELL IS Willow Grove, a bunch of trees?" Earl
Mullins asked.

Instead of pointing out that there were countless
things Mullins had never heard of, soap likely among
them, Finch replied, "People who live there claim that
it's a town. I'd say a village is more like it."

"What's the difference?" Reed Dyer asked.

Bert Fitzer answered back: "Are they redskins? Do
white folks live in villages?"

Finch let that go, saying, "The census takers differentiate by size. I couldn't tell you what the cutoff is, but
a town is bigger than a village, and a city's bigger than
a town."

"Still just a bunch of stores and houses, right?" said
Mullins, seeking clarity.

"Not many of 'em, though," Shel Gretzler said.

"The only one we care about will be the livery,"
Finch said, hoping to put a lid on it.

It seemed to work, with Dyer asking him, "How
much you think we'll pocket altogether?"

"With any luck, between one-fifty and two hundred
dollars each."

Reed made a show of counting on his fingers, screwing up his face while multiplying in his head. "About five thousand, is it?"

Amos didn't bother to correct him. "Pretty close, I'd say," he answered.

"So, about a thousand each, then?"

"You're forgetting my end, which is two-thirds," Finch reminded him.

"Oh, yeah." A sullen tone that time, less optimistic. "So about nine hundred each, then."

Fitzer snorted. "Reed, how far you get in school?"

"What school?" Dyer replied. "I learned my numbers playing cards."

"You win much?" Mullins ragged him.

"Bet your ass I do!"

"Next time you want a game, make sure to deal me in."

More laughter, mostly at Dyer's expense. Finch interrupted that, telling them, "Listen up. I need to fill you in on Willow Grove, mostly what you should do and *not* do, once we get there."

When he had their full attention, Finch went on. "We know they've got no lawman, but that doesn't mean they're helpless. Most of 'em that live there keep their guns close, just in case of trouble. Absolutely *do not* stir up any needless trouble, mixing with the locals, and ignore their women, whether they be wives, daughters, or grandmas. What we wanna do is sell these horses, not touch off a fight that gets us killed."

"By sodbusters?" The question came from Mullins.

"Sodbusters, shopkeepers, or whatever," Finch replied. "Expect a fight if you go looking for it and remember that we'll be outnumbered thirty-odd to one, not counting kids."

"So, we're just riding in and out?" asked Dyer. "How about a decent meal, maybe paint our tonsils some or catch hold of a hooker?"

"They've got a saloon with women there, but they likely make their own pop skull and I won't vouch for it. As for the painted cats . . . well, let's say you'll have good odds of catching clap."

"Can't even stop and get a decent steak, I guess?" Bert Fitzer groused.

"I'd focus on the money first," Gretzler chipped in, "and worry about chow or booze once we unload these animals."

"Shouldn't take long, a town that small," Earl Mullins said. "Hell, everybody needs a decent horse out here."

"Let's wait and see," Finch cautioned. "Take it one step at a time."

CHAPTER SIX

THE HUNTING PARTY had five members. Mr. Dixon rode one of the chuck wagon's two horses, a rose gray, with Isaac Thorne aboard the other one, a tobiano. Toby Bishop rode his snowflake Appaloosa, with Whitney Melville on a pinto mare, Deke Sullivan riding a yellow dun.

Bill Pickering had argued that he should tag along, but Dixon shut him down, insisting that his foreman stay behind to mind the herd and double-check for any steers that might have strayed due to the gunfire overnight. The foreman didn't like it, but he was a man who followed orders, ranking duty over happiness.

Bishop had wondered if the rustlers meant to lay a false trail, riding west when they were harried out of camp, then settling on a new direction once they'd put some ground between themselves and hot pursuit. It wasn't all that hot, of course, four hours and a smidgen wasted while the Circle K team waited on sunrise.

In that amount of time, Bishop supposed the rustlers could have traveled ten miles easily, escaping to the north or south, as well as west.

But it was not to be.

Tallgrass might be resilient, but it still bore traces of some forty horses passing over, holding steady on a westbound course. They'd never found the animal left riderless when Bishop shot its owner, but at least it wouldn't starve while wandering across the prairie. Predators might ultimately take it down, but that was out of Bishop's hands and he dismissed it from his mind.

After some ninety minutes on the raiders' trail, Dixon declared, "Looks like they made for Willow Grove, all right."

"You reckon they've got friends there, boss?" asked Sullivan.

"I doubt it," Dixon said. "The burg is no great shakes, I grant you, but the folks that I had dealings with seemed fairly honest. I can't see them laying out the welcome mat for straight-up outlaws."

"How about buying a bunch of rustled horses, boss?" asked Thorne.

"They might do that," Dixon allowed. "Last time I passed through there, a blacksmith name of Leon Moon was owner of the livery. He traded stock from time to time. A deal like this, I guess he might not ask too many questions."

Melville cleared his throat. Began to say, "But if they're sold already—"

"Then we take 'em back," said Dixon, interrupting him. "Lawman or no, he can't buy stolen animals and hope to profit from it."

"What about the 'good faith' angle, boss?" asked Sullivan.

"To hell with that," Dixon replied. "What's mine is mine unless I sign a bill of sale."

"With all respect," said Sullivan, "this Leon Moon

might take a different view of it. The other folks in town might side with him."

"And that would be their last mistake," said Dixon. "I don't reckon it'll come to that, but be prepared for anything."

Bishop stayed out of it, but he was thinking back to Mason County and the Hoodoo War. He'd wandered into that thinking the sides were cut-and-dried, right versus wrong, but when the gun smoke cleared, he wasn't all that certain.

If they had to fight a town he'd never heard of till last night, how would it end?

"How many people are we talking in this town?" asked Sullivan.

"Can't say for sure," Dixon replied. "My guess would be about a hundred sixty, seventy. Might run as high as two."

Could be a lot of guns, thought Bishop. *And a lot of innocent civilians caught in a potential cross fire.*

Still, it was too late now. Dixon was right about the stolen horses. If they couldn't fetch them back, Bishop saw no way for the drive to forge ahead or turn back, either one. Five drovers—whittled down by two unless they ditched the chuck wagon and starved themselves— would never keep two thousand steers in line with all their other hands on foot.

They only had one course of action open to them: moving straight ahead and taking back what had been stolen from them overnight. If blood was spilled, he reckoned there'd be plenty of it.

DAYLIGHT WAS NEARLY an hour old when Amos Finch led his surviving bandits into Willow Grove. The town wasn't fully awake yet, but some of its folks were getting on about their business, mainly at a restaurant called Slawson's for the breakfast service, while some early-rising merchant types were sweeping off their wooden sidewalks.

"That's the livery, off to your left," Finch said. He nosed his grulla toward the rambling structure, checking out the town's main street meanwhile, noting the broom-wielders who paused to eyeball new arrivals in their midst, trailing more horses than five men would likely need.

No women on the street so far, and he supposed the doxies at the town's saloon—the Gem, according to its sign—were doubtless in their cribs and sleeping off last night. None of the men he saw so far were packing guns where Finch could see them, but that didn't make them harmless by a long shot.

Cautious faces, not quite sullen, but he figured that could change in nothing flat if they felt threatened by a pack of seedy newcomers.

The livery's large door was standing open, muffled noises emanating from inside. Finch recognized the sound of horses being fed and raised a hand as they approached the building, signaling for his companions to rein up. Around them, fanning off to either side, the stolen mounts were glad to rest but eyed the men who'd snatched them with uneasy eyes.

Finch called out to whoever was awake and laboring inside the livery. "Hello in there! We've got some stock to sell."

A young man—more a boy, late teens at most—came out, wearing a union suit under bib overalls. He had a shock of red hair topping a round, freckled face and blinked once at the sight of strangers on his doorstep, with three dozen horses sweaty from their all-night run. He singled Finch out as their seeming leader, asking, "Help you?"

"You can take this cavvy off our hands at a fair

price," Finch said. "Turns out we've got more than we need, and less cash than we'd like."

"I hear you," said the kid. "Wish I could help you out."

"What say?"

"I ain't the owner here. That's Mr. Moon, the blacksmith. He's off on early visits to a couple of the farms this morning. I can't make an offer on your animals unless I wanna end up roasting in his forge."

Finch fought an urge to scowl, asking the boy, "When will your boss be back, you think?"

"He didn't say, but shoeing nags on two spreads that I'm sure of, it could take 'im three, maybe four hours out and back."

"Dammit!" Earl Mullins muttered, loud enough to wipe the kid's smile clean away.

Finch cut a sour look at Earl, then turned back to the boy. "Three hours sounds all right, I guess. You got someplace where we can stash these ponies while we're waiting?"

"Ain't got room for all of 'em inside, but there's a fenced corral out back. You wanna leave 'em there awhile, I reckon it's okay."

"They could use feed and water," Finch advised.

"The water's not a problem, mister. Oats or hay, now, I'd be forced to ask the going rate."

"Which is?"

"Four bits a day," the boy replied.

Finch worked out the arithmetic, which came to eighteen dollars. Frowning, he asked, "How about we write that off against the selling price?"

"You'd have to work that out with Mr. Moon. I can't say what he'd offer you, supposing that he wants to buy at all."

"Well, let's just water them for now, then. If he wants to deal, your boss can feed 'em on his own dime."

"Fair enough," the kid replied. "No promises about that sale, remember."

"I heard you the first time," Amos said.

The kid walked them around to the empty corral and held the gate open until the animals were all inside, then closed and tied it up. The rustlers left their own mounts with the rest, still saddled, hauling long guns from their scabbards as they left the pen.

"You want to, I can let you put your rifles in the livery."

"No, thanks," Finch said. "I find it's best to keep 'em close at hand."

"Okay, then."

"Is the grub at Slawson's any good?" Shel Gretzler asked the boy.

"It's fair, I'd say, in quality and price. Unless you're hauling cookery and want to build a fire back here, it's pretty much the only place in town."

"Guess it'll have to do," Finch said, and tucked his Henry underneath his left arm, leading his companions back onto the dusty street.

GAVIN DIXON MISSED his brindle mare but didn't mind the rose gray from the chuck wagon too much. At least he had his old familiar saddle under him, with his Winchester '73 in its boot to his right, muzzle angled down and toward the front.

He figured that might come in handy yet, before the day was out.

The rifle was chambered in .38-40—a .401-caliber cartridge in fact, with a bottlenecked case, hurling an eighty-grain slug downrange at just a smidge over eleven hundred feet per second. It weighed nine and one half pounds, had a twenty-four-inch barrel, and a striking range of right around one hundred yards.

For close-up fighting, though, his weapon was a Remington Model 1875 revolver, essentially a takeoff on the '58 percussion model with its cylinder bored out to fit metallic cartridges. It took proprietary .44 Remington Centerfire ammo and Dixon could hit what he aimed at within decent range, be his target a rattler, coyote, or man.

As to the prospect of gunplay over the stolen horses, he had a divided mind. Dixon was furious at being robbed, wasting more precious time, and would have liked to see the rustlers swing for it, no question. On the other hand, the prospect of a shooting match with outlaws, risking drovers in the process, put him off.

His mind was mulling over that, when Whitney Melville, scouting up ahead, called back, "We've got another dead one here."

They rode up on the corpse, sprawled in the tall-grass flecked with dried blood-colored rusty red.

"Another Mexican," said Sullivan. "You reckon that means something, boss?"

"Who knows?" Dixon replied. "Maybe losing the first one put him out of sorts and they got tired of it. Maybe he didn't like their leader's plan and bit off more than he could chew. It doesn't matter now."

"Except we're after five, not six," said Melville. "Closer to dead even."

With the emphasis on "dead," thought Dixon, but he kept it to himself. Instead, he noted, "And again, no horse."

"The first one likely ran off when his rider dropped," Thorne said. "This one, I'd suspect the others took it with 'em. One more to unload for cash, after they divvy up his gear."

"Whatever," Dixon answered. "Killing this one slowed them down a mite. Not much, maybe, but every minute helps us. Willow Grove it is."

"And if they ain't there, boss?" asked Sullivan.

"We might be up the creek," Dixon allowed. "Reckon we'll have to wait and see.

So they rode on westward, with the sun climbing behind them in a washed-out sky.

F INCH LED HIS men into Slawson's, following the smell of frying bacon that had reached them from a half block out. He counted eight diners ahead of them, most paired at tables, two men at the counter with their backs turned toward the street.

But not for long.

Strangers appearing in their midst surprised the locals, all eyes turning toward the unfamiliar faces, some blanching as curiosity contended with alarm. Five customers in gun belts might not raise eyebrows, but five men toting rifles, with revolvers tied down to facilitate fast draws, was something else again.

A waitress with her dark hair tied back from a round face, set atop a decent body, did her best to smile as she approached them, saying, "Gentlemen, good morning! Welcome to Slawson's." She couldn't help but glance down at their long guns dangling, but she held the smile.

"Don't fret about the rifles," Finch advised her. "We've got business at the livery and didn't want to leave them sitting unattended."

"Probably a good idea," she said. "My name's Corinne, and you-all must be new in town."

"Just passing through after we have a word with Mr. Moon."

"His day for visiting the farms," she said. "Well, just a second while I get a couple tables pushed together for you, and—"

"We'll help with that," Finch said, passing the job to Mullins with a nod. It took less than a minute, by

which time the other diners seemed to reckon there
was no cause for alarm and turned back to the breakfast plates in front of them.

Corinne directed their attention to a chalkboard on
the wall, with menu items listed in block capitals with
reasonable prices written after them, then came back
with five coffee mugs and filled them from a pot, not offering a choice of milk or sugar. Three of the rustlers
leaned their rifles up against a nearby wall, the other two
depositing their long guns on the floor beside their chairs,

The menu offered fried or scrambled eggs, sausage
or ham, with johnnycakes and fried potatoes on the
side. The weary riders mixed and matched their favor-
ites while Corinne wrote them on a little pad of paper
and retreated toward the kitchen once again. Each
man was using pocket money for his meal and the supply of cash was running low.

Eyeing the small change in his hand, Gretzler said,
"This looks like my last meal, lest we turn to stealing
chickens."

"All we have to do is wait for this Moon fella," Finch
replied.

"However long that takes," Fitzer grumbled.

"If we get outta here too early," Finch said, "we can
always stop at the saloon."

"Sounds better," Mullins told them. "But I only got
enough scratch left for one, maybe a couple beers."

"Until we sell the horses," Finch reminded all of them.

"And if this Moon don't want 'em? Then what?"
Dyer asked.

Finch shrugged. "Then we persuade him. Did you
ever know a businessman who didn't keep some cash
on hand?"

That got them laughing, Corinne smiling with them
as she brought their plates, although she'd missed the
joke.

* * *

Y OU GOT A fix on how much longer, boss?"
The question came from Whit Melville, a couple of the drovers murmuring to show that time was on their minds as well. Not sounding angry yet, but all aware that they should have been on the trail by now, another mile or so behind them and the herd.

Without checking his timepiece, Gavin Dixon said, "I make it right around another hour, more or less."

"I hope it's less," Deke Sullivan averred. "Them boys we left are gonna have a rough time managing the steers on foot."

"And once we get to Willow Grove," Thorne added, "we still gotta hope we find the horses and whoever took 'em."

"Horses first," Dixon reminded all of them. "I want to settle up those responsible for this as much as you-all, but our first priority is taking back what's ours."

He put it that way, rather than saying "what's mine," in hope that they all shared some sense of investment in their mission, even though most of the stolen animals belonged to him alone.

"Still wouldn't mind some payback, boss," said Sullivan.

"Let's play the cards we're dealt and see what happens," Dixon answered.

"Sure," Deke said. "Just like you say."

"But just in case," Dixon allowed, "before we get to town, all of you need to check your hardware. Wouldn't do to come up short of rounds if we start making smoke."

Dixon knew he shouldn't have to tell them something elementary like that, but didn't reckon they would take offense at him stating the obvious.

And if they did, to hell with 'em. A boss gave orders and expected them to be obeyed.

He glanced across at Toby Bishop, sitting easy on his snowflake Appaloosa, nothing on his face or in his attitude to show he was the least bit edgy. Dixon was impressed with Bishop, how he'd dropped one of the thieves last night and waited with him while the other hands on watch pursued the dead man's cronies. Killing was a part of cattle-driving sometimes, and he had no further doubts concerning Bishop's personal efficiency in that regard. Conversely, Toby didn't act like he'd enjoyed it either, telling Dixon that he wasn't hiding loco underneath a bland façade.

More like a soldier, Dixon thought, able to turn it on and off—although he'd known some veterans of the last war who'd come back home . . . "infected" was the best word he could think of for it, so inured to killing that they missed it when they came back to civilian life.

Some learned to bury that inside. Others went out looking for any lame, half-baked excuse to draw more blood.

To live through that—and live *with* it, managing not to lose yourself—decided if a man could face the future without breaking down.

And when they got to Willow Grove, Dixon supposed they'd put that standard to the test.

WITH BREAKFAST CLEARED away and paid for, Amos Finch led his surviving riders out of Slawson's and surveyed the sunlit thoroughfare of Willow Grove.

The burg's half-dozen stores were open now and doing business, a sodbuster's wagon passing by, the bed heaped up with surplus squash and ears of corn. A woman moving down the sidewalk with a basket on one arm, her long calico dress buttoned up to her neck, shifted her eyes away from them and said, "Excuse me, gentlemen," as she edged past them, carefully avoiding any accidental contact.

They all watched her go. When she was safely out of earshot, Mullins said, "You know, I reckon we could take this whole damn town."

"And I already told you once why that's a bad idea," Finch said. "We're here to sell them bangtails, not to get ourselves all shot to hell and gone."

"I heard you," Mullins answered back. "But still . . ."

"Still nothing. Who else wants a drink?"

They all agreed to that and started ambling toward the Gem. It was the town's only two-story building meant for human occupancy, since the livery's top floor was nothing but a hayloft.

The saloon was open when they reached it, causing Finch to wonder if it ever closed. There was no telling when a townsman or a traveler might crave a drink or something else to get him through the night, the latter need accommodated in the cribs upstairs.

The downstairs bar was quiet as Finch pushed in through its batwing doors, letting the men behind him guard against a rude slap in the face. Off to their right, an old upright piano waited silently for someone to sit down and tap its keys. Two wagon wheels suspended from the barroom's ceiling had been rigged up with three lanterns each to light an area complete with card tables and chairs, no players presently in evidence.

The bartender was somewhere in his forties, Finch decided, gray shot through his beard and thinning hair on top. He sipped coffee while swabbing down the bar's top with a well-worn towel and met them with a smile that stopped short of his eyes.

"G'morning, gents," he said. "What can I pour you?"

"Beer for me," Finch said, and nodded toward his men. "We're going dutch."

"One beer it is," the barkeep said, pulled it from a tap, leaving a foamy head on top. "Ten cents."

Finch slid a dime—his next to last—across the bar and waited while his men counted out change for their own drinks, whiskey or beer, and one of each for Gretzler, who was obviously feeling flush or extra-thirsty.

"This your place?" Finch inquired, after a sip of beer.

"Not hardly," the barkeep replied. "I manage things most times, but Mr. Grover Botkin owns the joint."

"Is he around, by any chance?"

"Sleeping upstairs. He keeps long hours, generally comin' down at noon or thereabouts. If you've got business with him, though . . ."

"Nothing like that," Finch said. "Just curious by nature."

"New in town." It didn't come out sounding like a question.

"Passing through. A little business at the livery before we move along."

"Silas goes round the farms Mondays and Fridays, if they need 'im."

"What we keep on hearing," Finch said. "Two, three hours was the last bid."

"That's about his usual. If you've got time to kill . . ."

The barkeep glanced up at the ceiling overhead, beyond which cribs were waiting, likely still smelling of last night's sweaty times.

"I reckon not, right now," Finch said. "We ought to keep an eye out for the blacksmith."

"This'll likely be his first stop when he's done," the barman said. "He likes to wet his whistle after shoeing horses or whatever. Says it helps him cut the dust after his rounds."

"Makes sense," Finch answered. "Maybe we'll get lucky. In the meantime, set me up again."

* * *

WELL, THERE SHE is," said Gavin Dixon. "Willow Grove."

There wasn't much town to admire from half a mile due east, and Toby Bishop thought the settlement would be no more endearing when they got up close. One-story buildings for the most part, with a couple of them one floor taller, casting longer shadows on the town's main street.

Dixon produced a spyglass, drew it out full length, and raised it to one eye. Bishop waited with all the rest, to hear what he'd say next.

"That building closest to us on the south," their trail boss said at last. "The one looks like a barn. It's got a pen of horses out in back."

"Yours, boss?" asked Sullivan.

"That's my surmise. I'll need a closer look to cinch it, though."

"We'd best get on, then," Sullivan suggested.

"Right." Their trail boss stashed the spyglass out of sight and made a clucking sound to set his rose gray moving forward.

Bishop, watching out for any human figures moving on the town's main drag and spotting no suspicious persons from afar, began deep-breathing, centering himself for whatever might lie ahead.

"So, what's our play, boss?" Isaac Thorne inquired.

"Ride straight up to the livery first thing," Dixon replied. "Confirm those horses came from our remuda, then talk to the man in charge."

The stable owner's sex could safely be assumed, in Bishop's view. He had no doubt a woman could administer a livery, keeping its books and all, but its persistent scut work would be dirty, sometimes backbreaking. Man's work, traditionally, though a wife and mother in these parts would also be acquainted with toiling around the clock.

Bishop guessed it was fifty-fifty that the rustlers had already sold their stolen horses and moved on. That meant Dixon would either have to buy them back at an inflated price, or else try taking them by force.

And if the gang was still in town . . .

Bishop hoped he wouldn't have to kill any more men today, but when in his life had wishes ever come true?

CHAPTER SEVEN

LEON MOON WAS forty-one years old and feeling every hour of it. Never mind that he was one of Willow Grove's most prosperous inhabitants. All things were relative and being well-to-do in a backwater prairie town would make him marginally poor if he lived someplace like Houston or even Galveston, in Texas.

Blacksmiths rarely starved, and he made money from his livery as well, but when he offset the expenses, Moon could count on feeling pressure mount inside his head until he had to take a slug of red-eye to relax.

Now, fresh off his morning farm rounds, he had Billy Campbell in his face, talking about strangers stopping by with animals to sell.

"They're back in the corral, sir," Billy said.

"The men, or horses?"

Billy laughed at that and slapped his leg, seeming to think the joke was better than it felt on Leon's tongue. "Horses, o' course! The men are downtown somewhere."

Can't have gone too far, Moon thought. *There ain't much town.*

He walked around to the corral and found it full. Moon counted forty animals in all, six of them saddled, all the rest bareback.

"Six strangers, was there?" he asked Billy.

"No, sir. Only five, but with another saddled mount. That cream dun over yonder."

"And how many were they after selling?"

"Didn't say, boss. All but what they rode in on, I guess."

"Would I be feeding 'em?"

"No, sir. I made that clear, regarding price. The man in charge said only water till he'd talked to you."

"That's something, anyway. Now where—"

Before Moon could complete the question, someone called out from the street. "Hello! Is anybody here?"

Now what? Moon asked himself, and started back around the livery to see. He hadn't recognized the voice, but when he saw five mounted men with hands close to their pistols, all of them were strangers save for one, whose face stirred something in Moon's memory. He tried to fetch a name, but it eluded him.

"You looking for your friends?" Moon asked the man with the familiar face, who seemed to be in charge.

"Our horses," said the front man. "Stolen out of our remuda last night, maybe ten miles west of here."

Moon told it plain. "I've likely got 'em. Strangers dropped 'em off while I was out on rounds. Looking to sell 'em, Billy says."

"Yes, sir," Campbell chimed in, prepared to say more until Leon shushed him with a glance.

"We'll need 'em back," the mouthpiece for the new arrivals said. "Hoping that won't cause grief for any of us."

"Not on my part," Moon replied. Then asked, "Do I know you?"

"Name's Dixon," said the talker. "I was through here sometime back."

"That's where I've seen you."

"Passing by, maybe. I never stopped in here before."

Moon nodded. Said, "I've got no problem handing back your animals, since they ain't cost me anything so far. Can't say about the six with saddles that was left off with 'em. I suppose the men that brought 'em may be wanting those."

The man called Dixon frowned at that and asked, "You know where we might find those fellas now?"

Moon turned to Billy Campbell, saying, "Well?"

"Yes, sir," Billy replied. "I sent 'em down to Slawson's for some breakfast. That was right around three hours gone. Unless they're real slow eaters . . . well, they ain't been back yet."

"Slawson's," Dixon said. "All right, then. Can we leave our horses here while we go have a look?"

Moon figured Dixon and his friends had more than simple looking in their minds. "Okay by me," he said. "How long you plan to be?"

"Long as it takes," Dixon replied, "and not a minute more."

A MOS FINCH FINISHED his second beer and told the bartender, "That's it for me."

His men picked up on that and started quaffing off their drinks as well, paying their tabs from pocket change.

"Back to the livery?" Earl Mullins asked.

Finch checked his pocket watch. Replied, "Seems close enough to me. If Moon ain't back yet, we can wait down there."

Shel Gretzler reached the batwing doors ahead of him, was halfway through when he stepped back, saying, "Whoa!"

Finch shouldered past him and didn't have to ask what the problem was. Five grim-faced men with rifles in their hands were coming down the middle of the street on foot, from the direction of the livery. Finch ducked back, hoping that they hadn't seen him, turning to his boys.

"Looks like we're out of time," he said.

"Already?" That from Reed Dyer.

"Couldn't swear to it," Finch answered, "but I'm no believer in coincidence."

"Made better time than I expected," Shelby said.

"What are we gonna do?" Bert Fitzer asked, just short of whining.

"Can't say if they're coming here directly," Finch replied. Not quite an answer, thinking fast.

"If they're not," said Gretzler, "we could line up at the windows here and hit 'em as they pass."

The bartender had seen them huddled by the exit. Now he asked them, "Everything okay, gents?"

"Mind your business," Finch instructed him.

"Hey, now . . ."

Finch raised his Henry rifle, asking, "Have you got a scattergun behind the bar?"

"Um . . ."

"Yes or no. Your life depends on it."

"I do. Yes, sir."

"Show me. Nice and slow, now."

The bartender did as he was told, produced a double-barreled twelve-gauge sawed off at both ends, no more than fifteen inches overall, counting the rounded pistol grip. He set it on the bar and stepped away, his hands raised shoulder-high.

"And nothing else?" Finch prodded.

"Just an ax handle."

"We won't need that. Shel, fetch the shotgun."

Shel did as he was told and brought the sawed-off back to Finch as he addressed the barkeep one last time.

"You need to go upstairs and wake your boss. Be quick about it and make goddamned sure you both come back with empty hands. If I see either of you heeled, I'm gonna stick this twelve-gauge where the sun don't shine and blow you inside out."

"Yes, sir!"

"Earl, keep 'im company. You have to kill 'em, try 'n keep it quiet."

Mullins trailed the barkeep to the stairs and then up to the second floor.

"The rest of you," Finch said, "get back from them windows. "We ought to see 'em passing in a minute. If they go by, let 'em."

"What the hell?" Reed Dyer challenged him. "You mean—"

"I mean exactly what I say. That kid down at the livery steered us to Slawson's. If he's done the same for them, it buys us time."

"For what?" Shel Gretzler asked.

"To make this joint the best fort that we can," Finch said.

WALKING THE LENGTH of Willow Grove to look for rustlers went against the grain for Toby Bishop, but he didn't have a better plan in mind. Passing each shop along the way between the livery and Slawson's restaurant put him on edge, particularly going past the Gem saloon, with all those windows, any one of which could prove to be a sniper's nest.

It wasn't his call, though. He'd seen nothing that

warranted him contradicting Mr. Dixon's plan or Billy
Campbell's information as to where he'd sent the rustlers for a meal.

And yet . . .

He carried the Winchester Yellow Boy in his left
hand, muzzle pointed to the ground, while his right hand
rested on the curved butt of his Colt. Wherever danger
came from, Toby would be ready to respond in kind.

And danger *would* be coming, that was certain. The
rustlers had to be somewhere in Willow Grove right
now. It was ridiculous to think they'd left their horses
at the livery, then wandered out of town on foot.

The question foremost in his mind, and in the minds
of his companions: Were the men they sought aware
that Gavin Dixon and his drovers had arrived in Willow Grove? Were they alert and watching even now?

And if they were, why hadn't Dixon and his men
come under fire so far?

No mind reader, Bishop couldn't supply an answer
to that question. He could only follow Mr. Dixon on
their trek downtown.

They reached the only restaurant in Willow Grove
and passed inside. Its diners, nine by Bishop's count,
looked up to see the new arrivals eyeing them and
broke off conversation while a waitress came to greet
them on the threshold.

"What a day this is," she said. "More strangers than
I've seen in months!"

"Where did the others go, ma'am?" Dixon asked.

"They finished up and left, sir. Are you looking for
them? Maybe friends of yours?"

"I'd have to answer 'yes' and 'no,'" Dixon replied.
"We missed 'em at the livery and didn't pass 'em on the
street just now. I don't suppose you'd have an inkling
where they went?"

"Well, now, I do believe one of them mentioned going to the Gem," she said. "You will have passed it on your way."

"We did. Roughly how long ago was that, ma'am?"

"Nigh onto an hour, I suppose. They stayed for breakfast first. If you-all want something to eat—"

"Maybe another time," Dixon replied. "I'd hate to let 'em leave without us telling 'em hello."

Before she had a chance to speak again, Dixon turned to his men and said, "Looks like it's time for us to visit the saloon."

H ERE'S WHAT YOU'RE GONNA DO," said Amos Finch. "Whatever gets y'all outta here the quickest," Grover Botkin said, "without nobody getting hurt."

"No one that doesn't have it coming," Finch amended.

"So? Just spell it out."

"You need to stay down here and greet who's gonna come along here pretty soon."

"And tell 'em what?" asked Botkin.

"You won't have to think about that. Just glad-hand 'em like you would with any other customer, then duck before the lead starts flying."

"Mister, this here place is all I got. Can't you just meet 'em in the street and settle whatever's between you-all?"

"Not in the cards, my friend. Do as you're told, and you should be all right, together with your barkeep and your working girls. Try any tricks . . ."

"I hear you, mister."

Shel chimed in, saying, "Mind you, no guarantees about your barroom, pal. It might end up showing some wear and tear."

To that, Botkin made no reply. Instead, he asked Finch, "Where are you and your men gonna be?"

"Upstairs feels right," Finch said. "A layout like you got here, I prefer to hold the high ground."

"And leave me with the mess," said Botkin.

"Thank your lucky stars that I don't make you part of it," Finch answered back.

"I feel no end of gratitude."

"That mouth of yours is gonna get you hurt someday, old man."

"Fool don't know when to shut his yap," said Gretzler, drawing back his pistol for a swipe at Botkin.

Finch stepped in between them, saying, "Easy, Shel. No need for that. If I came in and commandeered your place of business, you'd be mad as a wet hen yourself."

Beating averted for the moment, Finch then faced the Gem's proprietor. "You wanna keep those teeth and see the sun go down tonight, be smart and just do what you're told. Think you can live with that?"

Their grudging host nodded, then said, "I reckon so."

Then back to Gretzler. "See, Shel? We're all friends again."

"Uh-huh."

"Best check them others and make sure they're all in place."

"On it," Shel said, and started toward the stairs,

"About that bartender of yours," Finch said to Botkin.

"He's my nephew. Lost his parents in a river crossing and I raised him as my own."

"Be a crying shame if something nasty happened to him, now he's come so far along."

"Just leave 'im outta this, all right?"

"You leave him out, old man. Just do your part and make the act convincing. All we need's a couple minutes and you can forget that we were ever here."

Or maybe not, Finch thought.

There was a good chance no amount of time or alcohol would ever wipe this day from Grover Botkin's mind.

T HE CIRCLE K'S men stopped a half block from the Gem, beside an alley's mouth, invisible from the saloon's windows, and Mr. Dixon shared his plan, such as it was.

"We're gonna split up here," he said. "Toby and Isaac, you head down the alley and come at 'em through the back door. Whit and Deke with me. We'll go in through the front."

"We sure they're even in there, boss?" asked Isaac Thorne.

"I doubt the waitress lied to us," Dixon replied.

"Don't mean they didn't lie regarding their intentions, sir."

"I hear you," Dixon granted, "but it's all we have to go on. I can't see them hiding out in one of these few shops."

"Fair point," Isaac conceded.

"So, that's it, then," Dixon said. "They either know we're coming, or they don't, in which case we might still be able to surprise 'em. Getting drunk or laid up with the whores, I'll take whatever edge they give us."

Sullivan replied, "But if they *do* know . . ."

"Then we're walking into shit without a shovel," Dixon said. "Whoever doesn't care to take that chance, step off right now."

None of them budged.

"Right, then. I hope to see you on the other side, men. Failing that, you have my thanks."

Bishop trailed Isaac down the narrow alley, gravel crunching underfoot. No one had bothered locking up the Gem's back door, maybe because its customers might come around at any time, some of the married men in town not fond of entering from Main Street, where the world could see them come and go.

"Get ready," Isaac said, but Toby had his Yellow Boy already shouldered, cocked and aimed to fire over his shoulder as he turned the knob and entered in a fighting crouch.

No shots to greet them, and no hollering to rouse the house. Bishop entered behind his point man, leaving the door open for retreat if it became essential.

They were standing in a short hallway with doors off either side. To Bishop's left he smelled a kitchen where most of the food was fried in grease. Across the way, Thorne tried the other door and bared the clutter of a broom closet. Ahead of them, beyond a curtain made of dangling beads on string, what they could see of the saloon's barroom was empty, lit from overhead by lamps.

Beyond that, Bishop saw nothing and no one, heard nothing except a muted scuffling sound of footsteps overhead, somebody moving on the second floor. He'd never been inside the Gem, but standard layout for a bar and brothel meant bedrooms upstairs for business, maybe an office set behind the bar, an unknown number of employees, male and female, on the premises.

And five armed outlaws who'd be glad to use the hallway innocents as human shields.

Bishop and Thorne eased down the corridor, shoulder to shoulder, stopping just before they reached the beaded curtain. They waited, listening and barely breathing, for a danger signal that would start the shindig.

Half a minute later, Mr. Dixon shoved in through the batwing doors, with Sullivan and Melville coming in behind him. Turning to his right, or Bishop's left, their boss called out, "Is anybody home?"

* * *

Finch used the stubby muzzles of his borrowed scattergun, giving the bar's proprietor a shove between the shoulder blades and hissing at him, "Get out there!"

"Coming right up!" called Grover Botkin as he cleared the office doorway, stepping out behind the bar. "What can I do for you fine gentlemen today?"

Only three gunmen visible in the saloon from where Finch stood, off to the side of Botkin's door and peering through the space between the panel and the jamb. That meant the other two were either waiting on the street outside, or else . . .

Circling around in back. Of course, goddammit!

"We hope to find some customers of yours," one of the new arrivals said. "Just missed 'em at the restaurant, I'm told, so—"

Amos fired one barrel of the twelve-gauge into Grover Botkin's lower back, bouncing him off the bar's backside to sprawl out supine on the polished floor. Finch aimed his second buckshot round in the direction of his enemies but doubted he'd hit any one of them, the way they ducked and dove for cover.

Gunfire suddenly erupted from the second story's catwalk set above the bar and gaming room, one bullet shattering a window facing on the street, another plunking into the upright piano, followed by a snapping, twanging noise of strings and hammers being torn apart. A heartbeat later, three rifles began returning fire from the barroom, one of their bullets buzzing like a wasp by Finch's ear.

He ducked and hunkered down behind dead Grover Botkin's desk, a solid piece of lumber, making ready to defend himself. First thing, he tossed away the useless scattergun and raised his Henry rifle, looking over iron sights toward the larger room beyond, already filling up with gun smoke.

He was cornered, dammit—or was he?

A hasty backward glance revealed a doorway he'd neglected to notice while he was giving Botkin orders in the crowded office, moments earlier. Where did it lead? Finch hardly cared, so long as he could flee in that direction, looking for a better vantage point from which to blast his enemies.

Or just to get the hell out of the Gem and double back to reach the livery. His grulla waited for him there; he could take whatever cash was handy for the road. It meant no profit from the stolen animals he'd risked so much to gain, but that was life.

You won some and you lost some. Ultimately, all was lost.

Cursing underneath his breath, Finch edged back toward the door and cleared it, stepping into the Gem's kitchen area.

G AVIN DIXON SQUEEZED off a round from his Winchester, caught one of the rustlers breaking from one upstairs bedroom to the next in line, and brought him down. No way of telling whether he had scored a killing shot, but when the outlaw didn't rise or start to crawl away, Dixon assumed he must be wounded bad enough to take him out of play.

One down and four to go, if he believed young Billy Campbell from the livery. He couldn't think of any reason for the kid to lie, but had he bothered counting accurately when the gang rode in that morning?

Probably. Six saddled horses, one without a rider on arrival, brought the total down to five. It didn't take a genius to cope with that arithmetic.

So, call it four now, even if the man he'd drilled was still clinging to life.

Melville and Sullivan were keeping up a steady fire, Whit crouched behind the barroom's vertical piano, Deke behind an upturned poker table made of pine that offered less resistance to high-powered slugs than Melville's choice of cover. Neither one of them was wounded yet, but if they couldn't reach the stairs and close in on their elevated adversaries, that could change in nothing flat.

Unbidden, Dixon thought about the herd he'd left behind to run this killing errand, wondering if he would ever make it back again. Presumably, if he was killed, it wouldn't matter to him anymore, but would that mean his life came down to bitter nothing in the end?

To hell with that. Staying alive meant taking each new moment as it came.

If Sullivan and Melville couldn't budge, with Thorne and Bishop nowhere to be seen so far, Dixon decided he would have to rush the stairs himself. Why not?

A few short yards across open floor with three or four men taking potshots at him. What could possibly go wrong?

More to the point, how could he *not* risk it, when failure meant the loss of damn near everything he owned.

No point in calling out to Whit or Deke, alerting their opponents to his plan. Dixon launched from a crouch into a full-tilt sprint, watching the catwalk overhead as he drew closer to the staircase.

A shadow stirred beyond one of the doorways serving cribs upstairs and Dixon winged a shot in that direction, his .38-40 slug peeling back floral wallpaper. Nothing to show for that, but then he reached the stairs and started climbing in a rush, energized by the fight and wondering if that alone would keep him on his feet and moving, should he catch a bullet.

Better not to test that proposition, if he could avoid it.

On the second-story landing, Dixon started moving toward the cribs, no longer running now, taking his time and watching out for ambushers.

A few more steps now, and the enemy would be within his reach.

A NOISE FROM THE kitchen behind him startled Toby Bishop as it was empty when he'd checked it only a moment earlier.

Thorne heard the sound as well, was doubling back when Bishop raised an open hand to stop him, pointing back toward the barroom and mouthing, "Go ahead."

Isaac cocked one eyebrow at him, doubtful, then shrugged and kept on going to the large room that had turned into a shooting gallery. Bishop retreated toward the kitchen door and paused there, listening as best he could without pressing his ear against the door itself.

Why give a lurking enemy the chance to drill him through his head?

The sound of scuffling feet repeated, drawing closer. Bishop took a breath and held it, gave the kitchen door a flying kick, and followed through behind his Yellow Boy, reentering the reek of frying fat and beans.

A man he'd never seen before stood facing him, a Henry rifle in his hands. He didn't say a word, just snapped the gun's butt to his shoulder, index finger slipping through the Henry's trigger guard.

Unlike the Winchesters it had spawned, the Henry had no wooden forestock to protect a shooter's hand from barrel heat in a protracted fight. Beneath the barrel lay its magazine, front-loaded—yet another deviation from the Winchester design—containing fifteen rimfire cartridges, allowing one more in the chamber for a start.

He didn't give the startled outlaw time to fire. As soon as Bishop glimpsed the man and saw he wasn't one of Mr. Dixon's hands, he drilled a bullet through his adversary's throat and slammed him back against the kitchen wall beside the entryway he'd used. The dying man spat blood and triggered off a shot as he slid down the wall, striking a copper pot atop the kitchen's stove.

Bishop considered shooting him again but didn't need to, once he'd seen the light of life wink out behind dull staring eyes. Out in the barroom, half a dozen shots followed his own, then tapered off to nothing.

Who'd come out on top?

He figured there was no time like the present to find out.

Pumping his rifle's lever action, Bishop eased into the corridor and moved down to the beaded curtain that made visions of the barroom shimmer like a fading dream. This time around, though, what he saw as he emerged was closer to a nightmare.

Everyone that he'd arrived with was alive and circling. Bishop saw some blood soaking through Sullivan's left shirtsleeve, but it didn't seem to bother him, and Toby took it for a grazing wound. Raising his eyes, he counted three corpses and saw a spot where someone had crashed through the catwalk's wooden railing. Shifting to his left, he found the last gang member lying in a heap behind the bar, next to an older unarmed man, his back blood-soaked.

"Looks like we're all done here," said Whit Melville.

"Not quite," the boss corrected him. "Let's fetch those horses and get back to work."

CHAPTER EIGHT

B REAKFAST ON THE fifth day of their second week
out from Atoka was the same as usual, with the
addition of some wild mushrooms Mel Varney had discovered when he went off to relieve himself last night.

After ribald joking as to whether he had watered
them himself, he'd certified that they were edible and
fetched a little book out of the chuck wagon to prove
it. Chopped and fried, they'd made a nice addition to
obligatory beans and bacon, with enough left over for
supper or breakfast in the morning.

Since the fight in Willow Grove, the herd had traveled thirty-odd miles farther to the northeast. They
were still roughly a hundred miles from the Missouri
border, but to Bishop's mind, their wasted day had
paid an unexpected dividend. Six horses formerly belonging to the rustlers they had finished off in town
were part of the trail driver's remuda now, with no one
to complain about them changing hands.

They'd left the mess for Willow Grove's inhabitants
to clean up, which mostly meant adding the outlaws

and one of their own citizens to a small cemetery situated west of town. There was no preacher in the settlement, but they had managed to attract an undertaker and a carpenter who built such caskets as the town required.

One thing that never came in short supply was stiffs in need of burial.

And when that wasn't feasible, as Bishop knew too well, nature supplied disposal workers of its own.

He'd given up on counting days that they'd been on the trail. There was no profit to that exercise, but he still had a sense of progress, even when each morning's light displayed more countryside resembling what they'd traveled over yesterday and all the days before. Ranges of hills rose and subsided as they passed, such streams as they'd encountered after crossing the Canadian were relatively shallow and slow-moving.

Overall, if anyone had asked him—which they hadn't—Bishop would have said they were proceeding at a decent pace, putting the miles behind them steadily, advancing toward trail's end and closing in on life's end for the longhorns.

Bishop didn't ponder that eventuality. He understood that steers were raised for slaughter, cows for milking, chickens to provide eggs or appear on Sunday's dinner table. When he thought of death at all, it would be lives that he had personally ended or the friends he'd lost to sudden violence.

And what did he achieve from time wasted remembering the dead?

Nothing at all.

He caught a glimpse of Graham Lott, remembering the prayer that Lott had offered over supper on the day of blood in Willow Grove. Such rituals, Bishop had long ago decided, served the living rather than the dear departed, whether they'd been "dear" to anyone or not.

Didn't the Bible tell survivors—in Ecclesiastes, he believed it was—that while the living know they're bound to die someday, the dead know nothing and have no reward?

The day Bishop first heard that message from a pulpit, he'd surrendered any dreams of heaven, guessing that the end of life was simply that and nothing more: The End.

And since he'd ended a few lives himself, he found that somehow comforting.

If true, that meant he wouldn't spend eternity lounging around on clouds above or roasting in a firepit down below, troubled by people traipsing by and asking why he'd killed them years before, thereby preventing them from marrying and watching kids grow up to spawn grandchildren, using their threescore and ten years or whatever it was, had they survived that long, to see more of the world or make improvements in the little corners they'd inhabited.

As far as Bishop knew, none of the men he'd killed were likely to contribute much of anything to friends or neighbors back on earth.

In fact, he'd likely done the world a favor, putting them to sleep.

B ILL PICKERING GLANCED at the sun and checked his estimate of time against his pocket watch. It logged the hour as 12:15, which meant his educated guess was close enough.

The chuck wagon was serving sandwiches, salt pork on buttered bread, as drovers circled past to claim theirs and moved on to keep the herd in line. The sky above was clear, no threat of any further storms as the day wore on.

They'd lost a full day's travel to the mess at Willow

Grove and left the townsfolk there stuck somewhere between dazed and grieving. Pickering felt bad about the owner of the Gem saloon, but there'd been no way to prevent his murder by the thieves who occupied adjoining slots in Willow Grove's bone orchard.

Pickering was focused on today and on the days ahead—still close to six weeks if their luck held out—until they reached St. Louis. It had seemed a distant vision when they'd left the Circle K, and truth be told, their destination seemed no closer now than when they'd started out.

Trail drives were like that, weeks of tiresome chores and heavy labor, interspersed with frantic action when some unexpected danger put the herd at risk. Most of the work would classify as boring, and it left a man bone-weary overnight, but Pickering would take the dull times gladly over crises where the stakes were life and death.

"A penny for your thoughts," said Gavin Dixon, riding up behind him on his brindle mare.

"You wouldn't get your money's worth on that deal," Pickering replied.

"Mind blank, is it?" the boss inquired.

"Drifting, more like."

"Still wishing that I'd let you go along to Willow Grove?"

"No, sir. I understand your reasoning, and you were right about me sticking with the herd."

"Worked out all right," said Dixon. "All you missed was shooting, and you've seen enough of that."

"I guess."

In fact, he'd seen enough to last a lifetime, but that didn't mean he'd be exempt from any killing yet to come.

"Maybe we dealt with all our bad luck early on," said Dixon. "Could be free and clear from here on in."

"I'd like to think so."

"But you don't."

"I don't take anything for granted, Mr. D. For me, a day's done when I wake up in the morning without staring trouble in the face."

"Guess I can't fault you there," Dixon replied. "It works out well for me, at least."

"How's that?"

"You're just the man I need in charge, Bill. Looking on the dark side like you do, the world won't disappoint you often. And when it does, hell, it's always a pleasant surprise."

"I never thought about it that way," Pickering allowed, smiling despite himself.

He didn't like to come off as a croaker, seeing doom and gloom in everything, but if it helped him do his job, nip trouble in the bud, there was a list of worse things he could be.

"That sandwich any good?" asked Dixon.

"Tolerable. And no kickback from the mushrooms yet."

"That's good. Mel sacked enough of 'em for dinner and another round at breakfast 'fore we see the last of 'em."

With that, the boss clucked to his mare and headed for the chuck wagon to grab lunch on the move. Pickering finished his and wiped his fingers on his chaps, scanning the herd for any wayward steers.

H EY, TOBY!"
          Bishop frowned unconsciously, hearing the voice of Graham Lott behind him, then put on his poker face before he half turned in his saddle, saying, "Hey, Rev."

"I don't really go by that, you know," Lott said.

"What? 'Reverend'?"

"I never went to school for it, like some who come out with a title tacked onto their names."

"And yet you preach."

"Just got the calling for it, ten, maybe eleven years back now."

Bishop didn't intend to ask him how that came about. "I suppose that happens."

"Did to me, at least. I thank God for it now, o' course, but at the time . . . well, I'd be lying if I didn't fess up to suspecting that I'd lost my wits."

"That happens, too," said Bishop, softening his observation with a smile.

"Don't get me wrong," said Lott. "I wasn't nothing like Saint Paul, riding along one day and getting dumbstruck by the Lord."

You can say that again, thought Bishop. *Dumbstruck is one thing you'll never be.*

Instead, he answered back, "No thunderbolts and lightning?"

"Just a wagon by the roadside, after some Apaches happened by in Arizona Territory," Lott said. "Stole the horses, I suppose. A man was lying scalped where he'd died fighting them. Inside the wagon . . . well, let's just say that his missus and their young ones fared no better."

"That's a hardy thing," Bishop granted. "Living it or seeing it, after."

"It changed me," Lot said. "Don't know how else to explain it. Rode into a little desert town the day after that mess. They had a tent revival going on. Turns out the preacher liked to pull a cork as much as quoting Scripture, but I took his words to heart and let the rest go by."

"Sounds fair. Whatever works for you."

"I've been meaning to ask you how you're holding up. After . . . you know."

"The killings?"

"If I'm prying, just say so."

"No prying to it," Bishop said. "It's nothing that I haven't seen or done before."

"You have my sympathy," said Lott.

"Don't need it. It's not weighing on me."

"Are you sure?"

Bishop reined his snowflake Appaloosa up and turned to face Lott from his saddle. "We don't really know each other, Graham, but I'm gonna guess you've never dropped the hammer on a man."

"And you'd be right. It's not a goal I've set out for myself."

"I hope you never have to, but out here . . ." Bishop's hand gesture swept the herd, the plains, the distant hills.

"I can't imagine how it feels," Lott said, a quizzical expression on his face.

"Like nothing," Toby said. "I'm facing down a man, knowing it's him or me and there's no other way around it, I intend to make it him. I aim to stay alive. So far, it's worked. And when it's done, I don't feel anything. Well, maybe some relief."

"And dreams?"

"I have 'em, just like anybody else, but ghosts don't visit me. Don't go confusing me with Ebenezer Scrooge."

Lott's eyebrows rose. "You've read *A Christmas Carol*?"

"Saw it acted on the stage in Denver, the Platte Valley Theater, I think it was."

"I've never seen a stage play," Lott confessed.

"Won't say it changed my life, but it was entertaining, even if you see the ghosts having a shot of pop skull afterward, at the saloon."

"The Ghost of Christmas Yet-to-Be," Lott said, and seemed to shudder for a second, maybe putting on an act himself. "It still gives me the creeps."

"Wait till you see it with your own eyes, dragging chains."

"No, thank you! I'll leave that one on the printed page."

"Might be a good idea," Bishop replied.

"Right. Well, I'd best be getting back to work before I get a shout from Mr. Pickering."

"That wouldn't do," said Toby, offering a wave of sorts as Lott rode off.

Afraid of ghosts in fiction, never faced a hostile enemy in combat. Watching Lott as he tried keeping the longhorns in line, Bishop could only wonder why he stayed out west at all.

And come to think of it, his brain chided him, *why do* you?

"Shut up," he grumbled, noticing the Appaloosa's ears prick up. "Not you, old boy," he said. "Maybe I'm going loco, talking to myself."

THE AFTERNOON WAS well advanced when trouble struck again.

In this case, trouble was a prairie rattler close to four feet long, brown markings on a lighter background causing some folks to confuse it with the larger western diamondback that rarely strayed this far to the northeast in Indian country. While it delivered smaller venom doses than its more notorious cousin—and less still than the eastern diamondback or deadly cottonmouth—the prairie rattler's bite was dangerous enough to man and beast alike.

This time, its target was a steer that failed to notice it while munching tallgrass, and it struck the longhorn on one cheek, exciting it and other steers around it into milling, lowing chaos. Bishop was the first drover to reach the scene and found the snake already lifeless, trampled into bloody tatters, but the damage had been done.

He calmed the steers as best he could, with aid from other hands who got there after him. Bill Pickering was third to ride up on the scene, asking nobody in particular, "What's going on?"

Bishop pointed to where the snake lay curled and torn.

Pickering scowled and said, "Goddammit! What's the damage?"

"This one," Boone Hightower told him, pointing. "Got a bite there on the left side of its face."

Pickering took a closer look and Bishop saw his shoulders slump. "I see it now. We'll have to cut him out."

Ironically, they would have had less trouble if the snake had tagged a person. With a human victim, certain measures could be taken—for an arm or leg, a tourniquet, and maybe sucking venom from the wound—but with a steer bitten around the head, all bets were off. A tourniquet around the neck would strangle it, and who could drain a longhorn's facial bite without the likelihood of being gored?

No, Pickering was right. The steer's left cheek was swelling as they watched, the pain from it increasing exponentially. It wouldn't be much longer till the steer—hurting, disoriented, maybe blind in one eye, with its balance suffering—would start to run amok, and that way lay disaster for the herd.

Cutting a steer out of the group was dicey, and especially with a longhorn already suffering. Step one was lassoing its head, no easy job itself with horns spanning an easy seven feet. Once Bishop and Deke Sullivan had managed that, one sitting off to either side, the tension in their lariats preventing the longhorn from charging one horse or the other, Pickering rode on ahead to clear a path through other ranks of animals, leading the dead steer walking westward, out of line.

When that was done, no further injuries to show for it so far, they needed distance from the herd, waiting and watching as the drive moved on without them. The delivery of gunshot mercy they intended could have spooked the other steers and set them running blindly from the pistol's echo, injuring who knew how many more with sprained or broken legs, more gouged by horns, maybe taking a horse and rider down with them.

Bishop put no faith in bovine intelligence, but as the other longhorns topped a grassy rise and started down the other side, he could have sworn the bitten longhorn—dazed and hurting as it was, venom encroaching painfully upon its eyes and brain—sensed what was coming next.

The animal let out a low and mournful cry, cut short when Pickering's Colt New Line revolver punched a .41-caliber hole between its wide-spaced eyes. Its legs folded and it collapsed, the sudden pressure on its lungs from impact with the ground driving a windy grunt up from its throat.

Bishop knew there would be no beef on their plates tonight. Mel Varney wouldn't risk it, with the rattler's venom coursing through the longhorn's bloodstream, powered even now by the last slow contractions of its dying heart.

Such waste.

They left it to the vultures and coyotes, riding back to join the herd.

THAT'S TWO," SAID Gavin Dixon.

"Yes, sir. Not so bad, all things considered, after traveling this far," Bill Pickering replied.

"One steer a week?" The boss stopped short of

shrugging. "Could be worse, I know, but every steer we lose means cash out of our pockets at the end. At this rate, if it holds, figure another half dozen to go."

"Both incidents were unpredictable," said Pickering.

"I know that. Just like snow in April. Just like rustlers making off with the remuda."

"We came out ahead on that, boss."

"Horse-wise," Dixon countered, "after killing six men and risking some of ours."

"Well . . ."

"Don't bother me," the trail boss said. "Same way I generally wind up in the hole at poker."

"But you've never had a losing year."

"Not since you signed on, anyway."

"I ain't no good-luck charm," said Pickering, and hoped he wasn't blushing in the shade cast by his hat.

"I'll be the judge of that," Dixon replied. "Don't sell yourself short, Bill."

The foreman glanced away, uncomfortable with effusive praise, and something on the distant skyline drew his eyes. "Oh, Lord," he muttered, without being fully conscious that he'd spoken.

"What?" asked Dixon.

"Off there to the west, sir. I believe that's talking smoke."

White puffs rising from elevated land, created by the manipulation of a blanket over open flame with fuel handpicked for smoking, green wood being best. Pickering knew it was the Indian equivalent of Morse code, used to send brief messages about subjects ranging from epidemic illness to victory in battle to the charted progress of an enemy.

"Dammit! You're on the money," Dixon said. "How far off would you say that is?"

"A couple miles, at least. Say close enough to see the herd but too far off for counting heads."

"That's too damned close for comfort. Can you tell the tribe from that?"

"No, sir. It ain't like marking on a lance or arrow."

"But there's gotta be someone on the receiving end."

"Agreed. No point in sending signals otherwise," said Pickering. "A scout, then, or a few of them."

"With the main party somewhere else. Not answering?" the boss inquired.

"Can't say. If they're behind that rise, another two, three miles away, we likely wouldn't see it."

Pickering knew that was the main drawback with smoke signals. If your friends could see them, so could any enemies with eyes. As for the meaning of those random puffs . . . well, that was anybody's guess who didn't hold the key to a translation.

"Looks like double guards at night for the next week or more," said Dixon.

"Yes, sir," Pickering acknowledged. "I'll go spread the word."

S UPPER WAS ON the glum side, despite Varney and his helper baking up two apple pies for a surprise dessert. Bishop enjoyed it, but he stayed out of the conversation unless someone spoke to him directly, then kept his responses short and noncommittal.

Graham Lott had settled in beside him, uninvited, but it hardly mattered. Even he was more subdued than usual, a reticence to speak that clearly went against his grain.

At last, the pie behind them, Lott could tolerate the lack of gab no longer. "So," he said to Bishop, "now it's Comanches."

"Looks like it," Toby granted.

"Do you figure it's a war party?"

"I wouldn't know. It was a good move, doubling the guards."

"I'm on the second watch," Lott told him, sounding hopeful that they might be thrown together.

"First for me," Toby advised.

"I've been trying to figure out which tribe it is. Weighing the odds of whether we're in trouble, or its just some hunters signaling their village."

"Since the reservations started up," Bishop replied, "officially, we're in the neighborhood for Cherokee from here on to the border. If a raiding party's off their reservation, though, it could be any one of six or seven others. Then you've got the smaller plots mapped out for tribes the army doesn't count as 'civilized.'"

"And any one of 'em could have it in for us," Lott said, clearly discouraged.

"In for us, or out for beef," Bishop allowed. "From what I hear, the vittles on a reservation aren't worth writing home about—that is, if any of the relocated tribes still had a home."

"I guess it's no surprise they hate us, eh?"

"Some do, beyond a doubt. Same way that one of us would feel if Uncle Sam showed up on our doorsteps and told we were moving out to the Mojave Desert or he'd kill our kin and make us watch."

"Reminds me of President Jefferson," Lott said.

"How's that?"

"Not talking about Indians, but slaves from Africa. He said, 'I tremble for my country when I reflect that God is just and that his justice cannot sleep forever.' Something like that, anyhow."

"Never stopped him from owning slaves himself," Bishop observed.

"Sounds like he was a complicated man."

"Most are, you peel enough layers off the onion."

* * *

Bishop wound up sharing the first shift on guard with Odom, Gorch, and Abel Floyd, the Circle K's horse wrangler. All of them were on alert; Mel Varney was keeping coffee on for anyone who needed it to keep his senses sharp.

As if the risk of being killed and scalped—maybe the other way around—wasn't enough to keep a man from dozing on the job.

Bill Pickering professed doubt that any raiders would attack tonight, but after Willow Grove, Mr. Dixon was taking no chances. Better safe than sorry, as they say.

Dividing his focus between the longhorns and the outer darkness that surrounded them, Bishop wondered if the smoke signals observed that afternoon meant anything to them at all. It might have been some solitary hunter sending word back to his village that he'd lost his horse or was returning with a fresh-killed deer for supper.

Might have been, but Toby knew they couldn't take that chance and let their guard down. If a raiding party struck, its members would be out for beef or white man's blood, maybe a bit of both.

It was a gamble, and a man who couldn't sleep with one eye open ran a risk of never waking up at all.

Time always seemed to lag on watch, and this night more than usual, when any night bird's call could be a painted enemy communicating with his fellow braves. In fact, Toby knew time was passing as it should, although wan moonlight wouldn't let him prove that by his pocket watch. He scanned the night until his eyes grew tired of it, then circled by the chuck wagon to grab a cup of hot jamoke strong enough to keep his senses keen.

On his way there, Bishop passed by Curly Odom,

sitting with his Colt revolving carbine clear of saddle leather, butt plate braced against his meaty thigh. He raised a silent hand in greeting to Bishop but kept his gaze focused on nothing, way off in the night.

Toby rode on to the wagon, lamplit from within. The only sound intruding on his consciousness was the normal and expected, sleepy susurration from the herd, as of some single giant creature slumbering in peace.

But if awakened suddenly, alarmingly, that beast could run amok in nothing flat, not pausing to determine if a threat was real or just the remnant of a fever dream. A single whooping red man could accomplish that, or whirring rattles on a viper's tail.

And if that happened, God help any cowboy standing in its way.

CHAPTER NINE

D AY EIGHTEEN OF the cattle drive, with six more yet
to go at least before they crossed into Missouri.
The longhorns were marching on toward an appoint-
ment with their executioner with a blue sky and warm
sun overhead.

Did any of them understand that trail's end really
was the end for them?

Doubtful. In fact, Bishop presumed it was impossible.

There'd been no repetition of smoke signals since
the first time they'd been spotted, six days back. A
man with less experience might have drawn comfort
from that fact, but Bishop had too much experience
under his belt to take a sanguine point of view.

Granted, the message they had seen less than a
week ago, untranslatable by white men's eyes, might
have pertained to something entirely unrelated to the
longhorn drive.

It *might* have, sure. But Toby Bishop wasn't buying it.
Whatever the intentions of whoever sent that air-

borne message, he assumed it had something to do with Gavin Dixon's herd. A warning of their presence on some reservation's hunting grounds? If so, the land had not been posted against trespassers.

Were members of some nearby village worried that the drovers would attack them without cause? While this was not impossible, given the history of white men versus red, it seemed illogical that cowboys would desert their herd to raid a native settlement that wasn't even on the map, risking their jobs and lives to boot.

The only answer left to Bishop, then, was that the messenger behind the smoke signals had spied the herd, taken note of it, and was deciding what to do about it.

Food was often scarce on reservations, and even when plentiful, its quality left much to be desired. Toby could easily imagine raiders cutting out some steers to feed themselves, maybe their families, willing to risk an armed encounter if their hunger pangs were sharp enough.

And they were smart enough to steal livestock for profit, too, within a lawless territory where the likelihood of meeting U.S. troops was minimal, civilian law enforcement nonexistent. That meant a trail drive's hands should stay alert and ready to defend their master's living property around the clock.

Business as usual, in other words.

Assignments for the night watch had been served with breakfast. Bishop had the graveyard shift, from 2 a.m. till dawn, which meant a longer day than usual tomorrow. That was nothing new; he pulled that shift in regular rotation, roughly once per week, and had grown used to it, but that didn't make the next day any easier. More coffee helped, but by the time they camped somewhere ahead, he might be having a one-sided conversation with his horse.

The good news: He could say most anything and Compañero didn't seem to mind.

While focused mainly of the moving herd, he still took time to scan the western skyline, watching out for any telltale smoke. It stood to reason that the watchers might have crept around behind them in the dark one night, to shadow Dixon's longhorns from the east, so he included that horizon in his scrutiny.

So far, nothing.

That should have put his mind at ease, but it did not.

A fairy tale from childhood came to Bishop's mind, about a mythic race of "water babies," something close to gremlins, written by an author whose name Bishop had forgotten long ago. That lapse aside, one pertinent quotation still stuck in his mind: "No one has a right to say that no water babies exist till they have seen no water babies existing, which is quite a different thing, mind, from not seeing water babies."

And it was the same with hostile Comanches.

You might not see them, but until you saw them not existing—physically impossible—a wise man kept his eyes open and weapons handy, just in case.

When you're up against red men on unfamiliar ground, your first mistake could be the last.

"What do you think?" he asked his Appaloosa. "Have you spotted any water babies?"

Compañero snorted back at him.

"That's what I thought," Bishop replied.

HUUPI PAHATI'S NAME translated into English as Tall Tree, although he wasn't standing tall just now. In fact, he lay prone in the tallgrass, staking out a low ridge-line. His brown-and-white pony—what Spanish speakers called *manchado*, meaning "stained" or "dirty"—stood

some thirty feet behind him, downslope, loosely tethered to a solitary hackberry.

Tall Tree wore a buckskin shirt and matching trousers, supple moccasins handcrafted from the same
material, a simple leather belt around his waist. His
hair, shoulder length, was decorated with a single
feather from a red-tailed hawk, symbolic of his role as
a Comanche war chief. At his side, a single-shot Sharps
rifle lay within arm's reach, its barrel pointing eastward. Upon his left hip, sheathed, a cut-down cavalryman's saber was suspended from his belt.

Tall Tree knew little of his rifle's history. If asked,
he could not have explained that early Sharps rifles
chambered .53-caliber rounds, later reworked to feed
.45-70 government cartridges used by American soldiers. He cared only for the weapon's range, rated effective to five hundred yards and capable of killing
men at twice that distance, with judicious use of its
"open ladder" sight, which helped a shooter calculate
his target's range.

In essence, if Tall Tree could see something with
naked eyes, he could send a slug weighing four hundred grams to destroy it, whistling downrange at a
quarter mile per second. Nothing that one of his bullets struck would ever be the same again.

He was not on a sniping mission now, of course. Today, he simply had to watch and wait, timing the trail
herd's progress between starting off in dawn's pale
light and stopping when the white men hired to move
the longhorns found a likely place to camp.

It would have been a simple task to creep among
them anytime over the past four nights, eliminating
one or two with no disturbance of the rest. In other
circumstances, acting on his own, Tall Tree might have
enjoyed that piecemeal slaughter, but a larger group of

warriors now depended on him, and he would not jeopardize their trust in him by acting so impulsively.

The war party was small, six braves besides Tall Tree. None had participated in the great Lakota uprising of two years earlier, when Lieutenant Colonel Custer and 267 of his bluecoats fell before thousands of Sioux under chiefs Crazy Horse and Sitting Bull. Now Crazy Horse himself was dead, murdered by soldiers in Nebraska barely seven months ago, and Sitting Bull was on the run, his army withered to a shadow of its former self.

No matter.

Tall Tree and his men had feigned surrender, acting docile long enough to learn their adversaries' weaknesses, prepare themselves for what must follow next. He knew that all of them were bound to die, no hope of final victory by any leap of the imagination, but if each man in his band could kill one hundred whites— two hundred, better yet—their sacrifice would not have been in vain.

And in the meantime, he could teach a lesson to the cowboys who presumed all land within their field of vision properly belonged to them.

Two thousand longhorns, give or take, would feed natives on the Comanche reservation for a year or more, and if the bluecoats came to take them back, perhaps that final push would be enough to bring his people back from humble poverty, recapturing some measure of their former pride.

But not today.

The herd had far to go yet. And Tall Tree would follow them until he felt the time to strike was ripe.

G AVIN DIXON DIDN'T like feeling distracted from a job at hand. Tomorrow it would be a week since he had seen smoke signals rising from the west of where his herd was passing, and while there'd been no further hint of any trouble on the wind, he couldn't get the brooding threat out of his mind.

If he was honest with himself, there was no clear-cut reason for concern. By choice, he lived in, raised long-horns in, and herded them to market through the heart of Indian country, bearing that name for an obvious reason. If he thought about it hard enough, Dixon could list six major tribes with reservations in the territory, and probably three dozen others penned on smaller areas within the district's boundaries. In fact, the only place without at least one tribe in residence would be the so-called Neutral Strip or panhandle—and that was theoretical, wandering red men likely to be found on any part of it, but none allowed by treaty to consider it as "home."

He'd built the Circle K and raised his stock on land supposedly belonging to the Chickasaws. On trail drives, the long route between Atoka and Missouri crossed their land, then trundled on through land the government had set aside for Seminoles, Muscogee, Cherokee, and Wyandotte. In point of fact, you couldn't take a step most places in the territory without leaving tracks on land the U.S. government had "promised" to some tribe, for all the good that did.

After a couple of uneasy years, until he got the feel of it, Dixon had worried about constant trouble from the Comanches. He knew they hated white men moving in on them, after they'd been uprooted from ancestral homes and planted here against their will. Who wouldn't, if the shoe was on the other foot? But for the most part it had been all right, the odd steer now and then donated to his closest red natives, cultivating friendship of a sort.

It was the renegades who worried Dixon, and you never knew where you might come upon them, young bucks for the most part, drawn from one tribe or another, sometimes even mixing in a band that had it in for whites.

God only knew what they were thinking, maybe dreaming they could change things back to how they'd been before cavalry and homesteaders infringed upon their sacred lands elsewhere. It was a hopeless way of seeing things, but what of it? Each year or two there would be what the fools in Washington called "incidents," meaning that people of all colors lost their lives while brooding animosity lived on.

No smoke signals today so far, and if they made it through a few more days without having to fight, they should be on Missouri's soil. Not "safe" by any stretch of the imagination, since that state had discontented Indians as well, and white outlaws aplenty, still enamored of the late Confederacy, but at least they would have passed a major milestone on their journey.

And then, assuming they could reach St. Louis with the herd intact, sell off the steers, and pocket decent money, all they had to do was turn around and make the trek back home.

Some of them, anyway.

There'd be Bill Pickering, of course, and likely four more year-round workers from the Circle K—Floyd, Hightower, Odom, and Mel Varney. Anyone of those was free to break away as he saw fit, of course, but Dixon thought they'd found a home of sorts with him.

As for the rest . . .

There were a few men that he wouldn't mind keeping around his spread after the drive was done. Bishop for one, who'd showed himself a cool hand under fire and handy with the steers, besides. Melville and Sullivan would be two more welcome additions to the ranch, to supplement the half dozen he'd left behind and look after things while he and Pickering were gone.

One that he wouldn't ask to stick around was Graham Lott. Dixon appreciated piety as much as the next man but was also partial to the peaceful sound of silence every now and then. Lott seemed incapable of laying off the gab, and Dixon was aware of him occasionally getting on the others' nerves, although the self-styled preacher couldn't recognize that bent toward irritation in himself.

No need to think about it now. Dixon had never shied away from telling men to hit the road after they'd done a part-time job; none of them had held a grudge so far—or none he was aware of, anyhow.

He'd handle that chore when the time came, in St. Louis, and if his new hires ran true to form from other drives, most of the rest would want to stick around the city for a while, spending their hard-earned cash until they woke one morning needing more.

By that time, Dixon would be gone and building up another herd five hundred miles away from what St. Louis citizens referred to as the Gateway to the West.

And then, with any luck, after another busy year he'd do it all again.

Just hold off on the smoke signals, he thought, *and give us time.*

A NOTHER PROBLEM CAME along late in the afternoon while Mr. Dixon had Bill Pickering riding ahead of the advancing herd, scouting a decent place to spend the night. This time a couple of the steers crossed horns, with one getting the worst of it.

Longhorns were known for being temperamental and contrary, sometimes lashing out with no apparent reason, on a whim. That might blow over quickly, but before the inner storm passed, horns and hooved could injure other horses, men, or, as in this case, other steers. Handling an animal that tipped the scales somewhere between fourteen hundred and twenty-five hundred pounds was challenging at the best of times, but when the critter had a mad on, it could plow through damned near anything before it like a wrecking ball.

Bishop had no idea what set the steers to feuding on this afternoon and didn't care. The good news: It was over quickly, without touching off a free-for-all among the longhorns—or, worse yet, a general stampede. He'd heard the bellowing, seen thrashing on the east flank of the herd, and steered his snowflake Appaloosa toward the scene of the commotion, conscious of a couple other drovers moving in to sort it out at the same time.

The bad news: while it lasted, one longhorn, a bull, had gored the cow that set it off. One of the winner's four-foot horns had torn a bloody furrow from the cow's right hip down almost to her hock cap, so that she could barely stand on that leg, much less keep up with the moving herd.

His grim work done, the bull had fallen back in line as if there'd been no trouble in the first place, four full inches of its left horn smeared with blood that would dry rusty brown before the herd had gone another quarter mile.

Mr. Dixon rode up just as Bishop and Whit Melville were maneuvering the wounded steer aside, Boone Hightower keeping a sharp eye on the bull in case he started acting up again. Their boss observed the damage, cursed, and said, "She can't go on this way."

"No, sir," Bishop agreed.

"All right. Toby, you ride ahead and tell Varney that there'll be beef tonight. I'll do what's necessary here."

"You sure, boss?" Melville asked. "I don't mind taking care of it."

"My loss, my job," Dixon replied. "Leave me your lasso and I'll get it back to you."

"Yes, sir."

Bishop rode on to do as he'd been told, thankful he didn't have to hang around and watch another steer put down. It might not seem like much, after the men they'd killed at Willow Grove, but it seemed worse to him somehow. Maybe the pained, confused look on the cow's long face had struck a chord with him this time.

W HY NOT TONIGHT?" Iron Jacket asked. His name in the old language was Puhihwikwasu'u.

Tall tree answered, "We have time and need more preparation."

"They are only cattle," Nadua observed. His name translated in the white man's language to Someone Found.

"That would be true if we were only after food for our small band," Tall Tree replied. "But to collect enough animals for all our people on the reservation, we must wait and test our plan."

"The white men will fight back," said Bright Sun, named Tabemohats at birth by his parents, both murdered on the Trail of Tears.

"I hope so," answered Bodaway—Fire Maker. "We ought to kill them all."

"Temper your rage with wisdom, brother," Tall Tree cautioned. "They have us outnumbered two to one."

"White men are cowards!" Fire Maker insisted.

Old Owl—born Mupitsukupu—added, "And murderers of women. They deserve to die."

"What of the black man who rides with them?" asked Tabemohats, Bright Sun.

"What of him?" came the challenge from Great Leaper, born Gosheven. "White men once enslaved his kin and now he works for them? He is a traitor to his people and to life itself."

"Enough!" The tone of Tall Tree's voice cut through their argument and silenced all of them. When every pair of eyes was upon his face, he said, speaking with one hand on his cut-down saber's grip, "If you desire another leader, say so. Challenge me according to tradition. Otherwise, we follow the plan all of you agreed to."

No one spoke. After a minute passed, Tall Tree said, "Well?"

"Hold to the plan," Iron Jacket said at last. "But make it happen soon."

"In due time," Tall Tree said, not backing up one inch from the position he had staked out for himself. "It works as well next week as if we tried tonight. Better, in fact, since the white fools will soon forget the talking smoke and fall back into carelessness."

"They still post guards at night," said Someone Found.

"As always when they move their animals to market," Tall Tree said. "When the time comes, we will dispose of them and shift the numbers to our favor."

"But soon, rather than later," Old Owl urged.

"Patience, my brothers. While I go to scout the herd again, see to your weapons. Be prepared."

A weapons check would keep them busy for a little while, at least, although they knew their arms by heart. No warrior could afford to enter battle unprepared.

Their mobile arsenal was motley but effective. In addition to their war chief's Sharps rifle, Iron Jacket had a foreign-made Albini-Braendlin rifle, Someone Found had a Mauser Model 1871, Fire Maker carried a Spencer repeater, and Old Owl packed a Greener double-barrel coach gun. Two others, Bright Sun and Great Leaper, were equipped with Colt revolvers, the Dragoon and Navy Model 1861. Each man carried a scalping knife, and most of them a tomahawk besides.

And if they failed despite all his preparation, having followed Tall Tree's orders to the letter, it must be the will of the Great Spirit who created all land, sea, and sky. At least, in that case, they could face their ancestors with pride.

S IX MORE DAYS to Missouri," Graham Lott remarked, his mouth half-full of pork and beans.

"That's if we're lucky," Bishop said, "and don't run into any other snags."

"I've got a good feeling," Lott said, after he'd swallowed.

"And I surely hope you're right," Toby replied. "Just don't go counting any chickens yet."

"You-all forgetting about the Injuns?" Leland Gorch asked from the far side of their fire.

"Hoping the Lord will see us through," Lott answered back.

Gorch stared at him a minute, as if Lott was eating locoweed instead of Varney's cooking, then dismissed him with a tired shake of his head. "Praying won't help you when the arrows start to fly," he said.

"If Joshua could drop the walls of Jericho by blowing on a horn," Lott said, "I reckon God can get us through most anything."

"Amen, señor," said Paco Esperanza, off to Bishop's left, and set a couple of the others laughing.

Lott leaned in, lowered his voice, and almost silently mouthed, "Infidels."

"It takes all kinds," Toby advised.

Bishop was almost finished with his supper, laying off the normal second cup of coffee so that he could turn in early and catch some shut-eye prior to being rousted for his turn on the late watch. If he was lucky, he could bank enough sleep in the meantime to get through his shift and face another long day without feeling too run-down by tomorrow's sunset.

That is, if they made it that far without more interruptions. Or maybe that was simply wishful thinking.

As for Indians, hostile or otherwise, he hadn't seen one yet since their departure from Atoka, and he hoped to keep it that way. During wartime, he'd gone west to miss the military draft and didn't feel the least embarrassed by his choice. Toby despised slavers but hadn't felt the need to die or kill somebody else to prove that they were in the wrong.

Ironically, the journey west had not spared him from killing men at all. Thoughts of the Mason County Hoodoo War intruded on his thoughts until he shut them down, returned his plate and coffee cup to Rudy Knapp at the chuck wagon, and told everyone around the fire a general good night.

If there was anything to praise about drawing the last night shift, he reckoned it must be the span of time when predators—human or otherwise—slacked off from hunting, once they'd either satisfied their appetites or given up, surrendering to the fatigue that burdened any organism as the clock wound down.

Coyotes might lie up away from daylight until sundown for the most part, in their hidden dens, but scavenging for sustenance all night would wear them down. They needed meat as soon as possible after they woke and wearied just like anybody else if they were forced to chase after any scrap of food.

Finished, he took his plate and coffee cup to Rudy Knapp and fetched his bedroll from the chuck wagon, bidding the other hands good night. From there, he walked to the remuda for a final word with Compañero, told the snowflake Appaloosa that he'd be back soon, and got a nuzzle in return.

The nights were turning cooler as they traveled north, but sleeping in his jacket never kept Bishop awake. As usual, he laid his weapons close at hand, not counting on a raid by night but ready for one if it came.

As if preparedness was even truly possible.

Bishop had heard stories claiming that red men wouldn't fight after the sun went down, for fear of being killed at night and their souls getting lost in darkness, looking for their "happy hunting ground." He didn't believe it and had personally viewed the aftermath of two nocturnal raids staged by Apache warriors out in Arizona Territory, killing better than a dozen settlers and kidnapping one child who'd never been retrieved, alive or dead.

"Enough," he muttered to himself, and closed his eyes, his right hand resting lightly on the curved butt of his Colt.

If anyone tried to surprise him while he slept, they would be in for a surprise themselves.

CHAPTER TEN

NIGHT TWENTY-ONE. THE drive had finished three weeks on its journey from Atoka and were camping one or two days from Missouri's border if their luck held out. There'd been no further incidents or loss of stock so far, no repetition of the talking smoke that had put everyone on edge a few days ago.

Most of the drovers thought they'd ridden out of danger's reach by now.

Toby Bishop wasn't sure.

He had the second watch this night, with Graham Lott and Estes Courtwright, whom the other hands had started calling "Slim." Bishop had no clue who had started that, but Courtwright didn't seem to mind, accepting the nickname for what it was, a label of belonging to the group at large.

Tonight, there was an intermittent breeze out of the east, bringing a chill along with it. Some folks supposed that springtime weather in the border states was always warm, but that wasn't the case at all. With sundown, temperatures fell much as they did on deserts farther west, making a watchman thankful for his coat and scarf, even a pair of gloves, before the sun arose.

Compañero didn't seem to mind.

Off to the east somewhere, a nightjar's warbling call resounded through the darkness. Bishop was familiar with the birds that spent nocturnal hours hunting insects, known to certain rural folk as "goatsuckers" after a superstition that they fed themselves on goat's milk stolen while the nannies slept in fields or stalls. Pure bunkum, but some people couldn't let it go, the same way they spun tales of goblins and the like.

Bishop had given up on fairy tales before he'd run away from home. By then, he knew the world was strange and dangerous enough without exaggerating its inherent risks or fabricating gibberish to keep unruly kids in line.

At least, it hadn't worked on him.

They'd left the tallgrass prairie now, and while the longhorns still found ample forage, they were forced to work at it a little more. No snagging mouthfuls on the move. They had to slow a bit and duck their heads to crop the fodder at their feet, which naturally cost the drive a bit more time each day.

It hadn't hurt them yet, but Bishop knew that every extra day tacked on to their long march meant twenty-four more hours when the herd and men attending it were vulnerable, out in open country, prey for anything from sudden storms to men with theft and murder on their minds. Men of all colors, nationalities, what have you.

None of that made any difference if they were armed and steady-handed, bent on raising hell.

The only law out here was holstered on his hip and riding in his saddle boot.

Bishop saw Graham Lott approaching, slowed his Appaloosa long enough for Lott to nod and softly say, "All clear so far."

That wasn't strictly necessary, since all hands would be alert by now if there'd been any trouble, but the preacher couldn't pass on any opportunity to exercise his vocal cords.

Bishop offered a salute of sorts, raising one hand to graze his hat brim as they passed each other, riding on in opposite directions, then lapse back into his private reverie. The nightjar called again—but no, it was another one, maybe a hundred yards off from the first he'd heard.

A budding avian romance, perhaps? Bishop proceeded on his way, wishing the feathered flirters well.

TALL TREE CUPPED his hands, mimicked the nightjar's call again, and heard Iron Jacket answer him in kind from fifty yards away.

The birds, called *colchoneta* in the Spanish tongue, were small but vocal, imitated easily with just a little practice. Cries aside, they offered sustenance to travelers, laying their speckled eggs on bare ground without nests. Once young nightjars were hatched, the parents moved them out of danger's way by carrying the hatchlings in their beaks—or so an old Comanche shaman once proclaimed, though Tall Tree had not witnessed it himself.

Tonight there were no nightjars within calling distance of the white men's herd. Tall Tree and his companions took their place in the nocturnal chorus otherwise composed of insects, bats, and owls. Their imitation was not perfect, but white ears—much like the brains to which they were connected—rarely paid complete attention to the sound of nature's voices.

One more critical mistake.

Tonight's excursion was to be a practice run. They would peel off three steers and make their getaway, if possible, without arousing any of the cowboys in the process. And if that succeeded, on their next visit . . .

A screech owl's cry echoed across the plains. Bright Sun doing his best impression, conscious that too many nightjar calls from different directions would mean taking an unnecessary risk. A second owl—Fire Maker, this time—answered from the far side of the herd.

Tall Tree waited another moment, then uttered his final birdcall prior to moving in, Sharps rifle slung across his back, the cut-down saber in his hand. If killing was required, against his will, he hoped to make it sudden and silent.

Unseen, his fellow warriors would be closing in upon the herd, six braves extracting three longhorns, while Tall Tree oversaw the operation, supervising, covering their clandestine retreat. He could not do that with his saber, but just now, when none of the white men had been alerted, he preferred the quiet option if he had to spill their blood.

And killing one of them, he knew from prior experience, would not disturb him in the least.

White men were prone to talk about their consciences, a built-in gauge of "right and wrong" instilled in them from childhood, but they never seemed to mind when they were robbing, raping, or killing "redskins." It had been the same with slavery, Tall Tree recalled, from when his father, Tosahwi—White Knife in English—had waged war against the blue-clad "liberators" led by Stand Watie in the War Between the States. Tosahwi had been killed during the Battle of Pea Ridge, in Arkansas, shot down by Union troops while fighting on the side supporting slavery.

And why not? Stand Watie's whole family were slave owners and took black servants with them on the Trail of Tears, establishing a successful plantation on Spavinaw Creek in Indian country. Those kidnapped Africans were only freed by edict during February 1863, a month after the proclamation of emancipation from the White House.

All that was ancient history, occurring when Tall Tree had barely made the transit into manhood. Now he put it out of mind and focused on the task at hand.

Three steers, and hopefully no killing.

But if that was unavoidable, he and his braves were equal to the task.

G RAHAM LOTT WAS running over Scripture in his mind as he patrolled the herd, holding the chestnut gelding's reins loosely in his left hand, his right close to the holstered double-action Starr revolver primed with six .44-caliber rounds.

Lott reckoned that rehearsing Bible passages helped keep his mind sharp, while suggesting messages he might impart to fellow riders from the Circle K next Sunday, over breakfast. Few of them paid any real attention but he felt obliged to try regardless, on the theory that a seed cast onto arid ground might still take root and grow if the Almighty willed it to be so.

Another reason that Lott wouldn't share with any other living soul: He simply loved to talk, even when by himself, and quoting Scripture was the next best thing to talking with another person. And a fair approximation of conversing with the Lord.

The prairie night was quiet so far, save for more birdcalls than Lott remembered hearing since they'd left the Circle K. Gavin Dixon's home and outbuildings were ringed by shade trees, oak and elms, where birds roosted and chattered all day long, sometimes into the night.

Proceeding on his way, Lott reckoned that the longhorns wouldn't mind him preaching to them—and in fact they might prefer it to his somewhat reedy, off-key singing voice. They couldn't understand a word of it, he realized, and had no souls to save or lose in any case, but neither could exposure to the Lord's word do them any harm.

That grim finale waited for them in St. Louis, at the slaughterhouse.

As long as it stayed quiet through the final ninety minutes of his shift . . .

And then, as if his hopeful thought had conjured trouble, Lott saw something that he didn't understand at first. One of the steers ahead of him, some fifty feet or so, had stepped out from the mass of longhorns either munching grass or dozing. This one seemed intent on going for a moonlight stroll—but what about that picture set his nerves on edge?

A shadow on the steer's far side away from him and keeping pace.

No, make that *two* shadows in vaguely human form, walking upright but with their shoulders hunched, as if to take advantage of the longhorn as a form of camouflage. Lott thought back to the rustlers who had raided Mr. D's remuda and provoked bloodshed at Willow Grove—a town he hoped never to see again—and realized that he had happened on a pair of thieves at work.

Lott drew his Starr revolver, cocked it even though he didn't need to with its double-action trigger, and called out, raising his voice, "Hold up there! Stop!" Then to his fellow hands on night watch: "Rustlers! Rally round!"

One of the shadows stood taller then and seemed to lean across the longhorn's crest with something long and angular in hand. Lott heard a *twang* and caught a hint of motion, something slender racing toward him, before impact on his breastbone pitched him over backward from the gelding's saddle, tumbling him to the ground.

In free fall, Lott still hung on to his pistol, squeezing off a wasted shot skyward before he landed on the turf and felt the wind knocked out of him. More pain lanced through his chest, as if someone was leaning on the object that had skewered him, and then there wasn't even time for him to scream.

He died not knowing who had killed him, how they'd done it, or why the Almighty had abandoned him.

L OTT'S CRY, IMMEDIATELY followed by a gunshot, prompted Toby Bishop to reverse directions, clucking to his snowflake Appaloosa as he urged it to a gallop. Hoofbeats coming up behind him made him look around, spotting Courtwright as he responded to the truncated alarm.

Beyond them, all around the fire and chuck wagon, drovers were scrambling from their bedrolls or discarding cups of coffee, drawing guns. Over that hubbub Mr. Dixon's voice rang out, commanding, "Everyone up and at it! Move!"

Bishop found Lott where he had fallen, with his chestnut standing off a few yards to the preacher's left. Even in darkness, Toby could make out the shaft protruding from Lott's chest, some three feet long and fletched with feathers at the skyward-pointing end. The preacher's hand still clutched a pistol trailing wisps of smoke.

"The hell happened?" Courtright demanded as he came up to the scene of Lott's demise.

"An arrow," Bishop said, pointing the muzzle of his Peacemaker while his eyes scanned the outer darkness.

"Injuns?"

"Don't know yet," Toby replied, knowing it didn't take red hands to wield a bow. "I can't see anybody yet."

Off to their left, a longhorn stood thirty feet or so apart from Mr. Dixon's herd, head down and grazing. There was something dangling from around its neck and trailing on the grass, undoubtedly some kind of rope.

Surprisingly, Lott's gunshot hadn't spooked the steers beyond causing the nearest ones to shift around a bit before they settled back to cropping grass.

"Where did they get to?" Courtwright asked, as if Bishop should know.

"Most likely that way." Toby pointed with his Colt again, then reconsidered it with range in mind and swapped it for the Yellow Boy Winchester from his saddle boot.

He still had nothing in the way of targets, but if one showed up at least he'd have a better chance of drilling it.

More horsemen were approaching now, with Mr. Dixon in the lead and foreman Pickering hard on his heels. The boss craned from his saddle looking over Lott, then asked, "You men seen anything?"

Courtwright was first to answer, letting Bishop off the hook. "Not yet, sir. Nothing but that steer standing apart. Looks like a rope around his neck."

"That tears it. Goddamn rustlers," Pickering declared.

"That arrow points to Comanches," said Dixon. "Or it could be white trash hoping they can fake it."

"Either way, they're murderers," the foreman said.

"And gone as far as I can tell. Bill, take some of these boys and scout around the herd right quick. Find out if anybody else came at 'em from another side and wasn't noticed in the ruckus."

"Yes, sir! Odom, Thorne, Melville! With me!"

The four of them rode off while Bishop and the rest waited for Dixon to pronounce his next order. Deke Sullivan was coming back on foot, leading the long-horn they had nearly lost, its tether dangling from one hand. "It's plaited buckskin, Boss," he said. "Looks more and more like redskins."

"All right," Dixon replied. "Three of you fan out— Paco, Deke, and Whit. Try picking up some kind of sign if you can manage in the dark. If not, we'll try again at sunup."

"And what about the preacher?" Bishop asked.

"We'll plant him after breakfast. If we don't turn up a clear-cut trail within an hour, we'll move on. The sooner we can get away from here, the happier I'll be."

TALL TREE RAN swiftly through the darkness, half a mile or more to reach the point where his raiders had left their tethered ponies. He arrived before the rest and watched them, looking disgusted with themselves and rightly so.

"Old Owl, what happened?" he demanded. "You and Someone Found were closest to the shooting."

"The white man surprised us," Old Owl said. "If there had been some warning—"

"No excuses!" Tall Tree cut him off. "Could you not see him coming?"

"Saw him, heard him," Someone Found chipped in. "He was talking to himself, some kind of *doo 'áhályą́ą́ da*." Meaning "idiot."

"But caught you anyway," Tall Tree observed. "And fired a shot to bring the others running."

"I was faster," Someone Found replied. "He fired his pistol falling, I believe already dead."

"So now they have an arrow," Tall Tree countered. "If they recognize its markings they can name our tribe. Do you consider that a victory?"

"The other choice was to be killed ourselves. Or else use Old Owl's coach gun."

"The *best* choice," their war chief reminded them, "was to obey my orders and avoid letting the white men see you."

"No one saw us," Old Owl said, sounding disgruntled. "If the one did, he is silent now. None of the others had a chance."

"So, you consider this a victory?" Tall Tree inquired rhetorically. He moved on without giving either of them time to answer. "What of you, Bright Sun and Fire Maker?" he asked. "I see no steer with you."

"The shooting spoiled our chance," said Fire Maker. "We had our line around its neck when—"

"When you left a second clue behind." Tall Tree made no attempt to mask his disappointment. "Iron Jacket? Great Leaper? What of your mission?"

"No longhorn," said Iron Jacket. "But at least we left no clues behind."

"As if they needed any more, with two ropes and an arrow. We may just as well have left a sign."

"We will do better next time," Old Owl offered.

"It could hardly be much worse." Tall Tree relented then, deciding he had scolded them enough. Whatever their mistakes might have been, he needed their cooperation in order to proceed. "And we *will* try again," he said.

"How soon?" asked Fire Maker.

"At least four suns and moons," Tall Tree replied.

"They will not have forgotten us by then but let them think the shooting frightened us away. White men are foolish. They prefer to think good things await them, what the Mexicans call *optimismo*. They would rather run away from danger than confront it, as the Sioux found out at Little Big Horn."

He saw no reason to remind them of what happened after that great victory, when Crazy Horse surrendered in Nebraska and was foully murdered there, while Sitting Bull retreated all the way to Canada, his army dwindling pathetically along the way. Of the other war chiefs present at the fall of Custer, Two Moons was defeated eight months later, in Montana, while Phizi—Gall—followed Sitting Bull's road north to Canada and still resided there today.

Snatching defeat out of the jaws of victory.

Tall Tree reckoned he might be killed sometime within the days or weeks ahead, but when it happened, as he knew it must one day, he would not be shot down while running from his enemies.

THORNE AND ODOM carried Lott's corpse back to camp, with Bishop following behind them at a slow pace, leading their two horses. Mel Varney had a piece of canvas laid out near the chuck wagon, his two pallbearers setting Lott on top of it, then rolling him inside and tying off the ends with twine, and finally leaving him there, a giant hand-rolled cigarette, while Varney stoked the campfire.

Bishop wasn't sure about the fire, considering there might be raiders skulking in the dark with bows or even firearms, but he kept that observation to himself. The blaze—and fresh, hot coffee to go with it—had been ordered up by Mr. D, presumably after he'd weighed the risks against keeping his drovers on alert until the break of dawn.

As if they could have slept now, or would perhaps sleep for nights to come.

Bishop retreated from the campfire with his Appaloosa, found a spot where Compañero was content to graze awhile, and stood by with his Winchester in hand. Though still on edge and likely to remain so, Toby thought the night felt different somehow—nothing that he could put his finger on, but safer, if that term ever truly applied to any trail drive.

Something told him that the raiders had retreated for the present, but he couldn't take that to the bank with any confidence. Withdrawing might have been a ruse, a wily stratagem, and he wasn't about to make himself a human sacrifice by letting down his guard.

Hence standing well off from the fire, trusting the chill to help him stay awake. When Compañero had consumed his fill of grass, Bishop would walk him thirty feet out to the babbling stream they'd camped beside and let the stallion slake his thirst.

If Compañero felt like dozing then, Bishop would stand guard over him, the same as he was doing for their camp. Tomorrow, still four hours off, would be a long, hard day for everyone, and no mistake.

When he was younger, at a time like this—and there had been a goodly few—Bishop had tried to puzzle out the steps he'd taken, leading him up to the brink of danger. Introspection had its place, but he'd abandoned that technique during the Mason County war, when death was all around him and his only choices were to forge ahead or turn tail and get out.

At one time or another in the midst of that, he had done both.

The Hoodoo War was settled now, from what he

understood, although to no one's final satisfaction. Lawmen and the threat of prison had dictated its conclusion—for the moment, anyhow. As for some future generation picking up the feud where it was dropped, Bishop supposed only a fool would bet against it.

No slight or injury was ever truly laid aside, forgotten and forgiven. Most people weren't built that way, to turn the other cheek and love their neighbors as they loved themselves.

Better to strike first, while the iron was hot. Or, as some others liked to say, dig two graves when you set out looking for revenge.

His Appaloosa whickered softly, telling Bishop he'd consumed enough grass for the moment, and they moved off to the creek, Toby at full alert. That done, they doubled back to camp and settled into watchful waiting for the first gray light of dawn.

BILL PICKERING WAS carrying another length of plaited buckskin rope when he found Gavin Dixon near the fire and showed it to him.

"Found this hanging off another steer, along the south end of the herd."

"Same as the other one," Dixon observed.

"I'm damned if it's not redskins, boss. White renegades could use a bow all right, but I don't see 'em taking time to make a rope, hoping to throw us off the scent, when they could buy or steal one easier."

"Saying you're right—and I agree you likely are—where would we find 'em now?"

"No telling. Maybe miles away, if they were spooked enough."

"They draw first blood, then cut and run?" Dixon was clearly skeptical.

"It's how they fight, most times," said Pickering.

"The way I read it, they came in for beef and weren't expecting anyone to catch 'em at it. Killed the preacher as a reflex when he called them out."

"I can't blame Lott."

"No, sir. Same thing I would've done, but maybe shoot first, then start hollering."

A nod from Dixon. "What's your thinking on them trailing us from here?"

"It could go either way, boss. Since they made off clean, nobody killed or hurt on their side, they won't have a grudge to settle. On the other hand . . ."

"They didn't get the beef," Dixon filled in. "Unless we've lost a steer or two we still don't know about."

"No way to get a head count in the dark," said Pickering.

"And I don't wanna spare the time tomorrow either," Dixon said. "We'd just be sitting ducks. Breakfast, then plant the preacher and move out."

"Yes, sir. Just as you say."

"Maybe save time. Pick out a spot and get a couple drovers started on the grave, since no one's sleeping anyway."

"I'll see it's done. You want a marker for him, boss?"

Dixon responded with a question of his own. "When Lott signed on, what did he tell you about family?"

"None living, as he told it. Way out here, they couldn't find him anyhow."

"Forget about the marker, then. I don't want savages to dig him up and take his scalp."

"One less delay," said Pickering.

"Same thing with building up a rock pile," Dixon said. "We'll keep it simple, yeah?"

"Sure thing."

Mel Varney was already planning breakfast at the chuck wagon, not that the same meal every sunrise took much in the way of culinary strategy. Pickering fetched two shovels and a lantern from the wagon's gear and walked back to the fire with them, asking the drovers clustered there, "Who wants to get a start on putting Graham in the ground?"

To his surprise, six hands went up at once. He chose Melville and Sullivan, two of the larger hands, and led the diggers off to find a good spot for the murdered preacher's grave.

CHAPTER ELEVEN

A QUICK BREAKFAST BEGAN their twenty-second day
out from the Circle K, immediately followed by
the funeral of Graham Lott. Without the preacher, no
one volunteered to speak over his grave as Isaac
Thorne and Paco Esperanza filled it in, so Mr. Dixon
did his best.

It wasn't much and seemed to make him cringe a
little as he voiced a memory from bygone Sunday
school. "Ashes to ashes, dust to dust," he said. "We
didn't get to know Graham that well, but he was affa-
ble and kept the faith. Whatever's waiting for him, I
suppose he earned it."

Bishop wasn't sure about that last part, but the
words were out now and there wasn't any way to edit
them. Nobody else appeared to see the ambiguity, but
Mr. Dixon frowned a little as he wrapped it up, as if
dissatisfied himself.

Varney and Rudy Knapp had the chuck wagon
packed up by the time the earth was tamped down
over Lott's remains. That done, it took the best part of

an hour for eleven hands to get the herd and its remuda moving north. The longhorns, maybe grateful for a longer morning break than usual, were docile as they started out, but handling nearly two thousand steers still ate into the day.

And while he couldn't swear to it, Bishop supposed staying alert for hostile red men trailing them slowed down the other hands a mite, dividing their attention from the task at hand.

How long until that pressure started fraying nerves, spawning quarrels and dissension among men whose best hope for survival lay in wholehearted cooperation?

One more thing that Toby didn't care to gamble on.

Ahead of him, he spotted Mr. D and foreman Pickering riding together, seeming deep in conversation. Bishop could imagine some of what they had to say, mainly the obvious, wondering whether they could stay ahead of any trackers till they reached Missouri's southern border, wondering if that would even make a difference.

It might, of course, but then again . . .

Crossing a line drawn on a piece of paper meant no more to renegades of any race than spitting in the wind. By definition, they were on the wrong side of the law wherever they set foot, geography being the least of their concerns.

Fort Leavenworth in eastern Kansas was the nearest military base of any size, complete with cavalry, artillery, and a substantial settlement established in the late 1820s to protect the Santa Fe Trail. Call it the best part of two hundred miles due north from where the Dixon herd would pass on its trek to St. Louis. Running into troops that far from home would be a fluke and offer little succor in their hour of trial.

Which meant they had to deal with any problems on their own, the way they had at Willow Grove. The clear-cut difference: red hostiles—unlike white outlaws—wouldn't seek refuge in a town along the route of travel, where they could be hunted down and brought to book. Likewise, while they'd be passing through established counties, each with an elected sheriff, finding one meant deviating from their course to reach the nearest county seat, then likely hearing that the top lawman had his hands full with local brigands and didn't regard pursuing hostile Comanches as part of his assignment's purview.

They were on their own and roughing it, as Mr. D and all the rest of them had known from the beginning.

Holding on to what they could with what they had.

Tall Tree rode out before his fellow warriors, starting with a good hour's head start on his *manchado* pony, estimating that the white man's herd would be at least that far ahead of him in turn.

There was no rush to overtake them with the sun climbing a blue sky; quite the opposite, in fact, so long as he could chart their route of travel, once they'd crossed into Missouri. It was farther to St. Louis than to Kansas City, both prime markets for disposal of their steers, but with the current state of banditry throughout the state, it might be wise to take the longer road and shy away from trouble on the western border with Kansas.

Tall Tree had little interest in the conflicts between white men. Anything they did to thin their own numbers was fine by him. But even as a party with no interest in the cause of white-on-white mayhem, he understood the feuds that had survived long rancor over slavery, relieved in theory—although not in fact—by the conclusion of their Civil War.

A wild-eyed zealot called John Brown had led his sons and bloody-minded stragglers in a private war against slave-owning farmers spanning three long years before Brown spent his force and lost his life with an attack on Harpers Ferry, where a U.S. arsenal was housed. Brown had led a force of twenty men, one-quarter of them former slaves, to storm the arsenal nearly nineteen years ago, in mid-October 1859. Opposed by officers who later led the Rebel army and marines, Brown saw half of his men shot down, including two of his own sons. The rest were captured, Brown and half a dozen others hanged for treason while slave traders cheered.

Tall Tree considered it a tragedy that either side had triumphed in the War Between the States. He would have liked to have seen them wipe each other out, the plague of their invasion excised from the continent from sea to sea.

Granted, he'd never seen an ocean for himself, but when he pictured it in his imagination, there were only red men and their families lining the beach, ready and able to repel whatever white invaders faced them next.

It was a shame that he would never live to see that day, but while he lived, Tall Tree would do his best to pave the way for others who would follow him. Another Crazy Horse or Sitting Bull, perhaps, but wise enough to shun surrender and fight on until red men across the continent were joined as one against their foes and killed them all or drove their fleeing spawn back to the lands from which they'd come.

If that occurred someday, however far off in the future, Tall Tree reckoned he would not have lived and fought in vain.

For now, though, he had limited ambition. With his small war party, he would strike the white men by attacking what they valued most: their property and wealth. The more steers he could rustle from the herd he was pursuing, turning them to food or profit for his people, the louder it would make his adversaries squeal. And when they squealed, the troops in blue would come.

That would be Tall Tree's time. Not throwing precious lives away to storm the white man's forts against mass guns, but waiting to waylay them in the countryside, where native stealth trumped set piece strategy taught in their distant military schools.

He could devise another Little Big Horn massacre, but on an even grander scale. Why not? That clash in Dakota Territory proved white troops were vulnerable, sometimes led by officers who valued reputation over training and sound tactics. If he could rally enough red men and lay the perfect trap . . .

Tall Tree dismissed that train of thought as premature, watching for any snares his enemies might have prepared for him as they rode north, driving their herd in front of them.

Claiming a long-term victory demanded patience, planning, and resolve.

Tall Tree would make that journey one step at a time.

A N HOUR ON the road assured Bill Pickering that Mr. D's longhorns were none the worse for last night's wear and tear. By this time during last year's cattle drive, they'd lost a dozen steers during a risky river crossing, so the foreman reckoned they were points ahead so far.

Unless they wound up being robbed and massacred.

Which, Pickering admitted to himself, was still entirely possible.

Most days he tried to ride up front, helping to lead and steer the herd, but since the raid last night and the death of Graham Lott, he'd found a spot back toward the herd's west flank, not eating too much dust, but still in a position to surveil the ground they'd covered since breakfast. He didn't keep a gun in hand but was prepared to grab his Winchester or Colt New Line revolver at the first sign of pursuers on their trail.

Their enemies already owed one life for Lott's, and in his present mood, Bill Pickering would just as soon kill all of them to end the nagging threat.

Distracted as he was, Pickering noticed Mr. D approaching only when the boss was within twenty yards, his brindle mare trotting along at a fair pace. When he was close enough to speak without raising his voice, Dixon inquired, "All clear back here?"

"So far, sir," Pickering replied. "I've got my eyes peeled, though."

"Maybe we got lucky. Scared 'em off last night."

"Do you believe that, boss?"

"Nope. But I wish I did."

"Me too. I can't help thinking they've still got us in their sights."

"Unlikely that they'd come at us in daylight, though."

"Agreed, sir."

Dixon frowned. Said, "You know you can call me Gavin when it's just the two of us, right?"

"Yes, sir. Force of habit," Pickering replied. "This way, I don't get used to slipping up."

"You've never let me down, Bill, and I don't expect you ever will."

"I hope not, anyway."

"Won't happen. You're too good at what you do."

"Thanks. But we're looking at a new day now, with hunters on our trail. I couldn't even guess how many of 'em there might be."

"We'll know that when they show themselves," Dixon replied. "And then we'll deal with 'em. No mercy once it's started."

"No, sir. Still sorry that I had to stay behind when you went off to Willow Grove."

"As I recall, that was my order."

"Well . . ."

"Well, nothing. We came through all right, I'd say."

"You did, and that's a fact."

"That Toby Bishop seems to have a knack for it."

"But doesn't love it, like some do," said Pickering.

"That's true. Helps keep him on the sunny side of sane."

"It's good to have him on our side."

Dixon nodded and wheeled his horse, called back over his shoulder as he rode away. "Keep on it, Bill. You're doing fine."

B ISHOP SAW MR. D returning from the back end of the herd, holding a good pace as he rode up toward the front rank of longhorns. From a distance he looked normal, but it would require one of those so-called mediums to probe his thoughts to know what he was thinking.

Even lacking psychic powers, Bishop had a fair idea of what was going on inside the rancher's head. A boss carried the weight of any enterprise, no matter how he delegated portions of authority to get things done. In the event of failure, Dixon would be hardest hit among them—not at all like Eastern bankers who could lose money and blame it on the government or on the New York Stock Exchange.

Beyond a certain point in wealth, he realized, it might become damned near impossible to topple robber barons without killing them outright, but at the ranching level anything could happen—lousy weather or disease, wildfires and rustlers, price manipulation by big-city speculators, not to mention hostile Comanches—and men like Gavin Dixon took it in the neck.

Cowboys might realize some measure of the weight their boss was shouldering, and they relieved a bit of that by being competent, but if a ranch went belly up, they could ride on to find someplace new and start from scratch. For someone with his life tied up in land and debt, stitched tight by pride, there would be no escape.

For Bishop's part, he had to focus on today and then tonight before he got around to thinking of tomorrow. Would the people who had tried stealing a few steers come back wanting more?

That led him into second-guessing strangers he had never seen, an effort that he understood to be a futile exercise. Brigands of different races acted out of varied motives, simple greed aside, and there was no point trying to imagine what they'd do in any given situation, but for one.

If cornered, most lawless types of any creed or color would defend themselves. Some might surrender but that wouldn't be the rule of thumb. Whether they'd break off contact with the Dixon herd after their first attempt fell through was something else entirely, maybe caution winning over pure raw nerve.

When they returned to try their luck again, *if* they came back, Bishop would play the hand that Fate had dealt to him. It could go one way if he was on watch, another way if he was caught napping.

But any way it played, Toby would stand his ground and do his level best for Mr. Dixon and the Circle K. He'd signed a contract for the cattle drive's duration, and for him, there was no backing out of that.

And if he died trying . . . well, some might say that it was overdue.

I AM NOT SURE that we can trust him," said Iron Jacket, keeping his voice down.

Riding beside him, with the other four some yards

ahead of them, talking among themselves, Fire Maker asked, "Tall Tree?"

"Our war chief," Iron Jacket said, letting a measure of exasperation show. "Who else?"

"He hates the whites as much as we do," Fire Maker replied.

"That's true. But hate is not enough, unless he has ability to lead."

"The failure of our first attempt was not his fault."

"I do not claim it was," Iron Jacket said, anxious to set aside establishment of blame. "But two more suns have passed, and all we do is watch."

"Awaiting time to strike," Fire Maker said.

"For how long, then? Another moon? Two? Will we let the whites and all their cattle slip away?"

"He says they're making for St. Louis."

"So? Suppose that's true. The farther north we go, the greater risk we face of meeting farmers, even being sighted from one of their towns. More miles to bring the cattle back if we even succeed in taking them."

"It won't be that long," said Fire Maker.

"Are you so sure?"

"What would you do?" Fire Maker asked. He sounded nervous now.

"You know the law," Iron Jacket said. "One of us has the right to challenge him for leadership. It is our way. You've seen it done before."

Frowning, Fire Maker asked, "And who would do that?"

Iron Jacket feigned a moment's hesitation, then replied, "Don't worry. I'm not asking you to fight him, brother."

They were not in fact related, but had both been raised together, nearly grown when the soldiers came and razed their village, killing everyone they loved.

How they'd escaped was still a mystery, though Iron
Jacket gave full credit to the Great Spirit for watching
over them. The others in their small band had survived
similar things and all refused to occupy one of the
white man's reservations while they aged and wasted
into nothing.

Stung by the remark, which cast doubt on his prow-
ess, Fire Maker paused before responding. "What of
them?" he asked, tilting his chin toward Old Owl,
Someone Found, Great Leaper, and Bright Sun. "Suppose they don't agree?"

"We must consult with them first," Iron Jacket said.
"If they prefer Tall Tree and trust his leadership, of
course, I would not challenge all of them."

"Because our band is small enough," Fire Maker
said, stating the obvious. "If we destroy it, anyone who
does not die fighting will be alone against the whites."

"I have already spoken to Bright Sun," Iron Jacket
said. "He feels as we do."

"We?"

Iron Jacket said, "I've only trusted you with this
idea because I sense you feel the same. You would prefer to *act*, instead of following these white men and
their stinking animals from one horizon to the next."

That much was true, but challenging Tall Tree to
combat over leadership still struck Fire Maker as a
grave, unnecessary risk. The more he thought about it,
the more he saw the hazards that would make their
plan more difficult.

"What of the herd, then?" he inquired. "Do we just
let it go? Has all this been a foolish waste of time?"

"I won't rush into anything," Iron Jacket said. "To
gain agreement from the others will require some
time. I need to speak with each of them in turn, alone,
to make sure none of them betrays us."

Us again, Fire Maker thought. *He tries to make me*

an accomplice, without waiting for me to agree. "How long?" he asked.

"Until we've crossed into Missouri, eh?" Iron Jacket said. "Another two, three days at most. If Tall Tree has no plan of action by that time, we need to make a change."

As if it were that easy, thought Fire Maker. *As if we would ever be the same again.*

But he swallowed his doubts. "Three days," he said. "If all the rest agree."

He hoped he had not just placed a target on his own back.

IT WOULD BE another day or two before they passed the line into Missouri, crossing the invisible line that geographers called parallel 36°30' north. It meant nothing to Gavin Dixon, something that mapmakers had dreamed up to make a wild land seem all nice and orderly, but once that goal had been reached, they'd have another month, approximately, to complete their long northeastern slog.

If Fate and Nature let them make it that far, anyway.

He'd started looking forward to St. Louis, with its buyers waiting at the stockyards, to money in his pocket and paying off the drovers who would leave him there, but Dixon realized that was a risky way of thinking. Advance planning was mandatory, true enough, but as the boss he had to bear in mind the dangers still awaiting them as they traversed the next two hundred and ninety miles or so.

The drive had been more costly than expected, as it stood. Seven men dead so far, and while he'd had a hand in killing five of them—all enemies who'd meant him harm—it weighed on Dixon's soul. Beside that weight, the loss of steers so far seemed negligible, even at a going market rate of forty bucks per head. If they could keep their losses down over the next four weeks, say ten head overall, he still might pocket close to eighty thousand dollars.

Strike from that the cost of raising them—not much, around three thousand—and another thousand paying off the drovers for their time, and it would have been a good year for the Circle K. Then all he had to do was build another herd from scratch and do it all again this time next year.

Thinking of salaries brought Graham Lott to mind, and eighty dollars Dixon wouldn't have to shell out at trail's end. The preacher had begun to grow on him, despite a tendency to run his mouth too much, but there was more to it than that.

Each hand that Dixon lost during a drive—none in a great year; four men on the worst he'd ever had—was like a body blow that left him feeling vaguely sickened. Not his fault, of course, but theft and worse were always at the back of Dixon's mind, a peril every rancher shared, contributing to gray hairs on his head and worry lines around his eyes.

He hoped they'd get along with no more losses on the trail.

And wondered why that felt like he was whistling past a graveyard in the dark.

B Y TOBY BISHOP'S estimate, the night's campsite lay roughly twenty miles south of Missouri's border, now within their reach inside of two, perhaps three days, depending on the trail. Another month or so, that was, and no end to potential risks ahead of them, whether or not the raiders who had murdered Graham Lott came back to try their luck a second time.

And was it wrong that Bishop hoped they *would* return, giving him another shot at them?

Was it irrational, this feeling that he owed Lott something, for the jaundiced view Bishop had held of him, however well concealed from Lott himself?

Or had he just, unconsciously, become the kind of man who could not only cope with violence, but sometimes welcomed it?

Taking the supper plate that Rudy Knapp held out for him, Bishop decided that he didn't feel like harboring such doubts about himself. He wasn't proud of his participation in the Mason County war, but it had been a paying job and he'd believed that he was on the righteous side when he signed up. Later, when he'd begun to doubt himself and the entire crusade, he'd gotten out, hoping he hadn't stayed around so long that he could never clear the stains left on his soul.

And then, there were the worst times, when it didn't really bother him at all.

Like back in Willow Grove.

Estes Courtwright had asked him something, Bishop realizing that he hadn't heard a word of it.

"Sorry," he said. "What's that, again?"

"You really must be looking forward to them beans," said Courtwright, with a grin. "I asked about them redskins, whether it was troubling you, them maybe coming back at us."

"Something to think about," Bishop replied.

"But has it got you worried? Me, I'm worried and I won't deny it."

"Well . . ."

"I've seen what happens when the savages are done with people, when they have a chance to take their time with it. If anybody asks, I'd have to say that preacher caught a lucky break."

"I doubt he'd see it that way," Bishop said.

"I don't mean dying. I mean by dying *quick*. Before they had a chance to really work him on him, you know?"

"I'd just as soon not dwell on it," said Bishop.

"Right. It's bound to make a person queasy. Just forget I brought it up."

And saying that, Estes attacked his pork and beans with gusto, showing no signs of a troubled appetite.

Seated to Bishop's right, Deke Sullivan spoke up, not pausing first to clear his mouth of semi-masticated food. "I haven't slept right since the raid. Planting the preacher didn't sit right with me. If we get another shot at whoever done that, I wouldn't rightly mind."

"Injuns, I tell you," Courtwright said, talking across Bishop. "Damned heathens. What they done to Custer and his boys, hell, I don't even wanna think about it."

Hasn't put you off your feed, though, Bishop thought, but kept it to himself.

Instead, he offered, "Maybe not the best time to be bringing all that up."

"Just saying. I plan to be ready when they come."

And that, thought Bishop, was the best that any of them could hope for.

CHAPTER TWELVE

D AY TWENTY-FIVE FELT like the rest preceding it,
few differences that Bishop could detect offhand
since they had crossed into the Show-Me State. It felt
like riding into Mexico from Texas, with the landscape
pretty much what he'd been seeing since he tried his
luck in Indian country.

The major difference was reservations.

While the territory they had just departed was consumed by them, Missouri kept the land supposedly re-
served for Indians spread out and broken up in smaller
parcels, mostly scattered through the state's southeastern quadrant. There'd been no major conflict between
white and red men since the Osage War of 1837, and
even that was provoked by raiding parties out of Arkansas and Kansas rather than by natives of Missouri
who had settled on their own preserves.

Bishop was hoping that the Circle K's trail drive
wouldn't upset four decades of relations that most folk
would classify as peaceable, but heading trouble off would
have to rest in someone else's hands.

Their first full day of travel on Missouri soil had gone all right so far, passing a few miles east of one small town while Mel Varney rode in trailing a pack-horse to acquire supplies. He'd managed that without a hitch, despite a taint of liquor on his breath when he'd returned, and Mr. Dixon hadn't chided him for that where any of the other hands could hear.

Bishop supposed they'd all have had a drink or three by now if given half a chance.

With fresh supplies on hand, supper added some rice to the expected pork and beans, with fried pota-toes on the side. They washed it down with coffee, as per usual, then Bishop started getting ready for his shift on watch, the first roundup with Paco Esperanza and Deke Sullivan.

It was a clear, warm evening so far, with no clouds to speak of threatening rain overnight. Each day that they put another nine or ten more miles behind them, Bishop thought their odds improved of shaking off the raiders who'd killed Graham Lott.

The rub was working out how Bishop felt about that fact.

The smart thing, he'd decided, was to set his mind on never knowing who had fired the lethal arrow when Lott caught them rustling. If the thieves never returned to try again, there'd be no justice for them, rough or otherwise.

And Toby reckoned he could live with that.

Not *like* it, true enough, but live with it.

And truth be told, how often did a man break even in this life, much less come out ahead?

Wherever he had wandered since the day he'd run away from home, the people Bishop had encountered were roughly divided into categories—two or three at most, depending on the time and place. First thing, you had the upper crust: your politicians, judges, well-off merchants, big-time ranchers, and the like.

The second tier consisted of people who served the first-class crowd, including lawmen in that number, since they followed orders from the ones who'd given them their jobs and paid their meager salaries. Steal chickens from a country farmer and you might wind up in jail. But ride off with a rich man's horse and you'd more likely be the guest of honor at a necktie party.

Then, dwelling at the lower reaches of society were all the rest: drifters and odd-job workers, gamblers, whores and town drunks, not to mention outright thieves and murderers. If what Bishop had read in newspapers was true, Missouri had more than its share of those, including remnants of the old James-Younger gang who'd returned home after they'd been shot all to hell at Northfield, Minnesota; Sam Starr and his wife, Belle; Bill Doolin; and a host of others spawned by border fighting that had turned into the Civil War.

None were averse to stealing livestock if the opportunity arose, but Bishop guessed they'd rather rob a bank, stagecoach, or train than match guns with a bunch of men who were counting on a herd's delivery to make ends meet.

And there were lawmen in Missouri, if you caught one when he wasn't tied up running errands for whichever top dog bossed his bailiwick. Avoiding towns along their route of march, however, made the badges few and far between.

Which meant, as usual, that Bishop and the other hands would have to look out for themselves.

TALL TREE INTENDED for the cattle raid to go ahead tonight. Surveillance of the longhorn herd grew tiresome over time, and thanks to Someone Found, he knew about Iron Jacket's plan to challenge him as war chief if he did not execute the mission soon.

After that was done, if they succeeded, he would have to face the would-be traitor in his own small band.

Dissension could destroy a group of any size—whole tribes had been disrupted in that way, as he knew all too well—but in a smaller, close-knit party it was even more corrosive.

Tall Tree had no reason to believe the others had already turned against him. They might have overpowered him with ease, acting together, but their sense of honor would demand another leader to assert himself and best Tall Tree in personal combat before they followed him wholeheartedly.

Tonight's work should solve that problem, weaken Iron Jacket's resolve, and give Tall Tree the chance to deal with him before Iron Jacket made his move. That changed the nature of life-threatening surprise and turned it back upon his enemy.

Raising a cupped hand to his lips, Tall Tree mimicked a whippoorwill's call. An answer returned from the darkness, affirming receipt of his order to close on the herd and begin.

Tonight, there would be no half measures, no attempts to lead a single steer away, not even three or four.

Tonight, if the Great Spirit smiled upon them, Tall Tree and his braves were going to make history.

I F BISHOP HAD been scheduled for a later shift on watch, he would have missed the start of near disaster for the herd. But as it was, he found himself immediately in the thick of it with Sullivan and Esperanza.

When it started, Paco was singing a *corrido*, one of those narrative ballads that served unlettered peasants in his homeland as alternatives to newspapers, bridging the gap between cantina entertainment and delivery of late-breaking events, protests, or revolutionary propaganda. Tonight's song, falling somewhere in the middle, was "La Cucaracha"—"The Cockroach."

That might sound funny, but it worked as music and the longhorns seemed to find it soothing. Bishop wasn't sure exactly why or how, but he still smiled along as Esperanza's lisping voice drifted across the herd and camp.

Bishop didn't understand it all, but he was still enjoying it when suddenly all holy hell broke loose.

It started with a warbling shriek that could have done a cougar proud, though obviously uttered by a human voice. Another cry responded, emanating from another spot some fifty yards away, and then a rifle shot rang out, apparently not aimed at anyone but fired into the open air.

Bishop spotted the muzzle flash and had his snow-flake Appaloosa galloping in that direction, shouting out to any drovers in the camp who weren't already scrambling from their bedrolls, when a second shot echoed across the plains, followed immediately by a third and fourth.

And Mr. Dixon's longhorns did the rest.

Whatever else the gunmen might have had in mind, they'd started a stampede.

Unless you had lived through one—not simply watching it but caught up in the very midst of it—you would have found it difficult to grasp the chaos and destructive power of a herd in total panic.

Anything could start a herd of longhorns running aimlessly: a rattler's whir, striking a match, a tumbleweed propelled by gusting wind, on up to lightning bolts and thunder.

Not to mention gunfire in the middle of a lazy night.

Once it began, a stampede could destroy most anything that stands before it—fences, man-made structures on the small side, not to mention horses and their riders or hapless pedestrians. Depending on geography, the mad rush could destroy a herd itself, cattle or mustangs charging off a cliff and plummeting through space or diving headlong into rivers where large numbers of them drown.

In short, utter catastrophe.

And sometimes that was planned.

When buffalo were still abundant on the plains, some native tribes stampeded them deliberately, as a callous form of hunting, claiming those that died or were disabled in the melee, thereby saving cartridges, arrows, and energy.

To slow or halt a stampede that was already underway, cowboys had to attempt to turn a dashing herd into itself, so that the stock began to run in circles, forced to slacken its pace and pull up short of lethal obstacles. Shouting and cracking whips or waving lariats could help; pistol fire was normally the best approach, shocking the frightened animals back to a grudging consciousness of time and place.

Of course, that didn't always work—like now, when hostile fire launched the panic in the first place.

Toby Bishop and his fellow drovers faced two problems now, at equal risk of death or injury from both. The raging herd was one. The other, getting shot by whoever in hell had started the stampede.

I RON JACKET RAISED and triggered his Albini-Braendlin rifle in a strong one-handed grip, the single-shot weapon angled toward distant stars.

He did not know the gun was made in Belgium—didn't know, in fact, where Belgium was or even *what* it was. The rifle had belonged to a white settler killed and scalped, his rural homestead looted afterward, and so far, it had served Iron Jacket well.

Tonight, perhaps, it would dispatch another white man to his ancestors.

The longhorn herd was running as anticipated, cattle making panicked noises, their hooves thundering like U.S. Army drums in a parade that had degenerated into raving lunacy. Riding his pony bareback, feeding the Albini's open breech a fresh 11mm cartridge—the equivalent of a .43-caliber—Iron Jacket watched for the other members of his band, spotting them by the muzzle flashes of their gun.

It would be relatively easy to assassinate Tall Tree in the stampede's confusion, but Iron Jacket was postponing the war chief's elimination; he was focused now on the successful culmination of their plan. When they had gathered up enough survivors of the white man's herd to suit their purpose, then and only then would he challenge Tall Tree and best him honorably, in accordance with their tribe's tradition, fighting to the death, hand to hand.

When he became war chief, Iron Jacket wanted no taint on his name.

Around the trail drive's chuck wagon, cowboys shocked from dreams were on their feet or seated on blankets and tugging on their boots. The faster ones among them were already racing toward their horses, none as yet saddled, most straining at their tethers, spooked by the stampeding cattle.

It was nearly perfect.

Iron Jacket saw his opportunity and seized it. With his pony standing almost placidly beneath him, well away from the stampede's direction, he shouldered his rifle, cocked the hammer with his thumb, and aimed along its thirty-four-inch barrel past the iron sights. He used the campfire as a backdrop, picked a shadow as it moved between him and the flames, and fired.

A hit!

The stricken cowboy lurched backward, his legs betraying him, and fell into the fire. His cry of pain was music to Iron Jacket's ears, three of his fellows rushing to extract him from the flames.

Reloading his weapon, Iron Jacket left them to it, satisfied that with the act of wounding—maybe killing—one, he had in fact prevented four from riding out to head off the stampede.

For now, it was enough.

Iron Jacket tugged his pony through a half turn, urged it to a gallop as he rode to join the other members of his war party.

I S HE ALIVE?" asked Gavin Dixon, watching three drovers deposit Boone Hightower near the chuck wagon.

"Hit bad, boss," Isaac Thorne replied. "And burned some."

Dixon didn't bother cursing. They were past that now, compelled to act immediately if he hoped to save the herd and rout whoever had stampeded them.

"Leave 'im to Mel and Rudy," Dixon ordered. "Anything that they can't manage is beyond us. Rest of you, get saddled up and run the stampede drill. Spot someone shooting who ain't one of us, try blowing off his goddamn head!"

They answered, "Yes, sir!" in a garbled chorus, sprinting off toward the remuda, lugging guns and saddles. Abel Floyd was there ahead of them, untying tethers, handing off the mounts first come, first served.

The air was full of thunder, longhorns running, bleating. Gunshots punctuated it, some fired by raiders still unseen, others by Dixon's three drovers on watch. The slug that had drilled Hightower, he supposed, had been steered by either dumb luck or some decent marksmanship.

Dixon felt suddenly exposed, a target in a shooting gallery, but ducking under cover never crossed his mind.

He had a job to do, a herd and ranch to save.

And failing that, he might as well just pick a compass point at random, traveling until he found someplace where he could start from scratch.

At forty-seven, pushing forty-eight, Dixon knew that the odds of that were slim to none.

Bill Pickering ran past him, tugging at his belt and gasping, "On my way, boss! Bastards caught me watering the bushes."

Dixon would have laughed at that in other circumstances, but he didn't have it in him now. "I'm right behind you," he told Pickering, jacking a round into the chamber of his Winchester '73.

He got to the remuda seconds after Pickering, found Abel Floyd holding their horses for them while the other cowboys scattered, galloping away to try turning the herd or to engage their enemies, whichever they could manage best.

Once both their mounts were saddled, Dixon and his foreman mounted up, and Bill looked to him for orders.

Dixon didn't hesitate. "The herd has got to be our top priority," he said.

"With people shooting at us, though—"

"I didn't say it would be easy." Dixon cut him short.

"No, sir!"

"We do our best. If someone you don't recognize gets in your way—"

"Kill 'im," said Pickering, without a heartbeat's hesitation.

"That's exactly right," Dixon replied, and steered his brindle mare off toward the head of the stampede, already better than a hundred yards due west, no sign of slowing down.

* * *

Estes courtwright hadn't dealt with a stampede before, blind luck perhaps, and now, caught in the path of one, he wished he could have put it off forever.

But his wish came too damned late.

Courtwright wasn't entirely sure how he had come to be ahead of the longhorns. His sable gelding was a swift horse, granted, and he'd spurred it close to top speed in the mad dash out of camp, trying to do what he'd been taught by older, wiser hands—namely, to get as far in front of a stampeding herd as possible and fire over their heads to slow them down at first, then turn them back.

To that end, he was brandishing his Colt Pocket Navy revolver, a .36-caliber weapon larger than its name might suggest. He held his fire until he'd caught up with the leading longhorns in the panicked herd, his hat blown back and slapping at his shoulders, dangling from its rawhide chin strap while the wind rush whipped his longish sandy hair around his face. Some of it slapped across his left eye, stinging him, but Courtwright wouldn't rein the sable back from running full tilt over moonlit sod.

So far, he was the only hand in a position to prevent the herd from rushing on to hell and gone.

Reaching the point position, Estes mouthed a curse and steered his mount across the path of onrushing destruction, only then cocking his Colt and squeezing off a shot back toward the general location of their camp. No problem there. His aim was high, and even when his slug eventually fell to earth, the other drovers should be well clear of its path.

And if some of them weren't . . . well, who would know the difference when this was all behind them, anyhow?

He didn't know who'd started the stampede, presumably the Comanche who'd tried to steal from them a few days back, but none of them seemed to be firing at him now, which was a blessing in its way.

Now all he had to fret about was horns, hooves, and the tonnage of some nineteen hundred steers and change, thundering toward him like a tidal wave.

And bearing down on him right now.

Courtwright got off a second shot before the wave of flesh and bone enveloped him. His horse gave out a squeal of pain as it was gored inside its stifle, roughly corresponding to a human's knee, ripping through muscle and tendons, snapping bone. Estes tried to bail out of his saddle as the horse went down but wasn't fast enough. It landed on his right leg, rolled, and then it was his turn to scream.

He'd never felt such pain but reckoned that it wouldn't last much longer. Trying for a third shot with his Colt, he found his gun hand empty, trigger finger curling uselessly around thin air.

And that was when the longhorns trampled over him, hooves staving in his gelding's ribs, snapping its neckbones, shattering its skull. One of those hooves came down on Courtwright's twisted pelvis, snapping it in two, before the longhorn flicked its head and gored him underneath his chin, piercing his soft palate and brainpan like a javelin hurled at a watermelon.

Courtwright didn't feel it as his corpse was wrenched out from beneath his fallen mount and carried off downrange, dangling and flopping from the horn that finished him as if he were some ghoulish ornament.

THE AIR WAS filled with leaden hornets, buzzing after Tall Tree and his raiders as they drove two dozen longhorns, traveling southwestward from the point where they had set the white man's herd fleeing in terror. Tall Tree had been hopeful for a larger haul, but under fire and riding pell-mell through the night, he settled for the steers in hand.

Aside from parting shots beyond effective range, the white men did not follow in pursuit. They would be more concerned about collecting their remaining stock, driving the winded steers back toward the camp they had deserted when the first gunfire surprised them out of drowsiness. That might require another hour, likely more, and it would still be dark when it was finished, every man still fit to ride on guard duty for the remainder of the night.

Tomorrow morning, when the sun rose, there would still be work for them to do collecting strays, tending to any injured men or steers, deciding who was fit to travel on. Some badly damaged cattle might be shot. Drovers in urgent need of medical attention would require an escort to the nearest prairie town, some fifteen miles away.

And through all that, Tall Tree's Comanches would be traveling, herding their stolen livestock back across Missouri's border and beyond the reach of local law. When the white men got their wits about them and decided what to do, if any of them cared to track the raiders who'd humiliated them, it should prove to be a futile enterprise.

And even if they *did* succeed in following the war party, what of it?

Most would certainly remain to tend the shrunken herd. The handful that gave chase might spend a day or more on Tall Tree's trail, only to find themselves outnumbered and outgunned if they made contact.

Free longhorns and dead white men. It would be reckoned as a double victory.

The only major problem facing Tall Tree now was Iron Jacket.

Victory against the trail drive would have undercut the traitor's popularity among the other braves. Tall Tree had planned the raid and seen it carried out as a cooperative effort. If Iron Jacket tried to press his case now, he'd be arguing from weakness, trying to present himself as an alternative to a war chief who'd proved himself in battle.

But Tall Tree had no intention of allowing it to go that way, much less allowing someone who had betrayed him to select a given time and place for settling their feud. When they had put enough miles in between themselves and the remainder of the longhorn herd, he would confront Iron Jacket, take him by surprise, and force the issue on his own.

Whatever happened next, tradition had decreed that only one of them should live to fight another day.

Tall Tree fully intended that the honor would be his and his alone.

Y OU KNEW IT was bad when seasoned cowboys cried. Not sniffling just a little, as at weddings when they'd had too much to drink, but when hot tears cut through the dust coating their cheeks.

Bishop was not among the weepers, and in truth he only counted two of them, but who was he to judge?

Their losses from the raid: two men, one horse, and an uncertain number of longhorns. Surprisingly, none of the steers had died or suffered crippling injuries, and while a head count couldn't be completed until after sunrise, once the final stragglers were retrieved, Bishop and Sullivan had both seen faceless riders breaking off into the night, driving longhorns ahead of them. They had fired after the escaping thieves, without success, but hadn't ridden after them since Mr. Dixon had arrived, bellowing orders that retrieval of the herd came first.

Their dead were Boone Hightower, shot through his right lung and scorched in places when he fell into the campfire, and soft-spoken Estes Courtwright, gored and trampled almost beyond recognition by stampeding cattle.

That meant two more graves to mark their route of travel, while the horse that had died with Courtwright would be stripped of tack and left behind to nurture scavengers, the prairie's cleaning crew.

And then what?

Mr. Dixon was addressing that subject right now, standing behind the bodies of his trail drive's most recent fatalities.

"The bastards put one over on us, men," he said. "Those close enough to see them reckon they were Comanches, likely the same ones from before who murdered Graham Lott. Now they've got three lives on their conscience that we know of—that is, if they even have a conscience they can divvy up between 'em."

"Are we going after them?"

"Some of you are," Dixon replied, "but only after daylight, when we've finished rounding up whatever stragglers from the herd that we can find."

Bill Pickering held up a hand, as if he were a boy in school. "Boss, when you say some of us . . ."

"It's exactly what I mean, Bill. You'll be riding point on that with two men of your choosing, while the rest of us push on northward."

"But—"

"Don't need to chase 'em far," Dixon pressed on, as if his foreman hadn't tried to interrupt him. "All of 'em mounted, with the steers they stole, it shouldn't be a problem picking up their tracks. But listen good now. If you don't catch up with 'em inside a day, or two at most, forget about it and we'll eat the loss. Ride back and join up with the herd fast as you can. I got a feeling we'll be needing every man and gun from here on out."

The foreman clearly didn't like that order, but he bobbed his head and swallowed it, saying, "Yes, sir. Just as you say."

"It's settled, then," their boss declared. "Mel, get some food on, will you? We'll have no spare time to waste come sunup, in between the strays and digging graves."

CHAPTER THIRTEEN

MOST DAYS, BILL Pickering enjoyed working for Mr. Dixon, even when that work was arduous. This morning, though, he couldn't make that claim.

He hated running out on Dixon and the herd when they were three men down already, with the best part of a month's journey still left to go before they reached St. Louis.

If they ever reached that city with its stockyard, paymaster, and slaughterhouses.

Mr. D, in Pickering's opinion, needed him now more than ever, but he understood the order he'd received and was determined to obey it, whether he agreed with it or not. Sometimes he dared to offer unsolicited advice on some idea of Dixon's, but not this time.

His mission on this early morning was twofold.

Reclaim the stolen cattle if he could accomplish that, of course. But even if he couldn't manage to retrieve them fit for travel and eventual auction, he had to punish those who'd stolen them and killed off two of Mr. Dixon's drovers in the process.

That meant killing work, and since he'd missed the Willow Grove action—another order that he'd disagreed with but obeyed—there was no skipping out on this assignment.

Absolutely none.

Given his choice of hands to ride with him, he'd called on Whit Melville for sheer imposing size and Toby Bishop for the skill he'd shown at putting gunmen down. Bishop had slain two of the rustlers from the first gang that attacked their herd, and there was nothing to suggest he'd lost his touch for it during the interim between attacks.

This time it looked like Comanches, but once a fellow's mind was set on killing . . . well, what difference did that make?

Between them they were packing three good rifles, three six-guns, and ample ammo for the job at hand, unless the raiders they were seeking led them to a village full of warriors spoiling for a fight.

It didn't feel that way to Pickering, but he'd been wrong enough times in the past to keep his fingers crossed for luck.

They left before the funerals in camp, Pickering mounted on a sorrel mare, Whit Melville on his pinto, Bishop on his snowflake Appaloosa stallion. Picking up the raiders' trail from last night didn't take a genius with a magnifying glass, and they were making good time, only slowing when they came in sight of hills, a stand of trees, or something else that struck them as a likely ambush site.

Two hours into the pursuit, none of those apprehensive moments had panned out, and Mr. D's order came back to Pickering. A day or two at most, then give it up and they would eat the loss.

Meaning that Mr. Dixon would be eating it, another slice out of his profits when they hadn't come within two hundred and eighty–odd miles of their final destination yet.

And three men down, he thought. *Don't be forgetting them.*

As if he could.

Ranching was risky at the best of times in Indian country, the same for trail drives moving interstate, where anything could happen, and it often did. They'd seen a fair bit of that *anything* so far, starting with April snow, then rustlers, now the raiding party. Starting off with thirteen hands, not counting Varney and his helper, they were down almost one-quarter of their workforce, with half of the journey still ahead.

It was the worst drive Pickering had served on yet, for sheer attrition, and he never hoped to see its like again.

But it was time to put such thoughts behind him, focus on the bloody errand he had been assigned. And if he lived through that, there would be time to think about tomorrow down the road.

TALL TREE ORDERED a rest stop at midmorning, with the sun three hands above the western skyline, climbing in a clear blue sky. The others did not argue with him, though he caught Iron Jacket cutting sidelong glances toward him when he thought Tall Tree was unaware.

He had no doubt that Iron Jacket expected trouble from him, coming soon. For now, it pleased Tall Tree to make the traitor sweat, trying to guess when retribution for his backbiting and scheming would descend upon him.

Soon enough. But not just yet.

Tall Tree required his full band to transport the longhorns they had liberated from the white man's herd last night, killing at least one cowboy in the process. An attack of that nature invited hot pursuit, no doubt in progress even as his men dismounted, drinking from their waterskins and chewing pemmican, eyes watchful on all sides.

Tall Tree was not aware of any settlements nearby, where hired hands from the cattle drive could log complaints of the attack they'd suffered or solicit help from other whites in tracking down their stolen steers. Law on the prairie, even in Missouri, was whatever men with weapons had the will and power to impose.

And if pursuers overtook his war party, it would mean war.

Which bothered Tall Tree not at all.

He had not counted coup on any adversaries yet this year, a task requiring physical contact, often without inflicting lethal injury. It was a show of bravery, quite different from firing arrows or bullets from a distance that precluded using knives, war clubs, or tomahawks. Each close approach from which a warrior managed to emerge unscathed enhanced his personal prestige, while being wounded was a strike against him.

The reward for counting coup—an eagle's feather— marked him as a man.

The single feather plaited into Tall Tree's hair commemorated an event from eight months earlier. It was high time, he realized, to prove himself again.

Perhaps against Iron Jacket, who planned to take his life.

He glanced across at Someone Found and caught the warrior watching him, one eyebrow slightly raised as if asking a silent question. Tall Tree moved his head the barest inch from side to side, a negative response, but only for the moment.

He could not afford a personal diversion at this moment, with white hunters likely searching for them.

When the time came for a reckoning with Iron Jacket, Tall Tree wanted time to do it properly and relish the event.

Judging that they had rested long enough, he called for the remainder of his war party to mount their bareback ponies and resume their southward journey. Moving ever closer to the territory where their captive people dwelt in poverty on barren land selected for them by the Great White Father in the East, they could consider options for disposal of the captured steers.

Tall Tree had not decided yet if they should feed the reservation's hungry souls or seek a monetary profit from the mini herd. One path would win them goodwill and perhaps a few recruits. The other meant cash for more sophisticated weapons, useful in the wider war Tall Tree had planned.

But there was no need to decide right now.

Particularly when they might be fighting for their lives before the sun went down.

TOBY BISHOP HADN'T asked to join the hunting party, but he'd offered no resistance to it either. It was clear he'd been selected because of the fight at Willow Grove, and because he had mentioned to Pickering that he had played a part in Mason County's Hoodoo War.

So be it. That was what a man could logically expect when he had shot folks in the past and made no bones about it.

Do it once, twice, even three or more times, and you were the fellow people turned to when they had to cope with dirty work.

The sad part, he supposed, was that he didn't mind so much, making him wonder if the kind and caring part of him was being chipped away.

Or did he ever have one to begin with?

Melville, riding beside him on the pinto, asked Bishop, "What are your thoughts on this deal, Toby? Meaning what should we expect?"

"Can't rightly answer that," Bishop replied. "No way of telling what we'll find if we catch up with the raiders we're chasing."

"Oh, we'll catch them right enough," Bill Pickering chipped in. "I gave my word to Mr. D."

And Mr. D had given them a deadline, but there was no point in a reminder to their foreman for the sake of argument.

"Take that for granted, Mr. Pickering," said Melville. "If we find 'em, put 'em down and all, that leaves a whole new job soon as the shooting's done. How long you reckon it'll take to overtake the herd again?"

Pickering shot an irritated glance at Whit and said, "No point in worrying about that now. Let's take it one step at a time, all right?"

"Yes, sir. No problem."

"Great. Let's get a move on, if you don't mind."

Melville glanced over at Bishop, shrugging with a wounded *what 'n hell did I say?* look on his tanned face. Toby could only answer with his own shrug and face forward, concentrating on the trail they had been following since dawn.

He knew their job was going to be tough enough without breeding a quarrel among themselves. A chase, perhaps protracted, almost certainly concluding with a gunfight, was enough to think about just now.

If they were hunting six or seven braves, that meant they were outnumbered two to one at least. If those raiders were headed for a larger village, you could multiply those odds until they made the score at Little Big Horn seem evenly matched.

And there was something else to ponder, if the raiders ran across other white men who disposed of them, then felt like hanging on to Mr. Dixon's longhorns for themselves. That took the problem to another level altogether, and he didn't even want to think about where it might lead.

G AVIN DIXON WATCHED the final shovelful of dirt tossed onto Boone Hightower's grave and tamped down with the shovel's blade. As when they'd buried Graham Lott, no markers stood above the mounds of soil where two more drovers had been laid to rest.

Instead of trying to quote Scripture now, Dixon simply declared, "These fellas weren't expecting to meet death out here, but it's a chance we all took, starting off the drive. We've still got far to go, and friends in peril elsewhere, as they try to put things right. Won't help these men, but if they had a voice, I reckon they'd tell us to get the herd moving."

Somebody said, "Amen," as if he'd led them in a prayer, but Dixon didn't try to pick out who it was. He settled for "Mount up. The day's going to waste."

His drovers had recovered all the straying longhorns they could find. A quick head count told Dixon there were nineteen hundred and seventy remaining, and he didn't bother double-checking it. If strictly accurate, that meant the raiders had escaped with twenty-seven steers, and he still hoped to get most of those back if Pickering and his two backup guns were lucky, but it wasn't something he could count on.

Profits dropped with every steer they lost along the way, but if they held the line with what they'd managed to preserve, the coming auction in St. Louis should still put him in the black for this season.

Next year, too far away for anyone to contemplate from where they stood right now, would have to take care of itself.

Dixon mounted his brindle mare and watched the drovers as they got the longhorns in formation, heading off to the northeast. A cursory examination showed no injured steers, though some were off their feed a bit after the wild night they'd endured.

No great surprise, and they could make that up over the weeks to come if they were spared any further incidents along the way.

Mel Varney put the chuck wagon in line behind the marching herd, no rising dust to speak of while they were traversing grassy plains. Dixon came last, watching for any strays drifting to east or west, prepared to intercede himself since they were down six hands this morning.

That put his thoughts in motion, soaring off southward toward Pickering, Bishop, and Melville, making tracks in hot pursuit of that war party that had struck them overnight. Dixon had no animosity toward any tribe of Indians per se, but if they crossed him, killed his men, or stole what rightfully belonged to him, they instantly became his enemies. They were the same as any other cutthroat rustlers.

And Dixon only knew one way to deal with them.

He would have led the chase himself, but he had laid that thought aside in preference to staying with the herd, his livelihood.

Prayers wouldn't help the trackers now, he was convinced, and didn't bother with them. Pickering and company already knew they had his trust, and while that wouldn't get them through a shooting scrape, Dixon supposed it couldn't hurt.

He hoped to see them all alive and well within another day or two at the outside.

And failing that, he told himself that he had done his very best to see they were prepared for trouble on the trail.

At some point Fate would have to do the rest.

* * *

THEY STOPPED HERE for a bit," Bill Pickering observed. "See how the cattle milled around instead of holding to their route?"

Bishop supposed that he was right but drew no inference as to how far ahead of them the stolen longhorns might be now. Scanning the landscape they had recently traversed while heading in the opposite direction, he saw no place where the purloined steers could be concealed while snipers lay in wait to deal with manhunters.

"Wish we could tell how far they've gone ahead of us by now," Whit Melville said.

"You and me both," Bishop allowed.

"No point in sitting here and jawing over it," said Pickering. "They ain't here now, and every minute wasted puts them farther out ahead of us."

Toby decided not to mention it was Pickering who'd called the trampled grass and other signs of steers briefly at rest to their attention in the first place. Nothing would be gained from setting off an argument, and Pickering was right. Their first job was to catch up with the raiders, then dispose of them as quickly and efficiently as possible.

This time he didn't look at Whit to see if Pickering's remark had struck a nerve. All three of them were on the prod, and rightly so, but Bishop knew they had to keep their anger focused on the enemies who'd struck them overnight, killing their friends and making off with Mr. Dixon's stock.

Toby had only dealt with hostile Indians one time before and hadn't killed any that time. He had been staying over in a little Texas town called Barrenburg that mostly lived up to its name. He'd been recuperating from a bender in a harlot's crib when a small raiding party tore through town, whooping and hollering, setting alight the dry-goods store, and by the time Bishop had reached his Colt, the braves had galloped off, leaving a haze of smoke and shattered nerves behind.

His one and only skirmish with red men—at least, before last night.

And now, whatever lay ahead.

BILL PICKERING TRIED to ignore Bishop and Melville talking back and forth behind him. They were keeping up a decent pace and hadn't held him back so far, hence he could find no call for snapping at them, even though his nerves urged him to outbursts of pique.

He worried first and most about the herd, with Gavin Dixon left in solitary charge. Nobody better, when he thought about it, but he'd worked for Mr. D so long he still felt like a shirker, leaving Dixon with an epic list of chores while he—the foreman hired to shoulder much of that—was riding off with two of Gavin's hands when they were needed most on duty with the drive.

It didn't matter that they were obeying orders, risking life and limb with only fifty-fifty odds at best of managing to pull it off. Deserting Dixon, as it seemed to Pickering, still went against his grain.

The hell of it: He knew that they were on the raiders' trail but couldn't say how far ahead his targets were, how recently they'd made the tracks that he was following. Each yard he covered on his sorrel mare led Pickering farther from Dixon and the herd that needed him.

Damned if I do, he thought. *Damned if I don't.*

They'd covered four, maybe five miles since leaving camp a smidgen after dawn. The only edge he had over his enemies so far was that the longhorns they'd appropriated from the herd were bound to slow them down. Whether the raiding party was composed of six or seven men—an estimate advanced by drovers who had seen them fleeing in the dark—they had approximately four or five steers each to watch and manage on their trail, wherever it was leading them. Steers generally weren't as bad as mules for balking when you wanted them to move, but neither were they little lambs that fell in line instinctively and did as they were told.

The trick, when Pickering caught up with them at last, would be eliminating six or seven armed, determined men without harming the steers or spooking them into another wild dash over hill and dale. He thought—hoped—that the first part of his task was feasible, though perilous. The second bit threatened to waste more time he and the trail drive couldn't spare.

To cover that, he slowed his mare a bit, reluctantly, and spoke as his companions fell in place to either side of him. "When we catch up to them," he said, "no hesitation cutting loose. The only way we win this thing is by taking down as many of them as we can before they have a fighting chance."

"You mean, like, shoot 'em in the back?" asked Melville.

"Back, front, any way you can," said Pickering. "They're thieves and murderers, remember. Being Comanche, or whichever tribe, they're also violating treaties with the government. Same thing as any other outlaw wanted by the law, dead or alive."

"But we don't give 'em to the sheriff, right?" Whit asked.

"What sheriff?" Pickering replied. "Do you know

where we are, what county, who he is, or where he's got his office?"

"No, sir."

"Right. So put the law out of your mind and concentrate on Mr. D's orders. Eliminate the threat, recover any steers we can, and get back with 'em to the drive."

"Yes, sir. Just getting that straight in my mind."

"And is it straight now?"

"As can be."

"And you, Bishop?"

"No problem. Put 'em down, collect the steers, and get back to the herd."

"Correct," said Pickering, but he was stuck on Bishop's first two words.

No problem, eh?

But problems and a risk of getting killed were all Bill Pickering could think about.

THE AFTERNOON WAS waning, sunset's first long shadows reaching out across the plains. After the best part of a day in transit, with miles between them and the herd they'd robbed, Tall Tree decided it was likely safe to stop and rest awhile.

Not spend the night, perhaps, but time to build a small and smokeless fire from dried wood, sleep in shifts for two or three hours, with three men down and four awake to watch the longhorns constantly.

And what about Iron Jacket?

Tall Tree did not trust him, could not truly rest until his enemy was laid to rest.

He felt uneasy doing that while they were on the run, armed white men theoretically pursuing them, but what choice did he have? As soon as Tall Tree dared to close his eyes, would Iron Jacket spring upon him, striking without honor in his urgency to lead the war party?

He called the others to a halt, saying, "We stop here for a time. Two men sleep at a time, two hours each, the rest on watch."

"That leaves an odd man out," Iron Jacket said.

"I have allowed for that," Tall Tree replied, drawing his cut-down saber from its sheath.

"What does this mean?" Iron Jacket asked.

"You plan to challenge me," Tall Tree required. "There is no reason to delay it any longer."

He could see Iron Jacket was surprised by the exposure of his plan. Traitors, devoid of honor in their hearts, sometimes have difficulty realizing they, in turn, might be betrayed.

"So be it." As he spoke, Iron Jacket drew his knife and tomahawk, one in each hand. "Your time is at an end."

"Let us find out," Tall Tree advised.

Before his saber's blade was shortened, it had measured three feet long, now half that, single-edged and sharpened almost to the keenness of a shaving razor. Its guard was made of brass, its handle wrapped with leather. Presently it weighed a little under two pounds on a white man's scale. Tall Tree had practiced with it to achieve an expert's skill.

Iron Jacket gripped his weapons almost casually, turning to regard the other faces ringed around him. "And these five?" he asked.

"Shall take no part," Tall Tree assured him. "If you wonder whether they will follow you, should you emerge victorious, that is a question best asked later."

Iron Jacket frowned. "At least one of them has betrayed me," he observed.

"As any faithless traitor might expect," Tall Tree replied. "Do you accept the challenge now, or will you leave us empty-handed?"

"I accept, of course," Iron Jacket said. "Let us begin."

CHAPTER FOURTEEN

I T'S THEM," BILL Pickering declared, and passed his
spyglass off to Toby Bishop on his left. "No doubt."

Bishop confirmed it with a glance and passed the
pocket telescope to Whit Melville, letting him have a
turn.

"You notice one man down?" Bishop asked Pickering.

"Looks like they had some kind of falling-out," the
foreman said. "His chest's stove in. One less of 'em for
us to deal with."

"Fighting when they're on the run?" asked Melville.
"That make any sense to you?"

"Don't waste time figuring how Injuns think," their
foreman said. "We need to move before they all get
mounted up again and turn it into a running fight."

That made good sense to Bishop. It seemed the
raiders—painted like Comanches—weren't aware of
being watched so far. With Pickering and Melville, he
was standing on a ridge of sorts with dusk falling behind them, stretching out its velvet shadows overland.

Their horses stood downslope behind the three cow-boys, waiting for whatever came next.

"Snipe 'em from here?" Whit asked. "Or do you wanna ride on over there?"

"We don't want a long-distance fight running the longhorns all over creation," Pickering replied. "Mount up and have your rifles ready when we're closer in."

They were a hundred yards or so out from their targets presently, shaded by the oncoming night. None of the braves still on their feet had spotted them so far, but that could change at any second, hence the urgency for them to make their move while clinging to a vestige of surprise.

Bishop swung into Compañero's saddle, drew his Yellow Boy Winchester from its scabbard, weapon in his right hand, reins clutched in his left. Perhaps he was imagining the snowflake Appaloosa's eagerness to run and meet the enemy. If so, Bishop was pleased to go with the illusion, taking it on faith.

His two companions were aboard their horses now, all facing down the slope toward six red men and two dozen longhorns that belonged to Gavin Dixon. At a sign from Pickering they launched themselves downhill, no Rebel yells or premature gunshots, only the sound of hoofbeats over sod announcing their attack.

Downrange, one of the warriors saw or heard them coming, barking something to the rest that put them all into defensive postures, five with guns in hand, the sixth holding a bow.

"That tears it, boys!" said Pickering. Raising his Winchester and sighting down its barrel, left hand dangling his sorrel's reins, he ordered, "Give 'em hell!"

Bishop required no urging on that score. He squeezed the Yellow Boy's trigger and felt its recoil buck against his shoulder as a puff of muzzle smoke obscured his chosen target. Riding through that tart gunpowder haze, he saw the Comanche he'd aimed for kneeling on the grass, a crimson stain marking his buckskin trousers, still fighting to aim the long gun in his hands.

A muzzle flash and puff of smoke downrange, the distance from their adversaries lessened by one-third or more. The warrior's bullet sizzled past on Bishop's right, somewhere between himself and Pickering, missing them both.

Bishop pumped his Winchester's lever action and felt the empty cartridge casing it ejected clip his hat brim and deflect away as he was lining up another shot.

"Hold still, you whoreson," he muttered. "Just one more second now."

IRON JACKET'S HUNTING knife had grazed Tall Tree's left shoulder as they struggled, just before the war chief's saber plunged beneath his enemy's breastbone and angled upward, skewering Iron Jacket's heart. That thrust had frozen him in rigid death, his brain a second late in picking up the message, then transmitting it to slack-jawed face and folding legs.

The fight, such as it was, had lasted barely fifteen seconds overall.

When it was done, and Iron Jacket was laid out on the prairie grass, the other braves had whooped as one, congratulating Tall Tree on his victory. They likely would have done the same if Iron Jacket had defeated him instead, but on the face of it he had no reason to dispute their loyalty.

Not yet.

But they would all bear watching in the future, if their band remained intact to plan more escapades.

He was about to call upon the five survivors to

mount up, preparing to resume their southward march, when Someone Found looked past Tall Tree, pointed, and warned them all, "White eyes!"

Tall Tree counted three horsemen, still outnumbered two to one by his raiders. Whether they had pursued his party from the scene of last night's clash or simply turned up by coincidence, he could not say and did not care. If they were riders from the longhorn herd, they would attack. If not, while they might turn and flee, they could report his party's presence to local authorities or hunters from the trail drive.

Either way, the only safe white men were corpses.

Tall Tree did not have to tell his men that they should arm themselves. In seconds, Old Owl, Fire Maker, and Someone Found had seized their shoulder guns. Great Leaper had his long bow in hand, an arrow nocked. Tall Tree retrieved his own Sharps rifle from the ground and raised its ladder sight, cocking the hammer with his thumb.

He did not feel the slash across his shoulder now, his full concentration focused on the three riders as they raced forward, drawing closer to his party and the steers they'd captured hours earlier.

The next few moments would decide whether their effort was in vain, or if they would be granted further time to make their getaway after these three white men were dead. Through victory, his warriors would obtain more horses, firearms, and ammunition for the war Tall Tree had planned.

They might not live to see it through, but each white man they killed was one less enemy for other members of their tribe to face in the months ahead.

One of the horsemen fired a rifle shot and Tall Tree braced himself, in case his adversary had the proper range, but then he heard a wet *smack* to his right and Fire Maker dropped one knee, leg wounded. Gritting his teeth, Fire Maker raised his Springfield rifle, steadied it to aim as best he could, and was about to fire.

Too late.

Another bullet found him, punching through his forehead like a drill bit, lifting long hair on the back of his skull as it broke free and took flight with a fistful of his mangled brain. Fire Maker got his shot off then, wasted against the fading sky as he sprawled over backward, his blood spattering the grass.

THE KILLING SHOT was Melville's, from his Henry lever-action, either fired at Bishop's wounded warrior by coincidence or consciously. In either case, they weren't in competition, and Toby didn't mind.

Whatever thinned the odds against them suited him down to the ground.

Instead of fussing over it, Bishop turned slightly in his saddle, picked another figure clad in buckskin, and triggered his second shot of the engagement. He scored yet another hit, surprising him a bit with Compañero at full gallop, but like his first hit, this one wasn't a kill.

The wounded brave staggered, recovered from it without falling down, and fired what sounded like a twelve-gauge coach gun from the hip.

The range was wrong for buckshot, twice the recommended distance for effective shooting with a sawed-off scattergun. One pellet could have caused a fatal wound, each one of them roughly the size of a .33-caliber bullet, but they spread so fast and lost velocity so quickly that a man-sized target farther out than forty feet or so would likely get away with a painful peppering. Beyond that range it was unlikely that the triggerman would score a hit at all.

Toss in a wound on top of everything, and Bishop

guessed the shotgunner would have had trouble hitting a barn door.

But others in the war party were armed with rifles, calibers impossible to guess from such a distance when he couldn't get a clear look at their shooting irons. The sounds the weapons made when fired told Bishop they could close the intervening distance well enough—and one of them boomed out the telltale echo of a Sharps buffalo gun.

That weapon, in an artist's hands, could be a sure-fire killer well beyond six hundred yards; call it eight times their present distance. Luckily, whoever had the Sharps wasn't in Buffalo Bill Cody's class of marksmanship or anywhere close to it, though the heavy slug passed close enough for Bishop's left ear to report its whistling passage.

Another twenty yards or so and Toby planned to leap from Compañero's saddle on the run, hoping he didn't twist an ankle on touchdown, and close whatever space remained between him and his enemies on foot. A man could duck and hide better that way, without risking his animal to hostile fire, and shooting from a prone position had its own advantages.

Stability for one. A smaller target profile for another, increasing his adversaries' odds of nailing him.

The fair fights, Toby knew from long experience, were those you walked away from without trailing too much blood.

A few more seconds now, if no one shot him off his racing animal or framed the larger Appaloosa in their sights. Bishop refrained from triggering another shot as he closed in, scanning the hostile firing line and noting two of the red raiders were wounded now, a third loosing an arrow as his enemies got close enough for aiming well.

And . . . now!

He rolled out of his saddle, giving Compañero's rump a slap with his free hand before dropping into a crouch on solid ground. In front of him, two lifeless bodies on the turf, one of them dead before Pickering's riders spied their enemies. One of the five red men still on his feet was wounded, courtesy of Bishop's second rifle shot, but all of them seemed fit to fight and anxious to get on with it.

Particularly the one who held the stubby coach gun, swinging it around to find its mark on Bishop's face.

TALL TREE REGISTERED the sight and sound of Old Owl dying, shot down by the drover he had covered with his shotgun, proving too slow off the mark to fire its second barrel when he could have done some good for the Comanche side.

The white man's rifle bullet entered Old Owl's throat above the so-called Adam's apple, lifting Old Owl off his feet as if snagged by a giant's fishhook from behind. His moccasins cleared grass before he came back down, his shoulders touching sod before his heels. Dying, he fired the shotgun blast that might have saved his life if he had been quicker with it, shattering one of his own feet with the buckshot charge.

Tall Tree wondered if that meant he would be limping in his next life, in the Happy Hunting Ground.

No matter.

Tall Tree fumbled to reload his single-shot rifle but dropped the cartridge—two and one-half inches long, dull brass and lead, weighing just over one ounce—into the stubby grass between his feet. Instead of stooping to retrieve it, he reversed the rifle in his grip, clutching its thirty-four-inch barrel, wielding it as if it were a ten-pound war club.

Three white men and little time to choose among

them, so he picked the closest, shrieked a warbling battle cry, and swung the four-foot rifle at the cowboy's head.

The drover saw him coming, ducked, and Tall Tree missed his skull, the Sharps stock knocking off his high-crowned hat. Beneath it, Tall Tree glimpsed a tangled mass of sweaty auburn hair above a snarling face, teeth bared as if to grip and rend his larynx.

And they call us animals, the war chief thought, before instinct took over in the struggle for his life.

Somehow, he'd caught the cowboy by surprise, though not enough to brain him where he stood. Ducking and mouthing curses, the white man dropped his Henry rifle and was groping for a holstered pistol when Tall Tree collided with him, both men sprawling on the turf with the Comanche uppermost. His knee pinned down the white man's arms, leaving him vulnerable, as Tall Tree leaned forward, pressing with his rifle's hammer and breechblock against his adversary's throat.

It should not have taken much time to strangle him, with Tall Tree's solid weight atop the Sharps. A few seconds at most, if he had time to—

Something struck him in the ribs, a sharp kick with the pointed toe of someone's boot, he thought, and Tall Tree toppled over to his left side, lost his purchase on one enemy, and saw another looming over him.

The war chief kicked out with both feet and struck his enemy's right shin, propelled him backward, limping, curses on his lips. Before he could recover with his rifle, Tall Tree vaulted to stand upright, snarling like a treed cougar, as he withdrew the cut-down army saber from its metal sheath.

B ILL PICKERING STAGGERED but didn't let the wild kick to his right leg topple him, retreating from the brave who'd been intent on choking off Whit Mel-

ville's life. A rifle shot behind him made the foreman
jump, but since he felt no bullet's impact, he refused to
turn away from the red man, who'd drawn some hacking
weapon with a curved blade from a scabbard at his hip.

Was that a cavalryman's saber?

Yes, by God, it was!

The size confused him for a second, until he realized the blade had been shortened for some reason,
perhaps broken in battle and converted to a smaller—
but still deadly—cutting implement.

The thing to do was shoot immediately, not waste
time playing the warrior's game of combat hand to hand.
Pickering took another backward step, shouldered his
Winchester, and squeezed the trigger, but to no result.

Cursing, he realized he'd failed to pump the rifle's
lever action after gunning down one of the swords-
man's fellow braves. The weapon's hammer rested on
a spent round in the firing chamber, useless to him as
the empty Sharps had been to the red man intent on
gutting him.

Except the Winchester was a repeater, dammit,
with a dozen rounds still nestled in the magazine beneath its barrel. All he had to do was pump its lever,
point the weapon's muzzle toward the foe leaping to
reach him now, and fire point-blank into the chest beneath that buckskin shirt.

If only he had time.

Before Bill Pickering could prime his rifle for another shot, the red man was upon him, his bright saber
blade descending toward the foreman's face. Sharp as
it looked to Pickering, he figured it would slice down
through his hat's crown, spit his skull, and lodge somewhere about eye level, killing him outright.

Unless . . .

He raised the rifle overhead reflexively, gripped in
both hands and praying that he'd done it right, to keep

the brave from chopping off a few of his fingers. The saber's blade made a resounding *crack* on impact with his Winchester's receiver, almost jarring it from his hands, but Pickering hung on for dear life—literally—and lashed out with his right foot.

The bootheel missed his adversary's private parts but struck his hip a solid blow, propelled the red man back a lurching step or two, just out of saber-swinging range.

Was that enough?

Pickering tried to pump the rifle's lever, felt an unidentified resistance from it, no time to assess the problem while the whooping brave in front of him was bent on lopping off his head. He tossed the briefly useless weapon at his enemy and saw it strike the buckskin-covered chest before Bill reached down to his hip and drew the Colt New Line revolver holstered there.

It was the perfect range for pistol fighting, no more than a yard and change between them as he cocked the pistol's hammer, lining up to drill his would-be killer with a .41-caliber slug. An easy shot at that distance, impossible to miss, but the saber whipped around once more and rang against the pistol's four-inch barrel, jarring it aside and nearly forcing Pickering to drop it.

He nearly lost the Colt, his fingers tingling, wrist smarting, but managed to hold on to it. The hammer wasn't cocked yet, but he backed away, two lurching strides, and got that done. The native warrior, maybe sensing victory, rushed forward for another swing.

Grinning without being aware of it, Bill Pickering triggered a shot into the red man's groin.

TALL TREE HAD suffered pain before, but nothing of this magnitude. It was debilitating, dropped him from an upright stance into a wounded fetal curl, clutching himself with bloodied hands.

Not dying, necessarily, but stripped of his ability to fight.

Or was he?

Wheezing through clenched teeth, Tall Tree stretched out one red-stained hand to reach the saber that had fallen from his grasp a moment earlier. The white man with his smoking Colt loomed over the Comanche war chief, peering down at Tall Tree with a visage of unbridled hatred.

"You ain't gonna make it, redskin," he observed. "I give you points for trying, though."

A fragment of a plan occurred to Tall Tree. Looking past the gunman, as if noting someone coming up behind him, he remembered to use English as he called out, "Yes! Kill him!"

Instinctively, the man who'd shot him half turned from his fallen enemy, to face a creeping adversary who did not exist. At once, Tall Tree lunged for his army saber, blood-slick fingers closing on its handle, with its branched D-pattern handguard, grasping it and using his free hand to push off from the ground.

That effort cost him more pain, and a spurting gout of blood below. He tried to get one leg beneath him, helping lift his weight, but that was too much effort, forcing him to cry aloud from agony.

As he slumped forward, head hanging with long hair fanned about his face, the war chief waited for his enemy to fire another shot and finish him. Gunfire crackling around them, two eternal seconds passed before he realized that something had delayed the cowboy's obvious next move.

But what?

Could it be weakness? Had his foe run out of ammunition? Had the white man's weapon jammed?

Tall Tree might be dying but he was not finished yet. He knew enough to seize the moment and react, even if he could not stand up and face his would-be killer as a man.

The saber in his hand could be of service to him yet.

Clutching its grip and calling on the minimal reserve of strength that still remained to him, Tall Tree prepared to hurl the cavalryman's sword from where he was, hunched on his hands and knees. The drover might well kill him, but one last act of defiance should assure Tall Tree's acceptance by his ancestors as one who'd fought defiantly to his last breath.

Drawing a deep breath he assumed would be his last, Tall Tree reared up, teeth clenched against another crippling wave of pain, and hurled his saber overhand toward the drover whose bullet meant the death of him.

But on that vital point, he was mistaken.

Even as the sword flew from his hand, twirling through the dusk blade over pommel cap, another bullet struck him from an unexpected quarter, slamming Tall Tree to the turf and through it, into darkness everlasting.

T HE LAST THING Toby Bishop had in mind during the fight was rescuing Bill Pickering from being skewered by a flying sword. Still, when the opportunity arrived, he couldn't let it pass him by.

The red man Pickering had shot was nearly down and out, but he'd recouped enough strength in his final moments to try taking down the Circle K's foreman. Bishop had no idea where a Comanche had obtained an army saber and it didn't matter as the warrior made his pitch from fifteen feet or so.

It would be hard to miss a man-sized target at that range, although Bill might survive a hit from the peened tang instead of being run through by the saber's blade.

No point in taking chances, either way.

Bishop was less than twenty feet out from the warrior when he fired his Winchester into the hostile's bloodied buckskin tunic. Impact slammed the red man over on his left side, shot through one lung, maybe both, and possibly his heart as well. He barely twitched on impact with the trampled grass.

Bill Pickering, by contrast, ducked and spun around, reminding Bishop of a man who's felt a hornet scrabble down between his collar and his skin. The airborne saber missed him by an inch or two and twirled off into prairie dusk, Bill nearly toppling over, saving himself at the last instant with a breathless imprecation on his lips.

Sudden silence signaled that the fight was over. Pivoting with his Winchester poised to fire, Bishop found Whit Melville the last combatant standing, other than himself and Pickering. Around them, scattered on the grass, lay seven warriors, only one of them still twitching through his death throes.

"Looks like they got into it before we found 'em," Melville said, jabbing his Henry toward one body marked by obvious stab wounds.

"No honor among thieving savages," said Pickering. "Hey, Toby—"

Bishop felt a thank-you coming and he cut it short. "Forget about it. You'd have done the same for me."

"Okay, then."

Was that disappointment in their foreman's tone at being interrupted? Pickering recovered in a heartbeat, saying, "We should round these longhorns up before they wander off to hell and gone."

As much time as he'd spent around them, cattle were inscrutable to Bishop. Last night, nineteen hundred of them had stampeded at the sound of gunfire. Now these twenty-seven, while disturbed a bit and wandering away at random, showed no vestige of their former panic from the hostiles' raid.

Bishop guessed that it would take them twenty, maybe thirty minutes to collect the steers and get them headed north, back toward the larger herd, which would have gained nine or ten miles on them by dusk.

Whit seemed to read his mind, asking Bill Pickering, "You wanna move them out straight off?"

"I do," the foreman said, "unless you'd rather spend the night among dead Comanches."

"No, thanks," Melville replied. "I'd just as soon let the coyotes have 'em."

"Right, then. Best we saddle up and get a start on it."

Moving off toward his snowflake Appaloosa, Bishop realized the latest killings hadn't fazed him, wondering if that said something bad about him.

Or, he thought, *maybe it just feels good to be alive.*

CHAPTER FIFTEEN

Iᴛ ᴛᴏᴏᴋ ᴀ full night and day's riding before Bishop,
Pickering, and Melville caught up with the trail
drive at its campsite, shortly after sundown on day
twenty-seven of their journey. Now, midmorning on
day thirty, they were making decent progress through
south-central Missouri, all the drovers in a state of
high alert.

Experience had taught them that they couldn't be
too careful this time out.

So far, they'd seen no more Comanches—nor another white man either, save for one slump-shouldered
farmer slogging over grassland, wrestling with his
mule-drawn plow. Bishop remembered plowing from
his youth and didn't miss it—though, if pressed, he
couldn't honestly describe cowpunching as a better,
more uplifting life.

One upside to it, though, was seeing great swaths of
America beyond the boundaries of a homestead claim.

Along with the steers stolen by the raiders, Pickering and company had come back with the war party's

firearms and four of seven ponies, having lost the other
three while battling their late riders. With the bodies,
they had left behind one longbow, sundry knives and
hatchets, although Pickering carried the saber that had
nearly cut him down, suspended in its metal scabbard
from his saddle horn.

A sort of trophy, Bishop guessed, for having felt
Death's cold breath on his cheek and lived to tell the
tale.

Other than the obvious recovery of Mr. Dixon's
stock, there'd been no great palaver as to how the Indians had fought and died. Pickering gave the basic
numbers to a campfire congregation mourning its own
losses, three men down from when they'd left Atoka
on a sunny April day.

One-fifth of what they'd started out with, already
dead and gone, while they were still the best part of a
month out from St. Louis. Already they'd exceeded
what was the normal length of a trail drive, where the
odds of losing steers exceeded any fear of leaving dead
men in their wake.

And murdered men at that. The worst losses of all.

As Toby reckoned it, without a map to verify it, they
were probably in Christian County, named not for
the church, as he recalled, but for a Continental
soldier from Virginia who had traveled west after the
Revolutionary War and service as an officer under
George Washington to stake his claim on virgin land.
That placed them some two hundred and thirty miles
southwestward of St. Louis, with at least three weeks
to go—and very likely more—until they reached their
destination.

Some boys of Rudy Knapp's age, Bishop knew,
joined drives with high hopes of adventure. Veterans
knew better, teenage dreams dashed by hard work's
reality, leavened by periods of boredom on the trail.

Ironically, the times that seemed least tedious were often those when cowboys ran a risk of getting killed.

Not me, thought. *At least, not yet.*

"Strays on the west," their foreman shouted. "Bishop! Thorne! Get after 'em!"

Bishop tugged at his Appaloosa's reins and started after three longhorns who'd paused to crop some grass, then struck off on their own as if they'd tired of traveling in lockstep with the herd. He saw Thorne riding back to join him, having traveled farther toward the drive's front ranks, taking the deviation from routine in stride.

Bishop supposed the crew that still survived was adequate to see their journey through, but if their numbers suffered any more attrition, it could wind up being touch and go.

Every man must remain vigilant, not letting down his guard on watch or any other time, except the hours when he slept.

And even then, if he could sleep with one eye open, he'd be better off.

T HEY'VE CALMED DOWN pretty well, I think," Bill Pickering averred.

Dixon kept his tone even, neutral, as he asked, "You mean the steers or the men?"

"Feels like both ways to me, boss. Course, you give longhorns time to walk a mile or so, they won't remember anything was ever wrong to start with. Drovers, on the other hand—"

"I hear you," Dixon cut his foreman off. "Only a fool would say we've seen the worst of it this time around."

"Kind of a gloomy outlook, boss."

"I'd call it common sense," Dixon replied. "What

we've been through so far . . . I know some people in Atoka who might say that snowstorm was a bad-luck omen."

"Messing with tarot cards, are they?"

"Not hardly. Most of 'em would say it's life experience."

"I'd say we've done all right," Pickering answered back. "I mean to say *you* have, keeping the Circle K on track and going strong."

"You've been a big part of it, Bill."

"Well . . . thanks for saying that. But there's a reason you're the boss. Keeping it all corralled together in your head."

"Maybe. One thing I know for sure."

"Which is?"

"If we lose any more drovers, I'll need to find a town somewhere and hire some men to see it through."

He half expected Pickering to naysay that but got no argument from his foreman. Instead, Bill simply cautioned him: "You know the risk in that, boss."

"Sure. Hiring ringers who'll smile to your face and stab you in the back."

"Not saying that it has to be that way, o' course."

"But *could* be. I'm aware of it."

"And best to do without them if we can."

"What did I just say, Bill?"

"Sorry. Can't help agreeing with you, boss."

"Appreciate it." Staring past his foreman, to the northeast, Dixon frowned and said, "Now, what in hell is this?"

Pickering turned and followed Dixon's gaze, spotting small shapes on the horizon. After taking out his spyglass, Bill extended it and peered in through its narrow end, taking a moment to recapture what he hoped to see in close-up.

"Riders, boss. Four of 'em."

"Let me see that," Dixon ordered, holding out one open hand.

He took the pocket telescope and found the riders, who were moving closer on an intercepting course with his longhorns. Three of the mounted men appeared to be in their late twenties, maybe early thirties, while the one out front looked at least fifteen years older, gray hair visible beneath his Stetson's wide, flat brim.

Dixon had seen that style of hat before, on men and in the Stetson catalog, where it was called "Boss of the Plains." A certain attitude seemed to accompany wearing that style of headgear, if not universally, at least in men Dixon had personally met, from Tucson right across Texas and into Indian country.

"Can't say I like the look of 'em," he told Bill Pickering as he returned the foreman's telescope.

"Trouble, you think?"

"I wouldn't want to borrow any, but we'd better go and find out what they want."

"I'll back whatever play you make, boss."

"Taking that for granted, Bill. Don't give offense if you can help it, but that said, keep your Colt handy."

"Yes, sir."

"And I'd suggest the other men do likewise, just in case."

"I'll spread the word," said Pickering, and galloped off to do just that.

Dixon reached down to free the hammer thong on his holster, freeing up his Remington six-shooter for a fast draw if the need arose.

Before he met the strangers riding out to greet his herd, most of the other hands should be easing into position for a fight. That was the last thing Gavin Dixon wanted, after all that they'd gone through to reach this point, but neither would he shy away from it if trouble wouldn't let them pass.

* * *

Hebron Stark was fifty-one years old, a self-made man, to hear him tell it, never mentioning the funds his Boston Brahmin father had provided when they'd split for good, thirty years earlier. Hebron had turned his back on the family's shipbuilding business, determined not to waste his life cooped up inside a State Street office, overshadowed by his forebears in a manse on Beacon Hill.

He hadn't spoken to his old man—long dead now—after they had split, each raging at the other, but for all his muddleheaded boasts of seeking independence, Stark had still been wise enough to take the minor fortune ceded to him as a kind of parting gift and insult rolled up into one.

His father was convinced that Hebron wouldn't last a month outside of Boston. Hebron took the payoff with the intent to make a go of it beyond the old man's reach or influence, convinced it would be easy.

Both, as sometimes happened in a quarrel, were dead wrong.

Stark hadn't glimpsed the sea in thirty years and didn't miss it—hadn't even gone home for his father's funeral two days before Fort Sumter pitched the sundered nation into civil war. He'd found a rustic backwater that needed cash and a strong guiding hand, staked out a massive prairie claim that covered much of Christian County, and began eliminating anyone who challenged him. For outsiders who didn't know the rules of play, he offered curt instructions one time only, then removed them from the world he'd made his own.

By now the process had become routine. Stark saw no reason to believe that it would ever change.

Today he reined his white Arabian stallion to stand

some fifty yards in front of the approaching longhorn herd. He'd been expecting it since Tuesday, when the first scout brushed against a radius of his extensive spider's web, reported by a tenant farmer who'd been paid five dollars for the news.

Now here it was. Stark felt his pulse quicken, prepared to start the game anew.

His three companions, chosen for their reputations and ability to back them up with action, sat astride their mounts ten feet behind Stark. All three were armed, as Stark himself was, but they kept their weapons holstered. None of them would speak or intervene unless Stark ordered it by word or with some gesture they'd rehearsed.

The stage was his.

Stark took for granted that the lead horseman approaching him must be the herd's trail boss. The other two would be employees of whatever spread the longhorns hailed from, doubtless ordered to stand by and listen while their leader spoke for them.

"Morning," the trail boss said.

"Closer to noon," Stark answered back.

The stranger let that pass. "Name's Gavin Dixon," he explained. "And you are . . . ?"

"Hebron Stark. I own this land you're trespassing across."

"That so?" The trail boss didn't sound impressed so far.

"It is. Ask anyone around the neighborhood."

"Can't rightly say we've seen a neighborhood," Dixon replied. "Nor any living soul the past day and a half. Nary a sign or fence, in fact."

"Don't need to fence or post what everybody knows is mine," Stark said.

"When you say 'everybody,' that would be the neighbors you referred to?"

"And the local law. Also the mayor."

"Anywhere I've ever been, a mayor requires a town," said Dixon.

"Same here," Stark agreed. "Five miles due west."

"What town would that be, then?"

"Cold Comfort."

"Not the most inviting name," said Dixon, "Meaning no offense."

"Well, that's Missouri for you. We keep to ourselves."

"No problem, then. We're only passing through."

"Across my land," Stark said again. "Without permission."

"How would we obtain permission, without knowing you exist?"

"You see me now," Stark said.

"And, so . . . ?"

"There are two ways you can proceed, Mr. Dixon. Turn back and find another way around or pay a toll."

"As far as turning back, how would we know the limits of your property?"

"Ride into town, maybe, and ask the mayor. He's got the paperwork."

"Which would mean camping here, I guess?"

"For a small fee."

"How small?" Dixon inquired.

"Two bits a head per day, cattle and horses both. On top of that, four bits a man."

"And if I was to choose the toll?"

"Same rate. A day or so of steady travel ought to see you clear."

"Round numbers, then, we're about five hundred per day?"

"I'd call that close enough."

"You'll understand if I prefer to verify your claim before I part with any cash," said Dixon, making it a statement rather than a question.

"Only sensible."

"Which means a trip to town and back."

"Take all the time you need," Stark said. "When you come back with it confirmed, rate stays the same. Starting from here and now."

"We'd best get started, then."

"Suits me," Stark said. "I'll leave a couple of my boys to keep you company. Head off a problem if your herd keeps moving by mistake."

B ISHOP LISTENED, TOGETHER with the trail drive's other hands, as Mr. Dixon summarized his conversation with the man who claimed to own the bulk of Christian County, closing with "So, men, that's where we stand right now."

"What are you gonna do, sir?" Isaac Thorne inquired.

"First thing, what he suggested," Mr. D replied. "Ride into this Cold Comfort place and find out if he's speaking truth or just spinning a yarn to pick our pockets."

Bishop didn't think an outright lie was likely, though he couldn't absolutely rule it out. More likely, he surmised, this Hebron Stark had cash and guns behind him, operating in cahoots with those he'd placed in charge to run the nearby settlement.

Cold Comfort, he supposed, would prove to be a fitting name.

"And if it's true, sir? Then what?" asked Deke Sullivan.

"Let's take it one step at a time," Dixon advised. "As you can see, he left his men to cover us while we're deciding."

Bishop knew that Mr. D was using "we" in the broad sense. Whatever choice was made, it had to come from him alone.

"Three men ain't much," said Leland Gorch. "We could just pick 'em off from here."

"And start a war," Dixon reminded him, "without knowing how many other guns we're up against. On top of that, we've got Missouri law to think about."

"Likely some paid-off fraud," Gorch said.

"You could be right," Dixon agreed. "But I'm not going up against the law until I know what's what."

"And if this mayor or marshal, whoever it is, stands up for Stark?"

"Same thing I said before. We take it one step at a time. First check on what he said and find out if he told it straight. If that's true, then we'll have to bite the bullet. Either pay to cross his land or turn around and find another way to go."

"And we'll be losing money either way," Curly Odom observed.

"Money or time. It all comes out the same," Dixon agreed.

"Who's going into town, sir?" the foreman asked.

"You are," said Dixon. "Pick one of the other hands to ride along and watch your back."

"Bishop," said Pickering. "You game?"

"Ready when you are, sir," Toby replied.

"That's settled, then," said Dixon. "Five miles due west should put you into town a hair before sundown."

"Yes, sir," said Pickering. And then, "Bishop, let's ride."

YOU LIKELY WONDERED why I wanted you along," said Pickering when they had gone a hundred yards or so from camp.

There seemed to be no point in feigning ignorance. "Figure you'd want a shooter handy if you run into a problem," Bishop said.

"I've done my share of shooting," said Pickering. "You've seen some of it."

"The Comanches. Not casting aspersions."

"But you've been around more, as I understand it. Mason County, Willow Grove, and all."

"It's not just knowing guns and when to use 'em," Bishop said. "When you get down to it, some people just aren't willing."

"To be killers."

"Say it that way, it's like speaking of a breed apart," Bishop replied. "I don't mean someone like Wesley Hardin or the James boys. People kill for money or the sport of it *are* different. Kill in your own defense or someone else's, that's another thing."

"Won't anyone do that?" asked Pickering.

"You'd be surprised."

Bishop saw nothing to be gained by saying that he'd hunted men for pay during the Hoodoo War, when able guns were running short. It didn't shame him, but he didn't talk it up either.

Changing the subject, he asked Pickering, "So what are we expecting once we get to town?"

"My guess would be that Stark told Mr. D the truth. He has that feel about him, Stark does. He's a man who loves his money and is always out for more. If he can get it making other folks feel small, that's icing on the cake."

"You reckon that these folks we're meant to see are in his pocket, then?"

"Most likely, but we have to run it past them anyway."

"Suppose they try to squeeze the money out of us?"

"Wouldn't make sense. Show up without the boss, they ought to know we're not worth much."

Speak for yourself, thought Bishop. But he said, "And if they're after hostages?"

"I guess we'll have to talk 'em out of it."

"Us two against the town?"

"Won't come to that," said Pickering. "Mainly, we'll have to watch the lawman—marshal, constable, whatever tag Stark hung on him."

"And what about his men watching the herd?"

"Just watching till they see which way it goes. I hope so, anyway."

The three men left on watch had been outnumbered three to one, not counting Rudy Knapp, when he and Pickering rode out of camp, but Bishop figured Stark could send out reinforcements if he felt the need. At times like this, it would be nice if he could read another fellow's mind, assuming any of that folderol was true.

"Reckon we're just wasting our time?" Toby asked.

"Going through the motions," Pickering replied. "Besides, long as he pays the tab, it's Mr. Dixon's time."

"Okay," Bishop agreed. "But I'm just wondering what happens if they try to slam the door behind us."

"Then we knock it down," said Pickering, "along with anybody Stark has guarding it."

"Does that include civilians?" Bishop asked.

"It covers anyone who tries to interfere with us, Toby."

"All right. Just so we're clear."

"That bother you?" asked Pickering.

"Not so you'd notice," Bishop answered him.

And worried that it might be true.

The afternoon was well advanced before they saw Cold Comfort up ahead. From a mile out they knew it was a small town, only three buildings above one story tall, and one of those a church, judging from its spire. Bishop supposed the other two would be a lodging house and a saloon, likely with cribs upstairs. The rest, even before he had a chance to read their signs, he reckoned would be shops and offices, with homes set back on dusty side streets.

Cold Comfort, indeed.

He reached down casually and released his holster's hammer thong. With any luck at all, he wouldn't need the Peacemaker in town. But if he did, an extra second could make all the difference between survival and a cold hole in the ground.

COLD COMFORT LIVED up to its name. Most of the buildings could have used fresh paint, and some of them were missing shingles, so their roofs resembled mangy skin. Signs on display had all been painted in block letters, fading like the buildings they identified, with a severe economy of verbiage. Hotel stood beside saloon; dry goods across the street from butcher and next door to doctor; lawyer next door to marshal.

By comparison, the church came off as nearly eloquent. Its sign read SWEET HOME BAPTIST.

"Sweet home?" Pickering asked, in a musing tone.

"'Cold Comfort Baptist' might not pack 'em in," Bishop replied.

"A town that speaks its mind," said Pickering, "what there is of it."

"No mayor's office, though," Bishop observed.

"Marshal's the next best thing. If he can't help us, or he won't, I guess we start going door to door."

"Making no end of friends," Bishop replied.

"This ain't a social call."

They reined in and dismounted at the marshal's office, tying their horses loosely to a hitching rail out front, where they had access to a water trough. Bishop eyed it for floating dust and algae, but it looked all right.

He let Bill Pickering precede him entering the office. A stout man, red of hair and face, was seated at a desk, boots propped up on one corner, star pinned to his vest. As Pickering and Bishop crossed the threshold, he was talking to a pair of men seated on straight-backed wooden chairs before the desk.

The younger of them also wore a badge, his labeled DEPUTY, the older, fatter man's proclaiming him as MARSHAL.

That left one fellow—forty-odd years old with hair graying around his temples, thinning out on top—still unidentified.

Nobody stood as they walked in, but conversation died and three sharp pairs of eyes—one blue, two brown—assessed the new arrivals. Lowering his feet and leaning forward, elbows on his desk, the marshal greeted them.

"You must be from the cattle drive," he said.

"New travels fast," Bill Pickering replied.

"You know small towns," the marshal said.

"Been through a few."

"We ain't like most of 'em," the lawman said.

"That so?"

"We run a tight ship here, although we ain't at sea."

The deputy coughed up a laugh at that. Bishop supposed one of his duties was to make the marshal feel amusing.

Pickering smiled a bit and introduced himself, remembering to tack on Toby's name without an explanation of his duties with the Circle K.

"I'm Marshal Tilton. Harley to my friends, but you won't be around that long." A statement, not a question.

"And these other gentlemen?" asked Pickering.

"My deputy, Luke Hazlet. And the handsome fellow there"—delivered with a pause for laughter from the man without a badge—"is Mayor Creed Rogers."

"Missed your sign on the way in, Mayor," said Pickering.

"It just says 'Lawyer,'" Rogers said. "Saved paint and everyone in town knows who I am."

"Makes sense."

"You've talked to Mr. Stark, I take it," Marshal Tilton said. "Come in to pay the toll?"

"Nobody mentioned paying it to you," said Pickering. "He thought it best to verify the claim to certain land."

"Who thought?"

"Your Mr. Stark. Said you or Mayor Rogers here could clear it up."

"Whatever Mr. Stark says is the gospel truth," said Tilton. Hazlet bobbed his head on cue. When Rogers didn't join in quick enough, Tilton prodded him. "Right, Mayor?"

"Hmm? Oh, yes indeed. The gospel truth."

"Right, then," said Pickering. "We'll just be on our way."

"About that toll . . ."

"From what I understand, it goes direct to Stark," Bill said. "If Mr. Dixon should decide to pay, that is."

"*If* he decides? I hear you right?"

"Seems like your ears are working fine," Pickering said. "No doubt he'll let you know how that proceeds if he needs your advice."

"The smart thing would be paying up," said Tilton.

Pickering ignored that, one hand on the doorknob when he paused to ask, "You're the town marshal, am I right?"

"I am."

"With jurisdiction limited inside the town's limits."

The marshal and his deputy both frowned at that. Tilton replied, "Except in cases of emergency. You know, like scofflaws trying to escape. No call to bother Sheriff Anderson in Ozark when we're short on time."

"Scofflaws. I hear you."

"What about your buddy, here?" asked Tilton. "He a mute, or what?"

"You'll hear him when he wants you to," said Pickering. "Good day, now, gentlemen. Or should I say, 'Good evening'?"

"Mayhap we'll meet again," the marshal said.

About to close the office door behind them, Bishop smiled and told Tilton, "Be looking forward to it, sir."

CHAPTER SIXTEEN

BISHOP AND PICKERING returned to camp in decent time, distance considered. They found three of Stark's men still watching the herd, one mounted and the other two hunched down around a fire they'd built, maybe for brewing coffee while the night dragged on.

"Same three, you think?" asked Pickering.

"Can't say for sure," Bishop replied. "I only saw them from a distance and it's darker now. One of 'em had a red shirt on, if I remember right."

"You do," the foreman said. "I watched 'em for a minute through the scope, but they'd have coats on now, against the chill."

"He could gave swapped them out, I guess, the length of time that we were gone."

"I should have asked that so-called marshal more about his boss. Find out how many men he's got on hand, for starters."

"He'd have lied to you," Bishop replied. "Stark tells him what to say. I wouldn't trust a word out of his mouth."

"Reckon you're right. The boss ain't gonna like hearing my news."

"It's not your fault, sir. Men with too much money on their hands run little towns like that all over, from the Mississippi to the coast. If decent lawmen aren't around to rein them in, they start to think they're little kings."

"My worry is, he's right," said Pickering, "at least as far as we're concerned. We're down to ten shooters, not counting Varney and the kid. They'd likely fight if pushed to it but wouldn't do much good."

"It might not come to that," said Bishop.

"Fingers crossed," said Pickering, eyeing the campfire and three men a hundred long yards north of them. "But if it doesn't, we're still screwed. Either turn back and waste who knows how many days riding around Stark's land or pay five hundred bucks a day to cross it without knowing how much there is to it. Either way, the boss is losing money and that trickles down to all of us."

"Can't say I like the sound of that," Bishop allowed.

Pickering glanced across at him. "There's no worry on your end. A deal's a deal with Mr. Dixon. He'll pay off for days worked on the drive, even if that means he winds up in the hole."

"Bad for the Circle K, no doubt."

"'Bad' don't begin to touch it," Pickering advised. "We count on new stock for the next year's herd, plus cash for getting through the winter. Lose that edge, it means we're begging at the bank for help and wind up paying through the nose on interest."

"Bankers," Bishop replied, and let it go at that. He'd notice Pickering said "we" when speaking of the Circle K, as if he had a stake in it beyond his steady job.

"Don't get me started," said the foreman.

"Anyway, if Stark tries playing rough—"

"We fight. No question. Everybody has a right to self-defense, regardless if the law's paid off by some slick operator rich as possum gravy."

"Funny that you never ran into this Stark fellow before," Bishop observed.

"Last three, four years we took the herd to Kansas City," Pickering replied. "It's closer to Atoka, but we kept on running into trouble."

"Worse than this year?"

"Hard to credit, I suppose. Still, Mr. D thought it was worth a try."

"Reckon he'll switch back after this?"

Pickering shrugged. "I gave up reading minds," he said. "No profit in it."

"I heard that," Bishop replied, and followed him into a camp bristling with guns.

THEY'RE ALL UNDER his thumb, then?" Gavin Dixon asked.

"I won't say *all*," Bill Pickering replied. "We only met the blowhard mayor, the marshal, and his deputy. Stark owns all three of them, no doubt."

"When he says, 'Jump,' they ask, 'How high?'"

"You got it in a nutshell, boss."

"What feeling did you get for how much weight Stark carries?"

"In the county or beyond it, I can't answer that. Big frog in a small pond would be my guess. Statewide, unless he's richer than he looked today, I'd reckon there are some who overshadow him. The banks and railroads, for a start."

"Does us no good," Dixon replied. "No state police or rangers, not that we'd have time to find them if there were any."

"Whatever you decide, the men are with you, Mr. D."

"Because I led them to a swamp and got 'em stuck in quicksand?"

"No, sir. They've been through a lot already, but my read is that they're standing firm."

"I wish to hell we'd gone another route, Bill. Hindsight. A lot of good that does us now."

"You're not a quitter, Mr. D."

"That's true enough. O' course it ain't like I could quit out here, supposing that I wanted to. Just up and leave the herd to Stark and run off with my tail between my legs? Screw that."

"When we were riding in, I wondered if he's switched out watchmen in the time Bishop and me were gone."

"I kept an eye on that," said Dixon. "One guy came from the northwest and sent another of 'em home. Since then, they've just been cooking supper, making coffee."

"Watching," said Pickering.

"Keeping an eye on nineteen hundred steers ain't hard. But no moves otherwise."

"Stark wants his payday."

"Sure he does. Money for doing nothing and it's open-ended. Bastard won't say how much land he owns or claims to own. We say yes to his terms, we could get dunned for five, six days. Who knows? And he'd have witnesses to back his play in court, if it came down to that."

"You think it would?"

Dixon could only shrug at that. "Or he could put the county sheriff on us for trespassing, maybe swindling him out of what he's owed and we agreed to pay."

"You think he'd try that? Suing in a court of law?"

"Why not, if he's pulled this before and got away with it? I'm guessing there's no court in town?"

"Not that I saw. They label everything, but there was no sign for a justice of the peace. One thing, the mayor's also a lawyer."

"Ain't that sweet? He files a case in Ozark, maybe gets the sheriff to attach the herd pending a resolution. Slip some money to the judge, and we wind up paying a fine besides his goddamned toll."

"You mean to turn around, then, boss?"

"I thought about it," Dixon said. "But there's no telling how much property he claims to own, how far we'd have to double back or veer off to the east before we're shut of him."

"Well, like I said . . ."

"You and the rest are with me. Right. Now all I have to do is figure out my own damn mind."

"Same watch as always, overnight?" asked Pickering.

"Keeping it normal," Dixon said. "If Stark's men venture any closer, treat them as you would a pack of rustlers."

"Understood, sir. "I'll go get the first shift ready now."

Dixon watched Pickering retreat, calling out names to take first shift.

And wondered how he'd face tomorrow when the sun came up.

JAY COTHRAN HAD been on the Stark payroll for nigh on five years now and liked it fine. The pay was good, and when his boss was in a mood to punish someone for offending him, Cothran was favored with permission to extend himself beyond the normal terms of his employment, working off his own grudge toward the world at large.

Nobody ever asked him how he got that way, what he was riled about much of the time, and if they did, it only would have led to trouble, probably a broken jaw or worse.

A few times—more than that, if he was honest with himself—it had been *much* worse. Warrants on him out of Colorado and the Territory of New Mexico were evidence that it could be much worse indeed.

The wonder of it was that Hebron Stark saw past that. No, better than overlooking it, he *valued* Cothran for his personal peculiarities and how his temper, once unleashed, could rage like wildfire in a prairie windstorm.

Most times, though, Jay kept himself on a tight rein and did as he was told.

Why not, when he was happy with the way things were in Christian County, managing the Stark spread, handling any dirty work his boss required?

Tonight, for instance. Mr. Stark had passed the trail drive's leader off to Mayor Rogers and Marshal Tilton in Cold Comfort. What a pair they were, so crooked they could swallow nails and spit out corkscrews, both of 'em. They followed orders, took their cuts from any game they played a part in, and never bitched about it.

Why would they? Rogers loved to pull a cork and smelled of red-eye half the time. In Jay's opinion, anyone who'd hire him as a lawyer must be stupid, never mind the sheepskin on his office wall from something called Straight University in New Orleans.

Cothran wondered whether that was meant to be a joke, as if a school named "Straight" would turn out such a low-life snake-oil salesman.

Harley Tilton, now, was something else entirely. Back before the war, he'd been an overseer on an Arkansas plantation, Franklin County, if you could believe a word he said. He liked to reminisce about the good old days of whipping slaves for this or that minor infraction, lording over them, and how he loved to get one of their women off somewhere alone. Teaching them the fear of God, he liked to say.

It was a comedown when he had to put his whip away and light out to avoid conscription in the Rebel army, ducking into Indian country for the duration, then drifting to Missouri and hawking his gun as a lawman to whichever backwater settlement needed a bully with a badge to calm things down. From what Jay understood, Tilton had never lasted long in any town, being too heavy-handed for the storekeepers and homestead types—at least, until he'd come to Mr. Stark's attention and they'd cut a deal.

The upshot: Tilton had a lot of free time on his hands, unless Stark needed him for something special—the fat man who liked to throw his weight around.

None of that mattered now. Jay had his orders, crystal clear from Mr. Stark's own lips. The mayor and marshal had no role in that, unless somebody had to step in afterward and swear it all was legal.

Meanwhile, Cothran had a job to do.

His tool of choice was a Whitworth rifle manufactured between 1857 and '65, favored by Confederate snipers and credited with killing at least two Union generals during the war, John Reynolds at Gettysburg in 1863 and John Sedgwick a year later, at Spotsylvania. Although a muzzle loader, only capable of firing two or three rounds per minute in skilled hands, it fired a .451-caliber slug from its thirty-three-inch barrel and could kill out to two thousand yards.

For sniping at that range, Jay had a William Malcolm telescopic sight mounted atop the Whitworth's barrel, thirty inches long, which magnified a target six times over from the shooter's point of view. The only difference with shooting after sundown was the requirement of a light source near the mark he planned to hit.

A campfire, Cothran thought, should do just fine.

Now all he had to do was pick a man at random, line him up, and put him down.

See how that played with a trail boss who didn't want to part with precious cash.

B ISHOP MADE NO complaint when Pickering assigned him to the first watch. He wasn't sleepy anyway and had an interest in keeping track of Hebron Stark's lookouts.

The word was out from Mr. D and Pickering: Any advance upon the herd would be considered hostile and treated as such. From there, they'd let the chips fall where they may. That meant more gunplay, probably more killing, and to what end?

Bishop couldn't answer that and didn't try. He had inked a deal to work for Mr. Dixon and the Circle K until they reached St. Louis and sold off the herd. Whatever he was asked to do during the drive—within reason, of course—fell under the terms of his contract and Mr. Dixon bore the ultimate responsibility.

Not that a paid-off marshal or his deputy would see it that way, much less some judge who might be on Stark's payroll or harboring a mad-on against people traveling around Missouri without living there. That was a crapshoot, and whoever claimed he could predict the outcome of it was either a liar of a fool.

Bishop was neither, in his own opinion of himself.

With all they'd been through since leaving Atoka, he believed the other Circle K hands would stand with their boss and fight if it came down to that. He wasn't wishing for it, but what good had wishing ever done him, anyway?

Before he went on watch, Bishop saw to his guns.
They didn't need another check-over, since Toby always kept them clean and loaded, but it helped to put
his mind at ease. Fifteen rounds in his rifle's magazine
and one inside the chamber, six more in his Colt, and
twenty more in loops around his pistol belt. That gave
him forty-two before he had to root around inside a
saddlebag for spare rounds in a cardboard box.

The trip had cost him some already, but Bishop still
had enough on hand to fight awhile, if he made each
shot count—and that had always been his goal. There
was more ammunition in the chuck wagon, although
he hadn't taken stock of it and couldn't say how long
the drovers could hold out against a full-blown siege.

With any luck, it wouldn't come to that. But if it did . . .

Then he would cross the River Styx when he got
to it.

When the shot came, rumbling through the darkness, Bishop thought it sounded like artillery firing
from miles away. There was a rolling echo, but it didn't
spook the longhorns like the close-range fire that
started their stampede five nights ago. He didn't hear
the bullet whistling past, but when a cry was raised
from camp, some thirty yards from where he sat at ease
on Compañero, Bishop wheeled in that direction, making for the fire.

Dixon and Pickering were armed and at the ready,
grouped with other hands around one drover lying on
the grass. A glance identified the wounded man as
Isaac Thorne, shot through the side above his left hip
from what Bishop could make out. Most of the men
were jabbering at once, till Mr. Dixon hollered for
them to pipe down and keep their eyes peeled for another muzzle flash.

That made them duck and scramble, with a *click-
clack* of their rifles cocking, all hands likely thinking

that they didn't want to wind up getting drilled like Thorne.

Isaac was bleeding, Varney keeping pressure on the wound site with a towel from the chuck wagon. Bishop didn't need a medical degree to know that Thorne was seriously hurt and needed expert help to make it through the night.

Almost before he knew it, Mr. Dixon was beside his Appaloosa, looking up at him and asking, "Do they have a doctor in that town?"

"I saw a sign for one," Bishop replied. "Can't promise he's a good one, given what they have for mayor and marshal."

"For a thing like this, he has to be more skilled than we are," Dixon said.

"Yes, sir."

"It's plain we can't be hauling Thorne to town. We'd have to send the wagon, and he likely wouldn't make it halfway there. You need to fetch him back here, Toby."

"If he'll come, boss."

"Make damned sure he does. Promise him silver first, then lead if that don't work."

"The marshal may try horning in."

"Uh-huh. Where's Sullivan? Deke?"

"Right here, boss."

"Get saddled up and go with Toby. Bring that sawbones back, no matter what."

"Yes, sir!"

And here we go, thought Bishop. *Back into the firing line.*

Y OU SAW ONE of them drop?" Stark asked.

"Yes, sir. No question," Cothran answered him.

Behind the foreman, Ardis Newcomb chimed in, "That's a fact, boss. I can vouch for it."

"Who asked you?" Stark inquired, shutting him up. Then, back to Cothran, "Could you tell if he was dead?"

"No, sir. Too dark and far away, plus all them others ganged around before I had a chance to see if he was moving."

"And you came straight back here?"

"Straight through town," Cothran corrected him, "then swung off this way."

"Better still. Too bad we couldn't leave the others back to watch awhile."

"You likely would've lost 'em, sir. The drovers were riled up, and no mistake."

Stark nodded, sipped dark bourbon from the glass he held, but didn't offer drinks to anybody else. What good was status if you shared it out freely?

"You played it right," he told Cothran. "No one can say who shot him, or who sent you."

"Nope. No way at all, sir."

"So, all we have to do is wait for morning now. See if the man in charge is leaning toward a deal or wants to make a run for it."

"And if they run?"

"That many longhorns take a while to move. I wouldn't be surprised if we inherited the whole damned herd."

No one was moving on the main street of Cold Comfort when Bishop and Sullivan arrived, no lights showing shop or office in the town aside from the nameless saloon. In there, an out-of-tune piano jangled, and subdued laughter was audible beyond the batwing doors, as from a relatively quiet party going on.

They led a third horse, saddled, just in case the doctor had no transportation of his own.

"What day is it again?" Deke asked Bishop.

"Friday."

"They don't exactly live it up, do they?"

Again, the town's name came to Toby's mind as fitting, but he knew it didn't necessarily mean anything. During his travels, he had passed through other settlements with quirky names, and he'd heard tell of others without laying eyes on them. Missouri had another town called Tightwad. There was Hell, in Michigan; Pray and Big Arm, in Montana; Rough and Ready, California; Cut and Shoot, Texas; on down to No Name in Colorado.

Some were jokes, he guessed, while others sounded like expressions of regret by those who'd put down roots and lived to rue the day. Right now, he couldn't say about Cold Comfort and he didn't care.

As far as Bishop knew, no one had spotted them when they reined in outside the building labeled DOC-TOR, dark up front but with pale lamplight showing from a window at the back, into a narrow alley to the south. Bishop left Deke watching their horses on the street while he walked down there, found a side door, loosening his holster's hammer thong before he knocked.

It took the best part of a minute for a male voice from inside to ask, "Who's that?"

"You don't know me," Toby replied, taking a chance. "I'm from the longhorn herd outside of town. We've got a man hurt bad."

The door opened a crack, to show half of a man's clean-shaven face. He was approximately Bishop's age, with dark hair drooping over his right eye, above a pair of wire-rimmed spectacles.

"Hurt how?" he asked.

Toby responded with a question of his own. "Are you the doctor?"

"Reuben Pratt. And yes. What kind of injury?"

"A rifle shot," Bishop replied.

"Some kind of accident?"

"Deliberate, from far off." Bishop rolled the dice again, adding, "From one of Hebron Stark's men."

"Goddammit!" Dr. Pratt stepped back and opened his door farther, letting Bishop see a modest kitchen with a dining table in it and a single chair, nobody else in evidence. "You brought him with you?"

"No, sir. Judged him hurt too bad to ride. May be too late already, but I've got my orders, Doctor."

"Which are?"

"To bring help double-quick. We brought a horse in case you don't have one."

"Who's 'we'?" asked Pratt, peering around Bishop into the alley's darkness.

"Me and backup from the camp, in case we ran into more trouble."

Pratt frowned. Asked, "Is this some kind of test from Mr. Stark? Trying to judge my loyalty, or—"

"No, sir." Bishop cut him off. "Stark doesn't order me around and he's no friend of mine, I promise you."

"All right. Where did the bullet strike your friend?"

"Right about here," Toby replied, brushing a hand over his side near the beltline. "When Mr. Dixon sent us, he was bleeding bad."

"And how long ago was this?"

"The time it takes to ride five miles from camp."

Doing the calculation silently, Pratt said, "You realize it may be too late as we speak?"

"My orders are to try, no matter what."

"Of course. I'll need to put some items in my bag."

"Quick as you can, Doctor."

"And coming back?"

"Can't let you keep the horse," Toby replied, "but one of us will see you home."

"No time to waste, then," Pratt said, moving quickly toward his office facing on the street.

As they drew near to camp and Mr. Dixon's herd, Bishop tried picking out Stark's watchers where he'd seen their fire before the shooting, but they'd either doused it, to stop making targets of themselves, or they had left entirely. Even so, he kept expecting shots out of the shadows, riding with his shoulders hunched in readiness, hand on his holstered Peacemaker.

A guard who sounded like Whit Melville called out to them when they'd closed to thirty yards. "Who goes there?"

"Sullivan and Bishop," Deke responded. "With the sawbones."

"Come ahead, then."

Half the drive's remaining cowboys had them covered from all sides as they rode in. Bishop supposed the rest were out minding the steers and watching out for snipers.

Mr. D and Pickering came out to meet them, Bishop introducing Dr. Pratt. Their wrangler, Abel Floyd, relieved Pratt of his borrowed horse's reins while Pratt dismounted and removed the doctor's bag he'd slung over the saddle horn. They walked him to the spot where Isaac Thorne lay underneath a wool blanket with bloodstains showing through it.

Bishop didn't care to watch while Pratt knelt on the grass, removed the blanket, and examined Thorne. At his direction, Leland Gorch stood over them, holding a lantern close to help him see.

Bishop found Curly Odom standing near the chuck wagon's tailgate, sipping a cup of coffee, with his free hand clinging to his Colt revolving carbine.

"What's been going on?" asked Bishop. "Any more shooting?"

"They quit after the first one," Odom said. "Seems like it satisfied them. Killed their fire and rode off to the west. After the first shot, we laid low, trying to keep from giving 'em a target."

"Any word on what the boss is planning?"

"Not a peep," Odom replied. "But he can't let this go, right? If the law won't lift a finger, don't we have to handle it ourselves?"

"Can't speak for anybody else," said Toby.

But he felt like there'd be more blood coming at them, down the road.

CHAPTER SEVENTEEN

DESPITE THE DOCTOR'S best efforts, Isaac Thorne died on the shady side of dawn. Dr. Pratt explained the damage, standing over his late patient. Thorne had suffered major damage to his liver, colon, one kidney, and stomach, all of them together bleeding out while spilling fluids on the inside of his abdomen that led to fatal sepsis.

"Considering the time elapsed," Pratt told them, summing up, "there's nothing more I could have done for him beyond easing his pain with laudanum. In fact, I doubt a well-equipped hospital would have saved him."

Bishop watched as Mr. Dixon, stone-faced, told the doctor, "You did what you could. As far as payment—"

"No, sir. I won't hear of it," Pratt cut him off midsentence. "I'm just sorry that your friend was put through this. If it's a consolation to you, I suspect he was unconscious, or the next thing to it, almost from the moment he was shot."

"Can't say that puts my mind at ease," Dixon replied.

"No, I guess not. It's what we call a 'bedside manner,' mostly blowing smoke."

"But in your case, I'm guessing it's heartfelt."

"Sometimes," Pratt said. "Though I can think of some who don't inspire much charity of spirit."

"Like your Mr. Stark?"

"He's not *mine*, sir. If anything, I and the other townsfolk of Cold Comfort would belong to him."

"And everyone puts up with that?" Bill Pickering inquired.

"Some of us feel embarrassed by it, even shamed. In fact, he holds an economic stranglehold over the town and the surrounding part of Christian County. When I hear that name spoken, I'm torn between laughter and tears."

"But never thought of leaving?" Dixon asked him.

Bishop saw bright color rising in the doctor's cheeks that couldn't be accounted for by early morning sun. "Despite Stark's influence, most of the citizens in town are decent people. They fall ill like anybody else and need my help. As far as packing up and leaving, I might manage it, though cash for starting over elsewhere would be sparse. For shopkeepers, farmers, and such, the cost would simply be too great—always assuming Stark would let them go."

"You saying he holds people hostage?" Pickering asked Pratt.

"Not with a gun against their heads per se, but he holds title to most of the town and land for miles around. The businessmen owe mortgages and other loans that bind them to him. One, a barber, tried to get away last year. Moved to the county seat, but our esteemed mayor filed a claim on Stark's behalf, as his attorney. Left the poor man with his wife and children destitute."

"Mayor Rogers," Dixon said, as if the name tasted of bitter gall. "I met him, and that poor excuse for law you've got in town."

"If they were gone, with Stark and his hired bully-boys, it might be tolerable in Cold Comfort. Even pleasant, I suppose."

"But no one's tried to root him out?" asked Dixon.

"None who lived. The rest of us prefer to live, if only in his shadow."

"I don't like judging strangers till they've done me wrong," said Dixon. "How you lived's your business, none of mine." He glanced at Isaac, shrouded by the bloodstained blanket now. "But this is murder, Dr. Pratt. I won't ignore it and move on, even if Stark agreed to let me go without paying his toll."

"That's new, from what I understand. Seems like each time we turn around, he has another plan for taking more. More money, more land, more of our self-respect."

Bishop was ready, waiting, when the boss replied, "It's high time someone put a stop to that."

B ISHOP AND SULLIVAN rode into town with Mr. Dixon when he went to drop the doctor off at home. Except for Pratt, they hadn't slept since roughly this time yesterday, while breaking camp, but Bishop wasn't saddled with fatigue yet.

It would catch up with him, he supposed, but for the moment rage was keeping him alert.

They dropped Pratt off behind his home and office before circling back to Cold Comfort's main thorough-fare and stopping at the marshal's office. Dixon led the way inside and Toby followed, leaving Deke to watch their horses at the hitching rail and water trough. No sign of Tilton's deputy this time, but the lawman was tacking "Wanted" flyers on the office corkboard when they took him by surprise.

"We meet again," said Tilton, trying for a smile that came off looking like a sneer instead. "What now?"

"One of my men was murdered last night, at our camp," Dixon replied.

"When you say 'murdered' . . . "

"I mean shot from ambush by some goddamn coward hiding in the dark."

"Shooting isn't necessarily the same as murder, Mr.—what's your name, again?"

Instead of answering that question, Dixon asked one of his own. "When would a sniping after sundown *not* be murder, Tilton? Are you gonna claim it was a hunting accident?"

"Nobody mentioned hunting, and it's *Marshal* Tilton."

"Maybe. When you act like one."

The portly lawman lumbered to his feet, red-faced. Bishop couldn't have said if liquor helped with that, or if the odor coming off Tilton had simply lingered from the night before.

"Fact is, some people in these parts take a dim view of trespassing on private property. You ever think of that?"

"What kind of private property goes unfenced and unposted? Stark claims he owns everything, far as the eye can see, and we were in the middle of negotiating passage."

"Passage isn't camping out and killing time," Tilton replied. "Some people tire of waiting, if you get my drift."

Half turned to Bishop, Dixon said, "You heard him, Toby. He's accusing Stark of having Isaac shot. In fact, I'd say he's talking like a damned accomplice."

"Hold on, now!"

"You think we ought to make a citizen's arrest?" asked Bishop.

"You sons of bitches can't buffalo me!"

Tilton was reaching for his pistol, but he never made it, finding two guns leveled at his face before his own cleared leather.

"All right, now." His voice had lowered to a whine. "Just take it easy, will you? We can talk this out."

"How 'bout we drop in on the mayor," Dixon said. "He had a lot to say before. Being a lawyer, maybe he can tell me how a murder in this county might be legal."

"We can try 'im, but I doubt he's in his office yet," Tilton replied.

"No problem," Dixon said. "We'll wake him up if need be. This won't keep."

CREED ROGERS LIVED only a half block from the marshal's office, in a four-room house, the privy out in back. Despite its proximity, Tilton only made the walk on rare occasions, mostly dealing with the mayor at his office, which held shelves of lawbooks and a landscape on the wall that looked like something painted by a child.

The trail boss and his drover put their guns away before they left the marshal's office, but the memory of facing them still rankled Tilton, left an itch between his shoulder blades where one of them could put a bullet anytime he felt like it. To ward that off, Tilton was careful not to let his right hand linger near his Colt.

Along the way, they passed Harry and Deirdre Keane, heading in the direction of their general store. They managed matching smiles that stopped short of their eyes while wishing Tilton a good morning, Harry reaching up to tip his bowler hat at Tilton's silent followers. Neither Harry nor Deirdre showed anything resembling suspicion as they passed along the sidewalk, likely taking Dixon and his friend for employees of Hebron Stark.

Arriving at the mayor's house, they mounted the porch—almost an ostentatious touch, considering the other houses on his street. Dixon stopped Tilton then and asked, "He live alone?"

"Long as I've known him. Used to have a wife, he claims, but I've seen nary hide nor hair of her."

"No problem, then."

Toby reached past Tilton, knocked briskly, and stepped back, waiting so that he and Dixon had the marshal in a sandwich. Either one of them could draw and pistol-whip him where he stood, or cover Rogers if he showed up in the doorway armed.

Instead, the mayor answered in his shirtsleeves and suspenders, with a kitchen spatula in hand, surrounded by the smells of breakfast cooking. Rogers blinked one time for each of them, frowning, and then addressed himself to Tilton.

"Harley, this is a surprise."

"To me as well," Tilton replied.

"You brought the cowpokes with you."

"They brought me," Tilton corrected him.

"On what business?"

"That's best discussed inside," Dixon said to Rogers. "Lest you want your neighbors eavesdropping."

"Alrighty, then. I'm making breakfast and I didn't plan on four."

"We ain't hungry," Dixon advised, and prodded Tilton through the open door ahead of him and his companion.

"It's unorthodox," said Rogers as he moved back to the stove, flipping an egg and strips of bacon in a cast-iron skillet with his spatula, "but you can pay your toll to me, if that's your preference. I'll give you a receipt and pass the money on to—"

"We ain't here for that," said Dixon, interrupting him.

"Oh, no?" Still with his back to them, Rogers inquired, "What, then?"

"One of my men was shot last night. Murdered at long range by a sniper in the dark. Your friend here reckons you can quote a law that makes it all legitimate."

"I have no knowledge of the shooting you refer to, or whoever may have done it—if, in fact, it *was* done."

"You can take a ride out to our camp and see the body," Dixon said. "Or you can talk to Dr. Pratt. If that's not good enough, we can come back and drop it on your doorstep, Mr. Mayor."

Turning from the stove as something in his frying pan began to smoke, Rogers put on a face approximating outrage. "If you think that I had anything to do with—"

"Save it!" Dixon snapped. "We know you're just the organ grinder's dancing monkey."

Tilton stiffened, thought about his pistol, then dismissed the notion. Rogers faced them, colored blotches flaming on his cheeks. "Damn you! I won't be spoken to as if—"

"You wanna shut up of your own accord or shall I help you?" Dixon challenged him.

"If you think—"

Without further argument, Dixon stepped forward, hit Rogers with a right cross, and knocked him back against the stove. The mayor yelped at contact with hot metal, flinched away, and in the process of retreating spilled his breakfast on the kitchen floor.

"That's assault!" he blustered, lisping as his lower lip began to swell. "Marshal, you witnessed—"

"Dammit, Creed!" Tilton cut through his whining. "Can't you ever just shut up?"

"We didn't come to hear your nonsense," Dixon cautioned. "Tell us where to find your boss, and we'll be on our way."

Rogers spat blood onto the ruined remnants of his meal. "My boss? Who—"

"And you *still* don't get it." Dixon sounded almost mournful, stepping forward with his fist raised for another blow.

"Stark! Yes, all right!" Rogers blurted out, hands raised to shield his bloodied face. "I'll take you there, just—"

"Telling is enough." Dixon cut through his blubbering. "Directions to his place, and I won't ask you twice."

"Three miles southwest of town, A big ranch house and barn, with other buildings. You can't miss it."

"See? Was that so hard to manage?"

"Mr. D, you want to leave 'em here like this?" Bishop inquired.

Dixon considered it, then said, "I don't believe I do."

"Jail ought to hold them for a bit, if we can find that deputy."

Tilton felt traitorous, but thought, *Screw it.* "Luke should be in the office by the time we get back there," he said.

"I hope you're right," Dixon replied. To Rogers then, "Damp down the stove, and let's go see if Marshal Tilton gets to keep his teeth."

B ISHOP WAS FEELING twitchy as they started back toward camp, trailing the horse that Dr. Pratt had used to visit, on his failed attempt to save Thorne's life. Toby was half expecting to be ambushed on their ride back to the herd from Cold Comfort and was surprised when they got there without so much as glimpsing any more of Hebron Stark's gunmen.

Tilton and Rogers were confined with Deputy Luke Hazlet at the town's jail, crowded into one of two barred backroom cells. The lawmen had been stripped of gun belts, all three forced to turn their pockets out before Bishop had locked the cell's door after them and stashed the key ring in a drawer of Tilton's desk. Leaving them there, Dixon advised, "I'd wait awhile before raising a ruckus, I was you. Could be we left someone outside and listening."

When they were at the door, the deputy called after them, "Bullshit!"

He backed off from the bars, into a corner of the six-by-eight enclosure, when Bishop took one step closer to him, offering, "Or I could shut you up for good."

Outside, Dixon asked Toby, "How long do you think that's gonna hold 'em?"

"Ten or fifteen minutes, if we're lucky, boss."

"A head start, then. Let's move."

Arriving back at camp, they found all hands alert and watchful. Some among them had pitched in to dig a grave for Isaac Thorne but left the blanket-shrouded corpse until Mr. Dixon returned. The funeral that followed was a simple ceremony, short on ritual, ending with Dixon garbling the first part of Ecclesiastes, Chapter 3.

"To everything there is a season," he declaimed, "a time to be born and a time to die, a time to weep, a time to rend, a time to mourn, a time to kill."

Bishop knew he'd left out most of it and scrambled up the rest—a time to heal, to plant, to love—but Toby didn't plan to take the place of Graham Lott and turn to preaching. For the moment, Dixon's words would serve the drovers as they went to war.

Some of them, anyway.

"You know we can't afford to leave the herd unguarded," Dixon said, once Whit Melville and Curly

Odom finished filling in Thorne's grave and tamped the loose dirt down. "There's eleven of us left, and I'll be leading half to Stark's place, now we've got directions. Mr. Pickering will stay here with the rest—I'm sorry, Bill, but that's an order. I'll count on every one of you to fight like hell if someone comes around trying to lead the steers away or run them off. As for the split, we'll draw straws, fair and square."

Bishop was selected for the hunting party, riding out with Dixon, Esperanza, Gorch, and Sullivan. Those left behind with Pickering included Floyd, Melville, and Odom, plus Mel Varney and young Rudy Knapp.

Three miles southwest of town meant close to eight miles total, riding overland and bypassing Cold Comfort. They had no idea how many men Stark had on hand, or when Tilton and Hazlet would be freed to join the home team, with whichever townsmen cared to tag along or feared not to.

It was a gamble, and the stakes were life or death.

H URRY, FOR GOD'S sake, will you?" Creed Rogers demanded of his two shamefaced companions.

"I'm moving as fast as I can," Harley Tilton replied. "Keep your shirt on!"

Luke Hazlet just glared at the mayor of Cold Comfort, taking a Winchester down from the office gun rack, stuffing his pockets with spare ammunition.

It was the undertaker, Silas Umbrage, who'd heard them shouting from their crowded jail cell, stuck his head in, smiling at first—a crime that Rogers was unlikely to forgive—then circling around the marshal's desk to fetch a key and turn them loose. Before he came, the trio had discussed their options and decided there was only one, assuming they were able to escape before all holy hell broke loose.

They had to ride with all dispatch to warn the puppeteer who pulled their strings.

Fetching three horses from the livery had taken precious time, first to rouse the proprietor, demanding animals, then getting their mounts saddled and ready for the road. Now, finally, they were en route to Hebron Stark's place outside town, with Rogers praying that his tobiano gelding wouldn't stumble, pitching him headlong into the night, breaking his damned-fool neck.

It seemed to take forever, covering three miles between Cold Comfort and the spread their lord and master called Stark Acres. Lights were burning in the house as they arrived, and some of Hebron's hands were circulating through the shadows, wrapping up their daily chores and smoking, hand-rolled quirleys glowing in the night.

One rangy shooter tried to stop them climbing up three steps onto Stark's elevated porch, but Tilton flashed his badge and glowered when the lookout tried to laugh it off. Reluctantly, they were admitted to the big house while a black butler went off to fetch the man in charge.

"Well, what in hell's the matter?" Stark demanded when he finally appeared, wearing a robe made from some shiny fabric Rogers didn't recognize offhand.

They had agreed beforehand that he'd do the talking, and he kept it short: the trail boss and one of his *pistoleros* barging in, first at the marshal's office, then the mayor's house, forcing their hostages to point them toward Stark's place. Instead of going off half-cocked, as Rogers had expected, Stark seemed calm and thoughtful, saying, "No one's seen them around here."

"Not yet," the marshal blurted out. "It didn't sound like they were joshing, though."

"I'm not disputing your account, Mayor," Stark replied, observing the formalities despite what Rogers viewed as an imminent threat. "I'll be prepared. You rest assured of that."

"And us, sir?" Hazlet interjected, making Creed Rogers scowl. What was the point of making plans if no one stuck to them?

Instead of telling Luke to shut his pan, Stark said, "It's your call. Head on back and wait it out or stick around and see it done. Just don't get underfoot."

"I'm staying put," Rogers declared, before the lawmen had a chance to put their two cents in.

Stark nodded. "I'll have Erasmus bring you one drink each, but that's the limit. You're not getting spoony on my dime when I may need you thinking straight."

J AY COTHRAN DIDN'T keep the old man waiting. That was never wise, and most particularly not when there was action in the offing.

Stark wasted no time in getting down to business. "Jay," he said, "it seems we might be having company tonight."

The foreman didn't ask how Stark knew that. He'd seen the three chuckleheads from town arrive, demanding time with Mr. Stark as though they had any authority beyond their phony jobs.

"How many, boss?" he asked instead.

"Can't answer that," Stark said. "They only had eleven men before you plugged the shine. Leaves ten all told, and I'd expect their boss to leave half of them sitting on the herd, in case we try something."

So, five, no more than six. Jay didn't speak the numbers. Stark was capable of counting on his own and didn't care for yes-men as a rule—as long as everyone in his employ did just exactly what he ordered them to do, without delay.

"We've got 'em four to one," Cothran said.

"Not counting household staff and green hands," Stark reminded him.

"So, two to one."

"Still should be good enough. I'll join you for the party."

"Yes, sir." Jay tried to keep his face deadpan, but something must have shown despite his best effort.

"You disapprove?" Stark asked, cocking one eyebrow at him.

"No, sir. Not at all. Just thinking about you taking a big chance on the firing line."

"I'm touched by your concern," his master said, not sounding touched at all, but working up to angry.

Cothran tried to head him off from that. "No disrespect meant, sir."

"And none inferred. Just bear in mind who built this place and who's in charge of it."

"Yes, sir."

"When trouble shows up at my door, I kick it in the rear."

IT WAS WELL past midnight when five horsemen made their approach to Stark Acres. They couldn't see the house or any other buildings yet, but knew they had to be within a mile unless they'd gone badly astray.

Riding a few yards back from Gavin Dixon at the point, Bishop was watching out for pickets, at the same time thinking about those they'd left behind, guarding the herd. Dividing up their forces was a risky play, but he'd have likely done the same thing if some twist of fate had placed him in command.

On balance, he preferred receiving orders to pronouncing them. That way, at least, if someone else got hurt or killed, it wouldn't be his fault.

Bishop had no idea what they were riding into, but

he took for granted that they'd be outnumbered and outgunned by men who knew their home ground inside out and how to make the most of it. In any deadly fight, offense and defense both had certain drawbacks, but attackers normally lacked cover, charging at an enemy who'd had time to prepare, plot interlocking fields of fire, and take advantage of familiar ground they lived and worked on every day.

The fight for Malvern Hill in 1862 came instantly to mind. Both sides were equal, call it eighty thousand men at arms, but General Lee's troops were attacking fortified Union positions, with three gunboats on the James River supporting General McClellan's troops on land. When it was over, there were nearly twice as many Rebels dead as Yankees. A lieutenant general on the winning side opined, "It wasn't war. It was murder."

Bishop hoped that wouldn't be their fate tonight, but there was nothing he could do about it now. Ahead of him Dixon had raised a hand to halt the drovers trailing him. They grouped around their trail boss, narrowing their eyes when they at last detected signs of human habitation on the plains.

Toby saw lighted windows but no movement on the grounds.

And here we go, he thought, drawing his rifle from its saddle boot. *No turning back*.

CHAPTER EIGHTEEN

JAY COTHRAN FINISHED tamping down the powder in his Whitworth rifle's barrel, followed it with a heavy bullet and a cotton patch to seal its hexagonal bore, and then stowed the ramrod underneath the weapon's barrel. Mr. Stark supplied repeating rifles but the Whitworth suited Cothran, reaching out to twice the normal range of Winchesters and Henrys, accuracy heightened by the William Malcolm telescopic sight.

The scope wouldn't help Cothran much at night, he realized, but if Stark Acres faced invasion, as the boss surmised, and if one of their adversaries passed between Jay's hideout and the barn or bunkhouse, where lamps cast their light, he should be able to reach out and knock them down.

And failing that, he'd use the Winchester that lay beside him or fall back upon the Colt Open Top pistol riding on his hip. Jay was prepared for anything and didn't plan on letting any cowboy get the drop on him.

Some of the other hands on Stark Acres seemed apprehensive over facing armed invaders, but the prospect didn't worry Jay at all. He'd been expecting this when Mr. Stark sent him to rile the drovers up and force their hand. When he had dropped one of them at their camp, all that had followed from it was foreseeable—and, in Jay's mind, a welcome consequence.

What was the point of working for a man like Mr. Stark if Cothran never got to throw his weight around?

Jay figured he'd get one shot, maybe two, out of the Whitworth before he was forced to set it down and turn his hand to the repeaters for whichever adversaries were still drawing breath. By then, with any luck, he would have dropped two men out of the five or six who meant harm to his boss and to the property over which Cothran exercised a measure of authority.

He'd prove his usefulness once more, and that would bring its own reward in terms of job security.

But if he failed . . .

That did not bear considering.

Jay had the roof of Mr. Stark's ranch house staked out, accessed via a ladder at the rear. The curved ceramic tiles beneath him radiated heat despite the hour, after soaking up the sun all day, making a pleasant contrast to the cool night breeze that brushed against Jay's face. He had no worry about sliding off the roof, positioned as he was, but backing toward the ladder when the time came would require sure-footedness.

All Cothran wanted was sufficient time to pick at least one target, preferably two, before he had to take the fight down with him to ground level and be done with it.

"Come on, you bastards," he muttered to no one. "Come ahead and get it done."

T HE LIGHTED HOUSE and barn were still three hundred yards ahead when Mr. Dixon halted them and dismounted. The others watched him from their saddles, waiting till he said, "We'll leave the horses here, tethered around those sugar maples yonder. Come back for 'em when we're done."

Or not, thought Bishop, *if they finish us.*

It wouldn't matter in that case, but he disliked the thought of Compañero falling into Stark's hands, either being worked to death or maybe shot outright. He decided then and there to tie a slipknot in the Appaloosa's reins, so he could pull it loose at the approach of strangers.

Bishop owed that, at the very least, to the friend who'd carried him halfway across the country.

When all their animals were settled and the men's weapons double-checked, they got final instructions from their boss. Dixon was going straight in, up the middle, with Deke Sullivan and Paco Esperanza. While they closed the gap, Bishop's assignment was to flank Stark's layout from the east while Gorch circled around the west.

Given the longer distances his flankers had to cover, Dixon gave them both a five-minute head start. His parting order: "If you come on any guards, try not to let them sound a warning."

That was open to interpretation, Bishop taking it to mean that they were on their own, relying on their personal initiative. A sentry taken by surprise could be coldcocked—a fist or gun butt should be satisfactory—but judging how long any given man might lie unconscious was a gamble. One measure of miscalculation could be fatal for the Circle K's riders.

The only "safe" alternative was murder.

Bishop mulled the possibilities: a killing blow, instead of one that sent an adversary off to dreamland. Otherwise, all he could think of was the knife sheathed on his belt, its blade six inches long and single-edged, or strangulation with bare hands. The more time it required to put one guard away, the greater risk his boss and fellow drovers faced.

Bishop had only stabbed one man—a drunk in Waco who had tried to knife him in a bar—and that wound wasn't fatal. He had used the drunk's own sticker, turning it against him in their tussle, and no charges had been filed, although the city marshal had suggested in the strongest terms that Bishop hit the road. He had a memory of seeing red, then rinsing crimson from his hands and feeling no regret to speak of as he put Waco behind him.

Knifing someone with intent to kill was different, but once he drew the knife there could be no other result. Leaving a sentry wounded, crying out in pain, would contravene his orders and most likely get him killed.

Do what you have to do, he thought. *Then live with it.*

HEBRON STARK BUCKLED his pistol belt, twin Smith & Wesson Model 3 six-guns holstered on either hip. Around behind, two dozen leather loops held .44 S&W American cartridges, polished with a chamois cloth until they gleamed by lamplight.

In his tanned, big-knuckled hands he held a lever-action Spencer carbine, seven .45-70 cartridges loaded into its butt magazine, one more in the chamber and ready to fire once he cocked the hammer. It measured forty-seven inches overall, the barrel just a smidgen under twenty-two, weighing eight and one-quarter pounds. Its maximum effective range, according to the manufacturer: five hundred yards.

If all of that firepower let Stark down, he had a Remington Model 95 derringer in a vest pocket, both barrels loaded with a .41-caliber short rimfire car-

tridge. Meant for close-up killing with its stubby barrels, the Model 95 had an effective range of only ten
feet, give or take.

If all else failed, Stark also had a bowie knife, its
twelve-inch clip-point blade honed to a shaving razor's
keenness with a whetstone, then a leather strop.

Each weapon in his private arsenal had drawn blood
in the past and, if tonight turned out the way it seemed
to be heading, would draw more yet.

That prospect did not frighten Stark.

In fact, it made him smile.

He had enough dependable gunmen on hand to do
the job without him, under Jay Cothran's direction, but
Stark realized that any shirking of participation in the
coming fight would undermine his personal authority
downrange. New hires would start to doubt him first.
Veterans who'd been around much longer, sharing
risks with Stark, would recall how he'd fought beside
them against Indians and outlaws, running squatters
off his open range. Still, seeds of doubt would put
down roots like weeds among the red tiles on his roof.

A reputation, once procured, had to be nurtured
like a garden, or eventually it would wither on the vine
and fade away. He dared not place the whole burden
on Cothran's shoulders, or before he knew it, Stark's
hands would begin to see Jay as their boss in all but
name.

And that would never do.

Stark moved along the hallway from his office, past
the dining room and parlor toward his home's front
door. Outside, the night was nearly still, his men under
instruction to keep quiet, on alert for enemies who
could appear at any time, from any quarter.

It had been years, Stark realized, since he had felt
so vital. So alive.

* * *

CREED ROGERS CHECKED his Colt Model 1855 Side-hammer revolver's load, confirming there were five .31-caliber rounds in its small cylinder, and wondered what in hell he was thinking.

He'd been wondering that same thing since he left Cold Comfort with Harley Tilton and Luke Hazlet, riding out to Stark Acres on a borrowed horse from the livery stable. The very last place he belonged was at the site of an impending mortal combat, yet he'd placed himself in harm's way and it was too late to back out now.

Rogers had never shot a man, had never even fired a bullet *at* another human being. Come to that, he hadn't been in any kind of fight at all since he was twelve, maybe thirteen years old, and wound up losing that one badly, carrying the shame of it until he'd left home to escape by studying the law.

The problem, he supposed, was goddamned greed.

He'd been confronted by a situation in which a man with wealth had promised him a measure of authority, albeit in a godforsaken piss-pot town, and he had grabbed for that brass ring as if his life depended on it.

Now, Rogers supposed, it might.

The Colt Sidehammer was a small weapon, suited in that regard to his dwindling courage. It measured just eight inches overall, including its three-and-one-half-inch octagonal barrel, and weighed one ounce over a pound. Colt's Manufacturing Company had produced forty-odd thousand of them between 1855 and 1870, carried most often as a hideout gun by men who put their main trust in some larger firearm. Its effective range was estimated at twenty-five yards, and the three times he'd fired it, Rogers hadn't hit his target once at one-fourth of that distance.

Pitiful.

Right now, he could be at home, waiting to hear who'd won the battle of Stark Acres—or perhaps he should have picked some compass point at random and departed from Cold Comfort altogether. With his law degree he could have started over somewhere else and tried to leave his past behind.

But now it was too late for that.

No one around him knew how many cowboys would be coming after Hebron Stark, or when they might arrive, but the conviction that they *would* come was a universal constant, from the Big Man down to his household staff and the old man who mucked his stalls. None of them seemed as troubled by that prospect as Creed Rogers was—except, perhaps, for Harley Tilton and Luke Hazlet.

Neither of the lawmen seemed to be anticipating all-out war with anything but dread, though Rogers saw that they were fighting to conceal their fear. As he thought of all the times he'd seen them throw their weight around Cold Comfort, lording over men and women who accepted Stark's will as judgment from on high, their apprehensive posture seemed ironic now.

In other circumstances, if he had been safe himself, Rogers might well have laughed at their discomfiture, watching them squirm and try to hide it, but having his own life riding on the line—the only thing he truly cared about—had stolen the mayor's sense of humor and replaced it with a brooding premonition of disaster.

Had he brought this down upon himself?

Undoubtedly, he thought, and pushed that thought away as if some stranger had addressed it to him with hostile intent.

If he could only live to see another sunrise, Rogers promised faithfully to change his ways, move on, and find himself another life.

But that required him living through the fight to come, and he supposed that only Hebron Stark's hired guns could save him now.

ROGERS MIGHT HAVE been surprised to learn that Gavin Dixon—whom he barely knew, but who had turned his small world upside down—was saddled with misgivings of his own.

Not that he ever seriously thought of turning back.

Dixon was a man of some influence back at home in Atoka, as Rogers was in Cold Comfort, though he seldom acted like it unless he perceived some danger to his livelihood. In that case, he would fight—*had* fought—against opponents of all colors of the human rainbow. So far, he had always triumphed in those struggles, though the cost was sometimes high, verging on terrible.

But Hebron Stark had left him no alternative.

If Stark had waited out the night, Dixon supposed he might have folded in the morning, paid the toll that Stark demanded, and deducted it from the profits earned upon arrival in St. Louis, but Stark's arrogance had forced his hand, compelling him to do more.

The death—murder—of Isaac Thorne demanded an accounting Dixon recognized as long past due.

Honor demanded that he fight, regardless of the risk to the other men who'd joined his drive to herd longhorns, not plunge into a shooting war. Tonight—well, morning now, although the sun was still in hiding—marked their third fight in a month, roughly, and he could only hope that it would be their last, whatever happened in the next few hours.

If he lost, then it would absolutely be his last, and Dixon would have taken good men with him as his final act on earth. If they won, whoever lived through it still had another ten, twelve days of driving steers to market, dwelling on the losses they'd sustained.

Four drovers dead so far at hostile hands, the only good news being that he wouldn't have to pay their salaries under the terms each had agreed to before setting out. Against that loss, they'd slain thirteen opponents, but that didn't balance out in Dixon's mind.

Not even close.

His first duty, after delivering the herd, was caring for the men who helped him on the trail, and he had failed at that with Thorne, Lott, Hightower, and Courtwright. Not through any weakness of his own, perhaps, but simply from the state of being human, which meant fallible.

Tonight, we end this, Dixon told himself. *We settle it, even if nothing in the world can put it right.*

T OBY BISHOP SCANNED the eastern skyline, waiting for the first pale blush of sunrise, but it wasn't time for that yet. Just as well, since daylight would expose them to their enemies as they approached.

Beyond that, he supposed their errand was rightly a job for darkness, after all.

He didn't think about how badly they would be outnumbered by Stark's men. Fretting about it wouldn't change a thing, except perhaps to weaken his resolve and spoil his aim when pinpoint accuracy was required. Bishop had no fear on that score—no real fear he could point to, if the truth were told—and some folks might have found that worrying enough.

At what point would he face reality, accept the fact that he was basically a killer, and decide what that foretold for the remainder of his life?

Or, then again, it might not be a problem.

Five men against three or four times that number,

presumably. He had no faith in winning just because they had "right" on their side. So, in their own opinion, had most of the men he'd killed during the Mason County war. He guessed the rustlers who met their deaths in Willow Grove had felt the same, doing what seemed the best for them. And the Comanches doubtless had a valid grudge against white men.

All dead now, and likely forgotten by this time next week, except by Willow Grove's survivors and the Circle K drovers who still had lives ahead of them.

Nature or Fate, whatever people chose to call it, didn't give a damn who won or lost a given fight. Of that, Bishop was reasonably sure.

So, when they met the enemy, he planned to fight as if his life depended on it—which was fact, not speculation. Beyond that, whether it was the long view that made their struggle right, wrong, or indifferent, he didn't care to think about it.

A task was waiting for him, and beyond accomplishing it, nothing mattered.

Not a blessed thing.

I WISH TO GOD they'd hurry up and get here," Harley Tilton said.

"Uh-huh," his deputy replied. He didn't sound sincere.

"What's wrong with you?" Tilton demanded.

"Nothing. I just wanna get it over with, the same as you."

"Sounds like you're going to a funeral," Tilton replied.

" 'Bout how it feels," Hazlet admitted.

"That's no attitude for winning, Luke."

"I've got a bad feeling about this, Harley. I mean 'Marshal.'"

"Never mind that. Any way you slice it, we've got numbers on our side."

"Maybe."

"You doubt it? Even if that Dixon fella brings all of his men—which we both know he can't afford to do—Stark must have two, three times as many gun hands waiting for 'em."

"Yeah. If all of 'em will fight."

"You doubt it?"

"Wait and see."

If fact, Tilton had doubts himself, but wasn't voicing them tonight while being sheltered in the home of Hebron Stark. He owed the Big Man much of what he was today—though, for the life of him, at the moment Tilton would have been hard-pressed to say exactly what that was.

A "lawman" in a poor jerkwater town, of course. He had the tin to prove it on his vest, for all the good that did him now. Most of the people in Cold Comfort had a healthy fear of him—or, rather, of the man he represented—but beyond that Tilton felt their simmering contempt. If Mr. Stark didn't exist, virtual lord and master of his little realm, the townsfolk likely would have ridden Harley and Luke Hazlet out of town on rails, maybe with a fresh coat of tar for their traveling attire.

None of that mattered now, of course.

There would be time enough to deal with that tomorrow, if tomorrow came and Tilton was alive to see daybreak.

"You check your guns?" he asked Hazlet.

"Hell yes. Three times. Much more, and I'll have blisters on my thumbs."

"Won't kill you," Tilton said.

"No, *that* won't. We got people coming wanna do that for themselves."

"And you know how to handle that."

"I do?"

"Idjit! You kill them first."

"Don't stand there and act like I'm the one who got us into this," Hazlet replied.

"I didn't say—"

His deputy talked over him. "Because I ain't. We both know who's at fault."

"Don't let him hear you say that under his own roof."

"Hell, what's he gonna do? Fire me?"

"The mood he's in right now, losing your job might be the least of it."

That sobered Hazlet and he shut his mouth, but he couldn't help the sour expression on his face.

Tilton was satisfied with that, under the circumstances. With his own life riding on the line, he had no time to spare for coddling Hazlet and his injured feelings—not that he'd seen Luke express feelings for anything beyond money, rotgut, and the whores who plied their trade at Cold Comfort's saloon.

Tonight, maybe he'd have a chance to see his deputy behaving like some semblance of a man.

And how would Tilton, on his own account, make out?

B ISHOP RAN INTO the first lookout when he came within three hundred yards or so of Hebron Stark's ranch house.

The guy was smoking, had a rifle tucked under his left arm backward, muzzle pointing down behind him for a cross-hand grab at need. He also wore a pistol on his right hip, holster tied down to facilitate a faster draw, which meant that in a pinch he'd have to choose between one weapon or the other.

If he picked the rifle, that meant swinging nine and one-half pounds around one-handed, measuring just

shy of fifty inches long from butt to muzzle, before sighting on a target. If he hadn't jacked a round into the firing chamber, add another two, three seconds to the
whole procedure before he could fire a killing shot.

Or, if he chose the handgun, he'd be fumbling with
the rifle, trying not to drop it as he drew and fired. Three
seconds minimum, no matter how often he practiced
shooting stumps, bottles, or cans.

And that was only if he saw Death coming for him
through the darkness.

Bishop was approaching from the watchman's flank,
careful with each step to produce no telling noise. It
seemed to take forever, but if Dixon's other drovers
started shooting first, that might help him, distracting
his intended target when the lookout needed to be
most alert.

And he could work with that.

Ten feet before he reached his adversary now, and
he could smell the sharp tang of tobacco on the night
breeze, hear the lookout's gun belt creaking slightly
when he shifted weight from one leg to the other.
Bishop had considered how to do this quickly, quietly,
and had decided on a double hit: a butt stroke from his
Winchester to put the watchman down and keep him
quiet long enough for Toby to unsheathe his knife, pin
the guy down beneath his weight, and do what needed
doing.

Now.

He closed the last eight feet in two swift strides,
swinging the Yellow Boy around stock first and slamming it into the stranger's face. A muffled *crack*
reached Toby's ears just as he saw the gunman's jaw
slip out of line, causing his lips to twist and form a kind
of sneer.

That might have done him in, but Bishop couldn't
count on it. He followed through, kneeling atop the

downed man's heaving chest while his knife flashed by
moonlight, vanished into flesh and gristle, came back
streaming blood that glistened jet-black.

Done, or nearly so.

He had to wait out shivering death throes, but they
passed in another minute, maybe less. Taking no
chances, Toby tossed the dead man's rifle out of reach
and pulled a Colt Peacemaker from the fallen sentry's
holster, tucking it under his belt around in back.

Another gun might come in handy when the shooting started.

And as if in answer to his thought, it did, crackling
around the ranch house in a flurry that a drunkard
might mistake for Independence Day fireworks.

If this turned out to be the last night of his life,
Bishop could only hope to meet the threat head-on
and do his best.

CHAPTER NINETEEN

W HEN THE GUNFIRE started, Hebron Stark moved
toward the sound. If any of his men had taken
time to focus on him then, in passing, they'd have been
surprised—and maybe even horrified—to see that he
was smiling like a cat sitting before a bowl of fresh,
warm cream.

Why not?

His enemies had done the stupid thing, coming for
him on his home turf, and he would break them there,
annihilate them. When he'd finished that chore, he
would ride out with his men to claim the longhorn
herd, ready to kill the rest of Gavin Dixon's men or let
them flee if they were smart enough to do so.

Whichever way that went, he'd finish up the day a
richer man than when the sun last set.

He couldn't tell how many men Dixon had brought
against him so far, but from spotting muzzle flashes
and listening to the reports of rifles, he had estimated
five or six all told. That would be all the rancher could
afford to spare without leaving his stock unguarded on

the prairie, every head at risk of being stolen or just wandering away and getting lost on unfamiliar ground.

So far, Stark hadn't fired a shot—no point in wasting ammunition on shadows—but he was looking forward to it, hoping he could draw a bead on Dixon in the flesh and be the one to bring him down.

Officially, he might have bent some law by levying a toll on Dixon's herd, but who was going to complain? Prior drives had paid up and gone on their way, avoiding Christian County if they made another trek across Missouri, but as far as Stark could tell, no one had griped about it to the law. State law, that was, and not the flunkies he'd installed to run things for him in Cold Comfort. If Tilton and Hazlet couldn't pull their weight tonight, he'd have to find somebody else to fill their posts.

Someone who wasn't just a brute, but who had a knack for thinking on his feet.

For thinking at all, in fact.

But first, he had to win this skirmish, then move on to win the war.

Just the thought of it bred more excitement in his gut than Stark had felt in years.

B ISHOP WAS CLOSING on Stark's spacious barn when two men came out of a side door, one behind the other, looking all around, each with a rifle in his hands. They didn't spot him right away, but Toby knew he only had a few seconds before that changed and he came under fire.

The answer: beat them to it.

Shouldering his Winchester, he framed the second defender in its sights, thumbed back the rifle's hammer, and squeezed off. The recoil wasn't bad, a pistol cartridge in a rifle weighing more than nine pounds, and his shot was true, slamming the second man in line against the door from which he'd just emerged.

That slammed the door and blocked it, while the first shooter who had shown himself was spinning, looking for the sniper who had dropped his pal. His eyes focused on Toby just as Bishop pumped the rifle's lever action and he fired again from forty feet or less.

Another hit, the ranch hand's Stetson taking flight and carrying a fragment of his skull along with it. Bishop had no need to confirm that he was dead— brains on the grass was proof enough of that—but he stood over the first man he'd shot, prodding the body with his Yellow Boy's muzzle, ensuring that he'd made it two for two.

So far, so good.

The gunfire was increasing now, but no one else had noticed Bishop yet, as far as he could tell. Some of Stark's men were firing from the house, at least one more crouching behind a privy, leaning out to blast the night, and now a muzzle flash erupted from the Big Man's roof, followed a heartbeat later by the echo of a large-caliber hunting rifle.

Bishop couldn't say who that sniper was firing at, or even if he had a target in his sights, but his position made him dangerous to all of Mr. Dixon's raiders on the ground below.

Toby decided he should try to fix that.

Cautiously, wearing night's shadows as his cloak, he closed in on the manor house.

"SON OF A bitch!"

There was no one around to hear Jay Cothran curse his wasted shot, and that was just as well. If there had been, he might have shoved them off the roof for watching as he let the darkness fool him, causing him to miss his first round of the battle from his Whitworth rifle.

Damn the William Malcolm scope mounted atop the Whitworth's barrel. It worked magic in broad daylight, but at night, with the illumination being poor to none, it didn't help him differentiate between a lifeless shadow and a man intent on killing Hebron Stark's defenders.

Still, he hadn't shot one of the ranch hands by mistake. That calmed him down a bit, but only slightly, as he manhandled the muzzleloader, feeding it more powder and another .451-caliber bullet.

Everyone below was firing now—or most of them, at least. Cothran supposed a few had run away, perhaps even before the shooting started, though he hadn't seen them riding off with horses from the paddock. If he had . . .

Well, gutless "friends" could drop as quickly as advancing enemies.

CREED ROGERS CURSED himself for lingering too long around Stark Acres—or for riding out at all, in fact, when Harley Tilton and his rat-faced deputy, Luke Hazlet, could have made the ride without him, to apprise their mutual employer of the risk he faced.

But no. Rogers had come along—insisted on it like an idiot, in point of fact—telling the lawmen that the news should come to Stark from their alleged superior, Cold Comfort's mayor.

Now, just when he'd decided to sneak off, ride back to town, and hope Stark didn't miss him, he had lost the opportunity. A battle was in full swing just outside Stark's house, and Rogers had no choice but to join in.

Unless . . .

Perhaps he could escape on foot, unnoticed. He

could walk the five miles back to town. It wasn't all that far, and daylight would be breaking soon to make it easier.

If only he could leave the mansion without being shot.

Clutching his Cole Sidehammer, Rogers moved from Hebron Stark's parlor to the kitchen, where the two cooks—one a Chinaman, the other Mexican— were huddled in the pantry, muttering in pidgin English with their heads together, almost touching. They fell silent as he passed, then started up again as Rogers reached a side door granting access to the farmyard.

Just another hundred feet or so to reach the barn, where he could either take the horse he'd ridden out from town or leave it there and start his trek back home.

And after that?

The best thing he could think of was another journey, this one taking him as far as possible away from Cold Comfort, from Hebron Stark, perhaps out of Missouri to some other state, leaving his sullied reputation in the dust.

But first things first.

Rogers was nearly at the barn, walking with head down, shoulders hunched, as if his posture would prevent an enemy from seeing him, when someone—just a man-shaped shadow in the night—stepped out to meet him from around the barn's southeastern corner.

"Leaving are you, Mayor?" the prowler asked.

Rogers did not reply. Instead, he raised his Colt, triggered a shot, and literally hit the broad side of a barn, missing his man by six or seven feet.

"Goddammit!"

As he cocked the Colt, preparing for another shot, the faceless figure fired a rifle, its orange muzzle flash imprinting itself on Creed's retinas. A sharp pain forced the air out of his lungs, then he was toppling forward, squeezing off his second wasted round into the dirt before the world leaped up to strike him in his face.

B ISHOP STOOD FOR a moment watching Rogers bleed out on the ground and waiting to draw hostile fire. When none came anywhere near him, he cleared the barn and kept on moving, ready to confront all comers, circling wide around the manor house.

He wasn't ready to try breaking in just yet. Out front, at least three men were firing from the mansion's windows, two with rifles and the other with a handgun by the sound of it. Cut off from his companions from the Circle K, he wished them well, deciding he could do no better than to look out for himself and drop as many of Stark's gunmen as he could.

Meeting Cold Comfort's mayor had come as a surprise, but if Rogers was there—or had been; he was permanently absent now from everywhere—it stood to reason that the town's marshal and deputy would also likely be on hand, defending Stark.

Or maybe, like the mayor, wishing that they could get to hell and gone away before their time ran out.

Bishop wasn't assuming victory, by any means. Not yet. He still counted a dozen guns firing, at least, and only four of them—if that—could be his friends. After dispatching two defenders on his own, or two defenders and one fleeing coward, he could not assume that all of those who'd ridden out from camp with him were still alive, uninjured, with so much lead in the air.

And he was still focused on taking out the rifleman atop Stark's house, if he could pull it off. No easy feat, that, when the eaves of Stark's home were approximately ten feet over Bishop's head.

He could jump up and grip the tiles, if they'd support his weight without cascading down and braining him, but that would mean leaving his Winchester behind to free both hands. He didn't like that plan a bit, but it was all that came to mind as he was circling the house, ducking below dark windows as he passed them, half expecting to be shot at any instant for his trouble.

Rounding the southwest corner of the house, he almost ran into another one of Stark's defenders, rushing headlong toward him. Bishop whipped his rifle's butt around and struck the running man a blow that sat him down, dropping a six-gun as he fell.

Before the guy could clear his head, Toby stepped in and kicked him in the face, then brought his rifle's stock down once, twice, three times, till the head below it made a kind of ruptured-melon sound and the gunman began to shiver spastically.

Enough.

He grabbed the fallen piece—a Remington Model 1875, closely resembling Colt's Peacemaker—and decided against tucking it under his belt. If he was forced to climb without his Yellow Boy, two pistols ought to be enough.

And if they weren't . . .

He dumped the captured weapon's .44-40 cartridges, then flung it overhand into the dark, useless to anyone. Off to the east, a faint hairline of gray was visible on the horizon, dawn approaching in its own good time.

Bishop pressed on, circling behind the house, hoping to find something—a packing crate, whatever—he could stand on to reach the roof without having to leap and hang on for dear life. Another loud shot from above him signaled that the sniper planted there was still picking and choosing targets in the yard below.

Was that one of his fellow drovers dying? And if so, which one?

No time to waste now. Whatever it took . . .

And there it was, in front of him. A ladder stood propped up against the roof.

He guessed the sniper must have used it for his own climb. It seemed fitting, then, for Bishop to avail himself of that same access, which permitted him to take his Winchester along.

But he would have to do it quietly. A sneak attack was pointless if he went up making a racket, giving his intended target time to turn and pick him off.

"Here goes nothing," he whispered to himself, and started on the climb.

G AVIN DIXON TRACKED a running gunman in the yard between Stark's barn and what appeared to be a shed for tools or maybe feed. He had nine rounds remaining in his Winchester, six spent so far, and two men dead to show for that.

The others he had missed, or maybe winged one, and he couldn't rightly say how many more defenders Stark had on the premises.

A fight like this, you had to take enemies one at a time, as they appeared.

He led the runner by a yard or so, mind calculating speed and distance for his shot. A bullet weighing thirteen grams and traveling around twelve hundred and fifty feet per second—just over a quarter mile—would strike his target with six hundred and ninety foot-pounds of explosive energy, but only if he got his calculation right.

The target wasn't standing still, but sprinting, so he had to think about where his intended mark would be, reach out to let the bullet greet him as he passed, and take him down.

Three feet should do it. And if not . . .

He fired and saw the runner stumble, reeling through an awkward turnaround, one hand rising to clutch his torso. Falling, Dixon's target rolled, then struggled up on hands and knees, gasping from pain that wracked his body.

But he wasn't out. Not yet.

Pumping his rifle's lever action, eight rounds now remaining in the magazine, Dixon sighted upon the gunman's face in profile, hatless now, and didn't have to lead at all this time. Another *crack*, and this time, when the ranch hand slumped, Dixon was confident he wouldn't rise again.

He was no Lazarus, just more dead meat.

And where in blazes was his boss?

W HERE IN THE hell are you going?"
Harley Tilton had separated from his deputy when the shooting started on the property outside Stark's house, hoping to find a vantage point from which to fight without immediately being killed. That part was critical. He had a duty to his boss, at least in theory, but all Cold Comfort's marshal really cared about was his own skin and keeping it intact by any means required.

Now he was back with Hazlet, and from how it looked, he'd found Luke none too soon. His deputy had almost reached a side door on the west side of Stark's ranch house—had one hand on the knob, in fact—when Harley spotted him, his question stopping Hazlet short.

Luke turned to face him, color rising from his shirt collar to stain his face, as if he were a little boy caught with his hand in Mama's cookie jar.

"Just going out to have a look around, Harley," he said. "Get in the thick of it, you know?"

"Bullshit! You think I don't know a deserter when I see one, boy?"

"Deserter? Are you serious? This ain't the army, *Marshal*, just in case you hadn't noticed. And this ain't my war."

"A goddamned coward's what you are, Luke."

"Yeah? We was supposed to ride out here and warn Stark, nothing more. That's done, in case you couldn't tell. Our co-called mayor's already out and gone. He didn't feel like dying over something that has naught to do with him, and I don't neither."

"If you think that I'm just gonna let you slink away—"

"Let me? *Let* me, you say?"

One second flat, and Hazlet had his pistol out. It startled Tilton. In their monthly practice sessions, he had never seen Luke try to draw and fire, presumably because Hazlet had never felt it was required of him.

But now . . .

"You lost your mind?" Tilton inquired.

"Saving my ass," Luke snapped at him. "My mind goes where it goes, and right now all of me is getting out of here."

Afraid to try drawing his own six-gun, Tilton mustered what dignity he could and told Hazlet, "In that case, you can leave your badge."

Luke fairly sneered at him as he replied. "No problem. Won't be needing it wherever I end up.

Hazlet removed the tin star with his left hand, leaving a small tear in his shirt where he'd pinned it on that morning. With a gesture of contempt, he flung the badge at Tilton's feet.

"Wear it yourself," he said. "Go on and call yourself a double marshal. See how well that flies."

"Don't let me see your face again, you yellow-bellied rat."

"A live one, anyhow," Luke answered back. "If you

had any sense, you'd get to hell and gone away from here yourself."

"I've got a job to do." Surprised to hear the words emerging from his mouth.

"I leave you to it, then," said Hazlet. "When you're gutshot, take a second to remember that I told you so."

And he was gone into the night.

Without Luke's pistol in his face, Harley drew his own piece and moved to shut the door his erstwhile deputy had left wide open to the night. That wouldn't do. No telling who or what would pop in from the dark outside.

Part of Tilton wished that he had gone with Hazlet, but he still felt that he owed something to Mr. Stark. As to exactly what that was, he couldn't say.

But if he planned to leave, the least that he could do was tell the Big Man first and thus absolve himself of any guilt.

Assuming that Stark didn't fly into a rage and drop him where he stood.

Or maybe, Tilton thought, there was another way to go. If it appeared that Stark was losing, as unlikely as that sounded, wouldn't people praise the officer who brought his despotism to an end?

Something to think about while he was searching for his boss and making up his addled mind.

L UKE HAZLET WAS still mouthing curses as he cleared the house and started for the barn. Echoes of gunfire all around him kept him moving, on alert for any threat that might come at him from the first pale light of dawn.

Another day, and it was starting badly. Still might be his last, but if he died on Stark Acres, Hazlet vowed it wouldn't be from lack of trying to escape.

To hell with Harley Tilton, Hebron Stark, Creed Rogers, and the rest of them. Luke felt as if he'd shed a ton of weight just taking off his cheap badge, although he hadn't been aware of the job troubling him before. In fact, he'd quite enjoyed it up to now, but that was done.

Time to move on.

He reached the barn, none of the airborne bullets coming close enough to worry him. Easing inside, he found the horse he'd ridden from Cold Comfort standing in one of a dozen stalls and munching hay. Luke had to find its tack and saddle, draw it from the stall, and get it ready for the road.

Inside the barn, though sheltered from the gunfire going on outside, Hazlet felt more nervous than when he'd crossed the yard on foot. Out there, he'd known the shots weren't coming close enough to harm him. Now he kept expecting someone to barge in and blaze away, either one of the raiders or a hand employed by Mr. Stark, unhappy with the former deputy trying to sneak away.

There'd be no sneaking when he left the barn, though, riding out through its broad entryway onto a battleground.

"Quit stalling!" Luke ordered himself, and climbed into the saddle. That belonged to him, at least, and if somebody from Cold Comfort's livery waited around for him to bring the borrowed horse back home, they'd wait a damned long time.

"Come on, boy!"

Hazlet snapped the reins and hunched a little lower in the saddle as he left the barn behind. It was positioned so that riders exiting immediately faced the manor house, and so it was that he glimpsed movement on the tiled roof, someone crouching down as if to aim a weapon from on high.

Before he'd covered fifteen feet, that rifle's muzzle blossomed flame. The bullet reached him before any sound, slamming Luke over backward, rolling off the horse's rump and sprawling on the ground.

No pain at first. Between the shot and fall that followed it, he just felt numb.

The large-bore rifle's sound reached him a split second later, and he wheezed a bitter laugh.

Whoever said you never hear the shot that kills you was a liar and a fool.

N OW THAT'S MORE like it," Cothran muttered to himself.

A clean kill, one shot up and one man down.

The horse, minus its rider, raced across the farmyard, weapons going off on every side, and disappeared toward the horizon showing pallid gray with just a tinge of rosy pink.

Jay reckoned he'd allow himself one more shot with the Whitworth rifle, then swap it for the Winchester and clamber down to join the battle at ground level. Picking up the powder flask from where he'd laid it, by the weapon's ramrod to his right, he poured a measured dose of gunpowder into the Whitworth's muzzle, chased it with a hexagonal bullet, and topped it off with a small cotton swab, tamping it all down with three strokes of the rod.

During the War Between the States, soldiers could recognize a Whitworth firing at them by the shrill whistling sound its six-sided bullets emitted in flight. That wouldn't always help them duck, of course, but such was life.

Or, more often, the end of it.

When he was ready, Cothran scanned the killing ground below without using the rifle's telescopic sight.

Once he'd picked out a target, then and only then would he attempt to aim the Whitworth for another kill.

And then a voice Jay didn't recognize spoke up behind him. Said, "You're done."

"Am I?" Jay inquired, still lying belly down, not making any moves.

"You doubt my word, stand up and turn around. See for yourself."

Might take a minute," said the rifleman. "Don't wanna take a dive off here and break my damn-fool neck."

"You seem okay with heights," Bishop replied.

"All right for lying down, but I'm not gonna dance a jig for you."

"Nobody asked you to. Get up and turn around now, or I'll have to shoot you in the ass."

"Tough customer, I guess, back-shoot an unarmed man."

"I count three guns from where I stand, and wouldn't bet I've seen them all," Toby replied. "Get up while you still can."

"Yes, sir. I'm getting up, boss. Keep a light touch on that trigger, if you please."

The ladder hadn't been a problem, but Bishop had worried about making noise once he was on the roof, maybe dislodging barrel tiles to rattle off the roof and smash on impact with the ground. His luck had held, though, and he'd been in time to see the sniper blasting a familiar figure from his horse down in the yard.

His adversary slowly rose, hands out to either side once he was on his feet, then shuffled through a turn until he wound up facing Bishop. The sniper was smiling in a way that sent a little chill down Toby's spine.

To wipe it off, Bishop said, "Gunning down a law-man likely qualifies you for a noose."

"Lawman?" The gunman snorted, not what you would call a laugh. "If he was any kind of lawman worth the name, I might pass for the pope of Rome."

"Is that a Whitworth rifle you've got there?"

"Good eyes, friend. Some folks might mistake it for a Sharps."

"Not if they saw you muzzle-loading it."

"How long have you been standing there?"

" 'Bout long enough to wonder if it was you who killed my friend Isaac."

"Can't say I recognize the name. But, then again, I might've never learned it in the first place."

"Killed so many, have you?"

Lazy shrug, the hands still raised to shoulder height. "Well, I don't like to brag."

"Why do I feel like that's a lie?"

"We met before?" the sniper asked.

"Not introduced," said Bishop. "But I've seen your work."

"This Isaac fella, so you say."

"That's right."

"Where is it I supposedly killed him, and when?"

"Last night," Toby replied, stone cold. "Out at the camp a few miles east of town."

"Dark fella, was he?" asked the rifleman. "That rings a bell."

"Orders from Stark, or did you do it on your own?"

"Sometimes I get carried away." Still smiling. "I confess that as a failing in myself."

"Next time you're carried off, it should be by pall-bearers."

"We gonna do this, then? Right here?"

"It seems as good a place as any," Bishop said.

"Well, since you put it that way."

When the sniper moved, it came without warning. He hunched forward, his right hand streaking for the pistol on his hip. Bishop had time to raise his Yellow Boy a fraction of an inch before he fired without properly aiming, but it made no difference. His .44 slug drilled the gunman's chest and punched him over backward, both arms flailing, boots sliding on barrel tiles.

One moment he was there in front of Bishop, fanning air as if he hoped to fly away, then he was gone—not upward like a bird, but plummeting below, dragged down by gravity. No cry or any other sound as he dropped out of sight.

Bishop approached the roof's edge gingerly, checked out the yard for any weapons aimed his way, then peered straight down. His shot had likely killed the sniper outright, but the fall had snapped his neck on top of that, his head twisted at an angle never seen in living men.

"If you run into Isaac, tell him Toby Bishop sent you," he called down.

The sniper wasn't listening, or if he heard the comment on some other plane of being, he was stumped for a response.

Turning his back, Bishop retreated toward the ladder and the fight still going on below.

WHEN GAVIN DIXON spotted Hebron Stark striding across the farmyard, big as life, armed to the teeth, it took him by surprise. He'd taken Stark for someone who would hire his killing done and only show his face when it was time to crow about his latest victory.

Not so, apparently.

That didn't raise Stark any higher in his estimation—

still a damned extortionist who preyed on anyone around him—but at least he scratched "coward" off the list of other insults that applied.

Deke Sullivan, standing beside Dixon, half whispered, "That's him, isn't it?"

"The man himself," Dixon replied.

"A nice, fat target," Paco Esperanza said, raising his Henry rifle, drawing down on Stark.

Dixon reached out and pushed the Henry's muzzle down, saying, "Hold up. He's mine."

He stepped out of the shadows, Sullivan and Esperanza hanging back to cover him, and called, "Hey, Stark! Looking for me?"

The rancher stopped and turned toward Dixon, putting on a tense smile as he started walking forward.

"That'll do," Dixon advised him when he'd come within twenty-odd feet.

"You come to my home raising hell?" Stark said, a question Dixon figured was rhetorical. "Some gall you have, mister."

Dixon replied, "You play games with my livelihood? I figure turnabout's fair play."

"Killing my men?"

"You started that as well. If you don't know about it, ask your sniper about firing on my camp and killing one of mine."

"Trespassing!" Stark replied.

"I'm here to settle that right now."

"I have the marshal here."

"So, trot him out. This doesn't look like Cold Comfort to me."

"Meaning?"

"I have it from his own lips that he's got no jurisdiction outside town."

"I guess we'll have to settle this on your terms, then."

"Whichever way it goes, you won't hold up another herd."

"My land, my rules!"

"Guess you're a nation all unto yourself, then. We can test that notion now and see how it holds up."

Around them, firing had slackened off to silence, Stark's survivors standing by to see what their employer pulled out of his hat.

"Running a herd that size," Stark said, "it stands to reason you can count."

"I learned my numbers young. What of it?"

"Look around you, Dixon. Even if you kill me, you'll still be outnumbered and outgunned."

Dixon considered that and raised his voice when he responded, made his words audible across the newly silent property.

"We'll take our chances, Stark," he said. "For your part, why not tell your men to stand down if you lose. Give some of them a chance to live that might not have one otherwise."

Stark's eyes narrowed at that, but finally he gave a jerky little nod and called out to his men, "All of you drawing pay for me, heed this! If I can't take this fella, you're released from any obligation to me, freed to go your own ways. Otherwise, wipe out this vermin when I'm finished with the rat in charge."

"You talk a good fight," Dixon said. "How do you shoot?"

Instead of answering, Stark half turned to his right, reducing his target profile as he raised his long gun for a killing shot.

Dixon saved time by firing from the hip, pumping the lever action on his Winchester to fire a second shot as Stark recoiled and staggered, lost his rifle, then dropped to his knees. You could have heard a mouse fart as he knelt there, grimacing, then slowly toppled over on his face.

Dixon remained alert for any hostile movement from the other gunman visible around the farmyard, but they made no move against him. Some of them looked stunned, others almost relieved.

"We're leaving now," he told them, voice raised to be clear. "I've got no further quarrel with any of you, lest you try to follow us and start it up again."

By then, most of Stark's men were turning, moving off, some toward the bunkhouses, others making a beeline for the paddock and their mounts. He watched them go, then turned to Sullivan and Esperanza just as Gorch and Bishop showed up, moving in from different directions.

"Nobody hurt?" he asked them all as one.

Headshaking all around, Sullivan adding, "Not a scratch this time. They couldn't hold a candle to Comanches."

"All right, then," said Dixon as the sun peeked over the eastern horizon. "Best get moving, then. We've got a herd to move."

EPILOGUE

*E*AST ST. LOUIS
  Day fifty-three. The stockyards teemed with bustling, lowing cattle, their aroma wafting from the holding pens breeze-borne and drifting beyond the National Stockyards Company complex, spreading its effluvium downtown to business offices, hotels, and restaurants, giving the city's upper crust a grim reminder of what underlay their fortunes.

Toby Bishop reckoned that he'd never seen so many cattle in one place before, and never might again.

As each new herd arrived, its drovers were directed to another set of holding pens where auctioneers awaited buyers, gearing up to praise the animals they'd never seen before and seek top dollar with a decent rake-off for themselves in the process. Buyers shouted bids or brandished cards with numbers inked upon them, sparing aggravation to their vocal cords. It seemed chaotic, but there appeared to be no arguments among them, no one feeling slighted, even if their bids fell short and they were disappointed.

One way or another, all the bidders would acquire the beef they needed, processed in the slaughterhouses ranged around the stockyards, uniformly drab and menacing, as you'd expect from citadels of wholesale death.

Bishop paid no attention to the prices being bandied back and forth. They made no difference to the payment he had coming after seven and a half weeks on the trail. There'd be no bonus paid for fighting rustlers, hostiles, or a would-be dictator like Hebron Stark, since none was mentioned in the contract he had inked when signing up to join the drive.

And just as well, he figured, since financial compensation for the killing might have made him feel like he was back in Texas, doing gun work.

He didn't wait around to see the Dixon herd sold off and routed into one or more of the smoke-belching abattoirs. That wasn't Bishop turning squeamish in the face of death or giving up on beefsteak, simply shrugging off the blood he'd spilled during the drive and not desiring any more of it.

He was about to leave the stockyard proper when a voice somewhere behind him stopped him short, speaking his name. Nobody but the other drovers from the Circle K knew he was in St. Louis, much just pinning down precisely where, and this voice struck him as familiar.

"Mr. Dixon," Toby said, before he turned around.

"None other," Dixon said. "You lighting out, young man?"

"Just going for a drink or three. I would invite you, but . . ."

"I've still got business here," Dixon allowed. "Could take another couple hours, maybe three."

"I'll leave you to it, then, sir."

"Where can I find you when I've got your pay?"

"I'm booked at a hotel, the Eden Arms. No garden I can see, which makes them liars for a start, but it's all right."

"I'll find it," Dixon said.

"Or I could meet you somewhere else tomorrow if you'd estimate a time and place."

"Back here all right with you? Say noon?"

"I'll be here," Bishop said.

"Before you go, Toby, I want to thank you for a job well done from start to finish. If it weren't for you, I'm pretty sure we would've lost more steers, and likely men besides."

"Don't give me too much credit, sir."

"Only what's due. And you can drop the 'sir.' That is, unless . . ."

"Unless what, Mr. D?"

"You'd care to spend the next six months helping around the Circle K and getting ready for another drive come spring?"

Bishop considered that, picking a point in space above Dixon's left shoulder, staring at it just a tad too long.

"No problem, son. I understand your feelings after all we went through."

"I'm not sure I understand them all that well myself," Bishop replied.

"I meant after your trouble back in Mason County. We heard of the Hoodoo War on our patch, too. No names, of course, and I'd be leery trusting all the details in Atoka's paper, but word gets around."

"You had to be there in it, Mr. D. To see it, even smell it when the breeze died down."

"I know that smell, from wartime and since then. It never altogether goes away."

"No, sir. It doesn't."

"Anyway, just think about it if your mind ain't dead

set to the contrary. I know you'd be an asset to the Circle K. For what it's worth, Bill Pickering agrees."

"Tell you tomorrow, one way or another?"

"Sounds all right to me."

"And thank Bill—Mr. Pickering, that is. I do appreciate the vote of confidence."

"Until tomorrow, then," Dixon concluded. "Have a drink for me while you're about it."

"I might do that very thing."

They shook hands, parting for a day at least, or who knew how long after that. Bishop might never see the man again, much less Atoka or the rest of Indian country.

But he wondered, walking back toward a saloon he'd spotted earlier, if staying put for just a while and drawing steady pay would be the worst idea he'd ever had.

Ready to find
your next great read?

Let us help.

Visit prh.com/nextread

Penguin
Random
House